BOOK ONE

BOOK ONE

MISHA McCORKLE

ILLUMIFY
MEDIA.COM

Published by
Illumify Media Global
www.IllumifyMedia.com
"We bring your book to life!"

Library of Congress Control Number: 2020921509

Paperback ISBN: 978-1-947360-58-7
eBook ISBN: 978-1-947360-59-4

Typeset by Jennifer Clark
Cover design by Michelle McCorkle

Printed in the United States of America

To my mom, who fought dragons for me.

Elleson

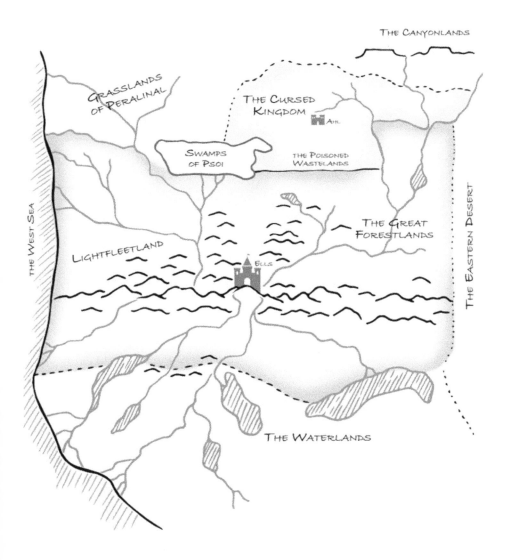

THE CANYONLANDS

GRASSLANDS
OF PERALINAL

THE CURSED
KINGDOM

ARK.

SWAMPS
OF PSOI

THE POISONED
WASTELANDS

THE WEST SEA

THE GREAT
FORESTLANDS

THE EASTERN DESERT

LIGHTFLEETLAND

ELLS

THE WATERLANDS

CHAPTER ONE

BROGAN COULDN'T BELIEVE what a great day this was. The sun smiled in beams of light; fall leaves blazed with color. The perfect-temperature air hugged him. It had taken two years for New York's Upper East Side to feel like home, but now he basked in its glory.

Bleep bleep. Bloop bloop. His cousin Emmy's special ringtone squeaked from his pocket.

He pulled out the latest mPhone-27 prototype, which his dad gave him after testing the display. It wouldn't be for sale on the market for another six months—one of the perks of having a father who was famous in the tech industry. "Hey Em."

"Just . . . no, Brogan!" Her deep breaths told him she was already out on the streets looking for him like this was an emergency. "I saw you hanging out with Davis at lunch. You can't. He was my boyfriend for two weeks in the seventh grade."

Brogan almost laughed. "Why does that mean I can't be friends with him again?"

"Because he's dumb like a box of rocks. You need smart friends to challenge you and set up mutual destinies and whatnot. Davis's whole family is dumb. His sister was caught cheating on her Calc AP test last year. How she ever got into AP in the first place—"

"*You're* sounding like a box of rocks, Em. If he had ten sisters who were caught stealing the Mona Lisa by trying to slip it under their shirts, it wouldn't alter my opinion of Davis." What he was about to say would appease her though. "But you're right. He *is* a little dim."

He pictured Emmy's satisfied smile. She was too concerned about the people he became friends with, but his dad would say the same thing about Davis. And how on earth did she come up with *mutual destinies* as a friend deterrent?

"Brog, dude, where are you? You have to run these things by me. I've known these kids since kindergarten. In eighth grade Davis told the whole school he had the president on speed dial. It was so dumb, because there are kids whose parents know the president, and it ended up becoming this huge deal . . ."

Emmy's chatter edged on the side of insufferable today. She wasn't stupid or anything, just focused on reputation, fashion, and what was it again? Right. This month she had been obsessing over perfect noses. She had it in her mind that Brogan had the most perfect nose, which was unfair.

By the time she'd rambled on about some uptown boutique with all the best clothes, he'd reached the foot of the Metropolitan Museum steps. "I'll talk to you later, Em." He hung up and pressed forward.

It was one of the few places he could sort himself out, and by now he could find it blindfolded, as if a siren's song guided him. He stepped into the Frank Lloyd Wright room and took a moment to let the perfectly designed space melt over him. This room always cleared his thoughts. Every detail formed a grand symphony of peace. It was almost an American version of the Japanese architecture he'd grown up with. If he could recreate it inside his bedroom, he might never leave.

What would that take? Blueprints? LED lighting behind fake windows on his interior walls? He would have to get help building wrap-around ledges and oak trim. Hire out leading for the glass. He didn't know how to use power tools, but maybe his dad would hire a master carpenter so he could learn.

He pulled out a sketchbook and a ruler, then began to take detailed notes and sketches. A familiar security guard rounded the corner. "You finally gonna build your own, Mr. Lukes?"

"As a matter of fact, Moira, I might."

The stout, middle-aged woman chuckled. "Impressive."

He liked her. Friendly, but not too nosy—despite knowing who he was, apparently. As she waddled off, he took to soaking in the atmosphere for a satisfying half hour.

"Ugh, I thought I would find you here. What is it this time?" Emmy shattered his sanctuary with her clamorous aura.

"Maybe it isn't a specific it. Maybe it's just a general nagging that never goes away." He eyed her, wondering if she would interpret his statement as a dig.

It wasn't, but her tilted head and questioning eyes assured him she didn't understand his existential angst.

"When you're done, Hollis and I will be at my house. She's totally obsessed with you, but you didn't hear that from me. So come over."

"Hot Hollis? I thought you weren't friends anymore." He couldn't keep the image of Hollis in short shorts from his imagination.

"She gets me into places. And since she's got a thing for you, it's leverage for me."

"I'm your bait? Geez, Em. You get in anywhere you want anyway."

"True, thanks for noticing." She winked.

"I'm not exactly *glad* I can help, but"—he bowed—"I'm at your service."

She beamed, grabbed his arm, and dragged him out of his place of refuge.

ON THEIR WAY out of the museum, several lights flashed bright in Brogan's eyes.

"Damn paparazzi," Emmy hissed, grabbing Brogan's jacket sleeve and pulling him past any wanna-be reporters asking annoying questions about his dad and whether he was considering a modeling career.

Brogan breathed hard as he and Emmy hustled to her place. They finally made it past the doorman into her elevator.

"They're getting worse, aren't they? Like more invasive?" she asked.

"Ever since your mom's ads went viral. I think I'm going to refuse ever filling in for her 'sick' models again."

"Yeah, I highly doubt they were sick. She just recognizes the hype of Leo Luke's son. Plus, you've got talent."

"Talent? You mean standing there and tilting my head in the right direction?"

"I told you your nose—"

"And I said I don't want to hear about my nose."

She smiled and booped his nose as he swatted at her hand.

The elevator opened into her parents' prewar penthouse. Emmy's parents had inherited the penthouse from great-grandparents who'd made their fortunes in New York in the 1900s. Before that, they'd lived in a modest home in Vermont. Emmy considered it her deep, dark secret, one she had Brogan swear never to tell.

He pulled out his tablet and threw his backpack on Emmy's bedroom floor. "I have to show you what I spliced together in Photoshop this morning."

"Yes, please, Mr. Artistic Genius. I hope you've made more animal mash-ups. The squirrelfalo is still my favorite."

"Can you imagine that monstrosity charging at you for peanuts next time we go to Yellowstone?"

"Nope, because I'm never going to Wyoming again."

"I thought you liked Jackson Hole."

Emmy flashed him a disbelieving glance. "Was that Wyoming?"

The doorbell announced Hollis's arrival. Emmy bounced from her bed and shimmered with joy as she turned to him in all seriousness. "Don't worry. She won't force herself on you if my mom is here."

"She would hardly have to force anything."

"Whatever, virgin."

Ouch. Brogan had never been in a relationship where "the next level" rested well with his conscience, but his mouth went dry when Hollis walked in to Emmy's room wearing a miniskirt.

She was by no means model-perfect, but something about her caught people's attention. Maybe it was her very white skin and dark hair that drew one's glance straight to her big, Armenian eyes. It didn't hurt that she chose clothes that accentuated her slender frame. Brogan knew he was staring at her long legs, but he couldn't stop himself.

Hollis's round lips parted as her silky voice pierced his malaise. "Emmy, go grab us some refreshments, will you?"

Hollis did command attention. Emmy almost bowed on her way out.

But it irked Brogan, treating Em like her little slave girl. Hollis's hubris made her large green eyes look cheap.

"I've been wanting to spend more time with you, Brogan, ever since we met at the Montjoy party. You were occupied by some game. Do you remember?"

He smirked. "I remember learning an awesome new card game. I guess you were there, too, weren't you?"

Hollis ignored this dismissive comment. She sat seductively on Emmy's bed, making sure to arch her back as she stared at the ceiling. "Come with me to Mardell's EDM party tonight."

Brogan shrugged. "Emmy and I were planning to go anyway."

Just then Emmy burst in with a tray of lemonade and fresh fruit.

Hollis stood and crossed her arms. "Fine. I'll see you there." She strutted from the room without a glance at the treats she had sent Emmy to fetch.

Emmy's eyebrows narrowed as she set the tray on her bed. "What did you do?" she hissed.

Seriously, Em had no idea what a sucker she was.

"I didn't do anything. But if we're talking about who we shouldn't be friends with, I'm nominating Hollis."

"Hollis carries weight."

5

"And diseases."

She laughed. "You're too clever for me to argue with. But we're still going to the EDM—"

"Yes, Emmy. You're dragging me there. My dad will be pissed if he finds out, but I'm going. I'll even dance with Hollis . . . at a polite distance."

She smiled triumphantly. "Pfft. Good luck. Her octopus arms are quivering at the thought of wrapping themselves around you. Now go *expunge* your school uniform. And don't wear something my mother gave you."

Aunt Dana was an up-and-coming fashion designer. She'd suckered Brogan into modeling her newest line, but as her daughter, Emmy dismissed everything she created.

"Wear that shirt you picked up at Numen-The-Human. I'm in a boutiquey mood these days."

"Am I your Ken doll?"

She threw a stuffed animal at him. "Ken dolls don't argue."

"They also don't have the equipment to interest Hollis."

Emmy was still cackling as he left her room.

LATER THAT EVENING, Brogan climbed into the back seat of Emmy's chauffeured town car as it pulled up to his house.

Emmy whistled. "You're definitely making that shirt look better than the runway did."

"Please don't tell me it's because of my nose." Brogan swatted Em's finger from booping it. "Off limits. You need a kitten or something."

"Agreed." She pursed her lips. "I'm thinking it's time to start interviewing for my next boyfriend."

"Make sure he likes nose boops."

"It takes a special nose to boop, Brog."

At the entrance to the club, Em took it slow, strutting in like everyone cared. Brogan, on the other hand, made a beeline toward the back, near the DJ, where he could lean on the wall, hands in pockets, and watch his trendy schoolmates let loose to the music.

Many of the kids he'd never seen before, but that was New York for you.

Brogan recognized Mardell, the host, next to him and said, "Fun party."

Mardell's face lit up. "Brogan!" He held out his hand and Brogan took it. "Welcome to the house. How did your biochem test go?"

"Nothing negative to report, as far as I know."

Mardell, competent and charismatic and one of the better students at school, grinned. "I aced it."

"Glad to hear it. Love the new haircut. How can I get that look?"

Mardell quirked an eyebrow and searched his face. "Be born black?" He chuckled.

"Ah. I'm already disqualified."

"You'll have to stick to your vanilla haircut. It goes with your dance moves."

"Ooh, that hurt," Brogan choked out as he covered his heart.

"I only hurt the people I like," Mardell said, which made Brogan laugh. Mardell put his arm around Brogan's shoulder and they faced the dance floor together.

"Geez, Mardell, how did you score this place?"

"It's my mom's club. She let me shut it down for the night so I could throw an under-age party. She's cool to the city, but strict to me." He craned his neck. "I snuck gin in somewhere though. You want?"

"That's okay. Emmy can find booze anywhere. Like magic. I think she squeezes it from rocks. I'm kinda over it, plus I have jiujitsu in the morning."

"Yeah, about Emmy. I've been thinkin' I like her big anime eyes."

Brogan followed Mardell's gaze to the group of jostling teenagers, where Em was having a great time owning the floor.

"I've never noticed that her eyes were cartoonish in size."

"They take up most of her face, like universes unto themselves.

But I guess it'd be weird if you paid too much attention to your cousin."

"Yep." Brogan eyed Mardell's nicely shaped nose. It would suit Emmy. "Looks like she could use an awesome dance partner. You should join her."

Mardell smiled wide and struck out across the floor.

Brogan snorted. *Universes unto themselves.* How long had Mardell been into Em? As soon as Mardell left his side, a delicate hand wrung itself around Brogan's bicep. Brogan turned and found himself starting down at beauty. He caught his breath.

Hollis winked. "Time to dance."

He followed without protest.

Her dancing wasn't overly seductive, just enough to make Brogan want to toss his relationship-only policy. Why he didn't like this girl?

Hollis glared over at Emmy dancing with Mardell. "Isn't he a little too cool for her?"

"For Emmy? You know she's my cousin." *And my closest friend,* he added to himself.

Hollis shrugged and pulled him into a deeper embrace.

He pushed her off. "Sorry, I'm done dancing for now." As he walked away, he didn't look back to see what kind of fury might be on her face.

How did he fall into that spell? His brain must have been addled for a hot second.

He made his way down a corridor, looking for a restroom. LED light strips surrounded all of the doors. Maybe the blue light was for the men's room and the pink light for the ladies'? There weren't any signs. He pushed his way through the heavy blue-outlined door and fell down a step, losing his balance and falling hard to the floor. The door banged shut behind him, leaving him in darkness. No music made its way in either. It was cold and still and silent.

Brogan stood and groped along a smooth, damp wall for a light switch or a door handle.

Nothing. Even the door seemed to have disappeared.

He reached for his phone—it was gone. Then he heard a tone-less, breathy chuckle from somewhere nearby, sending his creep-o-meter through the roof.

He lowered his voice to sound commanding. "Who are you?"

Something cold slid along his palm and gently tugged at his fingers.

He drew his hand back. "Turn the lights on."

A whisper responded between sniggers. "But I don't need the lights."

Brogan's temple thrummed a steady heartbeat and his senses heightened. If he could see this weirdo, he could fight back. He had never felt vulnerable like this before.

Suddenly the door flew open and the rhythmic beat of the music poured in. A tall, muscular man pulled Brogan out of the room.

The door clanged shut behind him. The man opened the same door again, and behind it was the men's restroom—well lit and full of random, normal-looking dudes doing their business.

"This what you were looking for?" asked the stranger who had rescued him.

Brogan couldn't make sense of what had just happened. "Yes? But how—"

"Shh . . . just be more careful next time."

Brogan stared into the blue lighting of the bathroom. He looked down and saw there was no step down into the room; it was perfectly level with the hallway.

He needed to get out of there. His head throbbing with adrenaline, he turned and made his way back to the DJ stand, where he grabbed his phone and texted Em. *I'm walking home. Have fun.*

He didn't know if it was the shock, but he couldn't remember if the man who had helped him had walked away or even what he looked like. He could only remember the cold caress on his fingers.

CHAPTER TWO

THE NEXT MORNING, Brogan found himself again in the Frank Lloyd Wright room. He didn't remember walking there. His concentration had clamped onto the events from last night—which he kept reliving, trying to figure it all out.

A door had opened into darkness. He had fallen into the darkness, where something sinister teased him. Then a stranger had come for him, pulling him back to reality. Then that stranger had reopened same door. The. Same. Door.

The second time the door had led right to the bathroom, filled with normal people and those crazy blue lights clubs use to keep drug addicts from seeing their veins and shooting up. And there had been no step down, like the one he'd fallen from a moment earlier.

His brain kept working to untangle the knot, even as he looked around at the symmetry and beauty of his favorite refuge at the Metropolitan Museum. This time, the orderly designs couldn't tame the chaos of his mind. Sure, being here helped when the only thing on his mind was school stress, self-doubts, or arguments with his dad. But to sort out space-time altercations he'd need something stronger—maybe twisty modern art.

He released a long breath. He hadn't been dizzy or confused last night. He hadn't misunderstood what he'd experienced. Either it happened or he hallucinated the entire thing.

He had never hallucinated before.

His back pocket vibrated. He pulled out his phone. "Hi, Dad."

"You missed jiujitsu. Are you okay?"

Brogan looked at his watch; its small hand sat halfway between eleven and twelve.

"I'm fine. I . . . I actually forgot it entirely."

"That's not like you."

"Yeah." He paused, not quite sure if the question he was about to ask would alarm his father or not. "Dad, is there schizophrenia in our family?"

"Not that I'm aware of. Have you been seeing things?"

He didn't seem too concerned, and that made Brogan feel a little better.

"Just a situation from last night," Brogan said, then wished he'd hadn't. If he said much more he'd have to tell his dad about the party.

"Don't assume you're crazy. This world hides mysteries. We can talk about it later, if you want. As for this missing jiujitsu, Coach Mark agreed to give us a private lesson at one o'clock. I don't want you neglecting any part of your MMA training. Your sword work looked great Tuesday, by the way. I posted that back layout on Instagram. I only meant for your grandparents to see it, but it got 400,000 likes."

Brogan's face grew warm. "Dad, please stop posting me on your Insta. And it got 430,000 likes."

His dad guffawed. "Now you really have to prove yourself. Hope you're good enough to beat your old man."

Dang it. Dad would probably work him hard in jiujitsu. He should have gone to class this morning. "I'll see you at the gym."

BROGAN BARELY HAD time to run home and change into his gi before sprinting to the small gym. He preferred working out in a

T-shirt and shorts, but all martial arts teachers insisted on the wrap-around jumpsuit. It trapped heat inside and by the time he pushed through the gym door, sweat trickled down his chest. A few women lifted weights in the back, but the sparring floor was clear for Coach Mark, Dad, and Brogan.

Dad sat up from a stretch when the door slammed. A bright smile overtook his face—an expression Brogan had only ever seen when his dad looked at him. It told Brogan he was the most important thing in his dad's world.

He stood at Brogan's approach. "I see you've already warmed up, son." He massaged the back of Brogan's sweaty neck. "Couldn't wait to throw down with your old man?"

Brogan grunted. Dad was anything but old. He had barely been nineteen when Brogan was born, so now at a very healthy thirty-six, he won every sparring match they had.

Coach Mark's voice broke in. "A lap of crab walks and bear crawls. Get your shoulders warm. We aren't sparring today."

Brogan's chest lightened.

"We'll do a few hours of mobility strength training instead."

This was actually worse. Brogan massaged his obliques. They'd only just recovered from last weekend's corestravaganza. And mobility strength meant a painful combination of stretching and extending muscles normally neglected—like hip flexors and traps. Might as well shed the gi now. He'd be more comfortable working in shorts alone.

His dad followed his lead, and a couple of the ladies at the weights stopped and stared. One took out her phone and snapped a photo.

Brogan knew his dad was attractive—and famous—but that didn't make the unwanted attention any less rude. Heat rushed around his head and neck. "Hey! Could you not?"

The woman tossed her dark brown curls in defiance, though her cheeks reddened.

"Calm down, buddy." His dad stepped between him and the woman. He made Brogan lock eyes with him. "It's tacky," he said loud enough for everyone to hear, "but no reason for you to lose your cool." He lowered his voice. "I've been very successful, and with that comes some annoying boundary issues with strangers. But let's be grateful, okay?"

"I just hate that people always take your photo, and now paparazzi are starting to take mine. Even at school. It's creepy. And last night—"

He couldn't finish. And when he saw the concern in his dad's eyes, Brogan wished he hadn't said anything at all.

"What happened last night, Brogan?" His dad crossed his arms —a sign that he meant business.

Brogan sighed. "I went to Mardell's birthday party."

His dad's jaw clenched. "Didn't I tell you not to go to places like that without a bodyguard? Don't you remember Prague?"

"Geez, Dad. How could I forget? I was the one who was lifted by my shirt collar toward that van."

"And if it hadn't been for Karel's quick reflexes, you might not be here." He pointed to the ground, accentuating the veins in his hand and forearm.

"But I was nine! And it's New York. There are way more important kids at my school and at that party. I'm just a CEO's son. Some of their parents are diplomats."

"You are an easier ransom than a diplomat."

Brogan was tired of this argument. "I can't always be babysat. I'm seventeen as of two weeks ago, and you've raised me to be a fighter. Besides, last night was weird. It wasn't normal. It wasn't *natural.*"

His dad cocked his head to the side, still breathing hard, but a softer, more fearful expression swept over his eyes. "What do you mean? How was it not natural?"

Brogan detailed the experience of falling into a darkened room, the creepy voice, and the bizarre alternate universe he was pulled back from by a stranger who somehow knew he was there.

His dad's eyes narrowed. "Okay. Let's get through this work-out, and I'll think about that further. I love you, son." He hugged Brogan tighter than usual and patted his shoulder. "Now twenty-five tricep push-ups. Go!"

. . .

ONE GRUELING WORKOUT LATER, Brogan found his quads giving way, making his gait awkward and unsure. His dad had no trouble marching home despite the extended squat sequences. His stride was actually faster and longer than usual. Brogan jogged every few steps to keep up.

Dad held the heavy townhouse door open for him but said nothing more. He strode straight to his office on the second floor and closed the door, which closed Brogan out of any further discussion into what he was thinking.

Brogan huffed in disbelief. Weren't they supposed to talk or something? The darkened door loomed over him—a symbol of his father's dismissal.

He swallowed his frustration and grief and climbed to his fourth-floor bedroom, onto the balcony overlooking Eighty-Second Street. He shed the gi, fell into his chaise lounge, and stared up at the clouds. A stray red leaf landed on his chest and stuck to the sweat. How did his father have the ability to make him feel so loved and so rejected all in the same day?

When Brogan was a child, his father's approval meant everything. Whatever it took—saying the right things, winning his soccer games, acting in a community play—Brogan lived for the light from his father's eyes. But lately, praise always seemed accompanied by criticism.

Loneliness began its familiar choke.

Bleep bleep. Bloop bloop. He pulled his phone to his ear. "Emmy. Thank God. I was about to spiral out."

"Brogan! Why didn't you call? I caught you in time?"

"Yeah." He swallowed hard, embarrassed, but he could trust Em. She was the only one who had noticed his periodic crashes, and since he didn't need to hide it from her, he welcomed her interference.

"Don't move. Just relax. I can be there in ten minutes."

He rested his head on the chaise's soft cushion, took deep breaths, and stared at the cloud formations. One reminded him of a character from *Moose Tracks*, the weird cartoon Emmy always snorted over and then made him watch ridiculous clips where the bunny died in a new gruesome way on each episode. Thank God Emmy was shallow. Who knew he needed a friend like that?

"Brogan!" Emmy called in a panicked voice from the door into Brogan's bedroom.

"Out here, Em." His voice sounded far away, even to him.

She burst through the balcony doors. "Here. Drink this." She pressed a cold water bottle against his bare chest.

He shot up. "Emmy!"

She snickered and leaned against the railing. "There he is."

"Was that necessary?" He laughed with her as he twisted the cap.

"It's just diagnostic." She pointed at his forehead. "You weren't lost too deep in there."

He grabbed her finger and twisted it enough to feign cruelty. "Yeah, you called at the right time. Tell me how things went with Mardell."

"Ow!" She yanked her finger free before her face lit up. "You saw that?"

"I *instigated* that, after the kid wouldn't stop staring."

"Really? At me? I always took him for the type that would go for—"

"He's a dude, Em. He goes for looks, at least at first."

"Yeah? I bet after hanging with you, I could interest a dweller of the deep at second."

Brogan chuckled. "Mardell is pretty light. Just smarter than you."

She hit him and giggled. Things must have gone well for her to smile like that. Then she added, "You left early."

He stood and walked inside, not wanting her to notice any angst over the event of the night before. "I wasn't feeling it. Sorry about the shirtlessness."

"Meh. You're too much like family for it to do anything other than disgust me a little."

He picked up a semi-clean shirt from the floor and pulled it over his head. "No need for either of us to be scarred for life."

She followed him inside, sank into his leather recliner, and draped her legs over the arm. "When are you going to a therapist, Brogan?"

He lay on the floor and let the cool marble tile draw the heat from his muscles. "Dad doesn't believe in them. He keeps saying a good workout fixes everything."

"I don't want you to become half-zombie like him, Brogan. We all love us some Uncle Leo, but he's never dealt with—"

"Yeah, I know." Brogan cut her short, not wanting to deal with his mom's death at that moment either. Adding a completely different trauma wouldn't bode well with the dark emo hole on whose edge he had been teetering.

She pulled out her iPad, plopped on the floor next to Brogan, and started an episode of *Moose Tracks*.

"Seriously, Em?"

"Shh. Just let the mindlessness take you." She propped the screen up and cackled over the fake animal cruelty. It was actually kind of funny, but he couldn't take more than three episodes.

"Are you missing a social event by being here?" he asked.

Emmy jumped up. "Yes. But you know"—she pinched his cheek—"family first. If you're done being needy, I'ma head out. No chance I can convince you to come to—"

"Bye, Em." He waved her out. "Thanks."

"Ugh. See ya, loser."

CHAPTER THREE

SEVENTEEN HUNDRED MILES AWAY, in small-town America, a normal teenaged girl with an abnormally scarred face made her way to school. There were no town cars or chauffeurs or towering buildings on the landscape.

Daisy's four-door junker choked at the last stoplight. Despite the occasional cough, a dent in her front fender, and the fact that her paint had faded beneath the scorching high-plains Colorado sun, this car just kept rolling through life. The car was her soul sister. So much so that she'd named her Maisie.

A sporty, silver two-door pulled up beside them. A girl with straight blond hair stared ahead without acknowledging Daisy, as if their mothers weren't best friends or they hadn't known each other since childhood.

Daisy rolled her eyes. Two more years and she'd be in college —somewhere far away from this depressing, six-stoplight town. In the meantime, she needed to get through each miserable day at Layton High School without letting herself adopt the insecurities that ran deep within the student body.

Yeah, okay, she'd already failed at that. But at least she *knew* and could address them with therapy later.

Her radio suddenly blared, "These boots were made for walkin," as if Maisie needed to communicate solidarity with her. The radio worked only at random, and when it did, Daisy couldn't turn it off.

If you can't beat 'em . . .

Daisy belted out the words to the song: "And that's just what they'll do. One of these days these boots are gonna wal—" The radio stopped mid-bellow, leaving Daisy to scream the last line unaccompanied.

Daisy turned toward Julie, who met her gaze this time. Julie's mouth quirked before she looked back at the road, punched the accelerator, and sped away.

Daisy and Maisie puttered on, eventually into the student parking near the back end of the school. Maisie shook as her engine died.

"Poor old girl." Daisy stepped onto the asphalt and limped toward the school's back doors—the ones right next to her locker. She'd figured out exactly where to park to shorten the distance she had to hobble each day.

When she pulled the door handle, it resisted. She checked her watch. It was 7:44 a.m., six minutes before lock time. She sighed. It would be a pain to limp all the way around the south wing just to go through the main doors. It would make her late for class too.

She pounded on the door instead. A boy opened it, laughing. Daisy wasn't sure who he was expecting to see, but it wasn't her. As their eyes met, his expression cooled and the smile stiffened on his face.

"Um . . . hey, Daisy. Principal Tecklenburg announced they would keep the back doors locked in the morning. You must have missed the announcement yesterday."

Yep. She must have been wearing her earbuds at the end of art class, as always. Since she avoided organized activities, announcements didn't typically pertain to her.

"Thanks, Dean."

He half-smiled—the kind of smile that just stretched one's lips out sideways and avoided exchanging any actual emotion—then walked away with his eyes focused on the ground.

You'd think, after four years, he could at least show a couple of teeth when he smiled.

SHE HEARD Dean's infectious laughter three times before lunch. Then he sat at the library table closest to her during study hall.

Agitated, Daisy avoided the hallway he typically walked through on his way to math. She'd had enough hopeless titillation for the day.

Finally, the blink of fluorescent lights greeted her for sixth period—her last class on Thursdays. She and Maisie would be cruising in exactly fifty-five minutes.

She stifled a deep-seated groan before it could escape her chest. Was it Dean Whitley day? Because he sat in the used-to-be-empty desk next to hers. Resignation slowed her hobble, but cruel fate still forced her butt into the seat.

"Settle down, everyone." Mr. Kobe waited for the kids to stop talking. "You may have noticed another student in our class. Dean transferred to our unit this afternoon so he could have fourth period for his local government internship. Congratulations, Dean."

Mr. Kobe grabbed a sheet of paper from his desk. "That means you have new group assignment partners."

Daisy tensed.

"Daisy Bloom, Julie Rampart, and Dean Whitley, you will present the Ming Dynasty."

She wanted to chuck something hard at Mr. Kobe, but opted instead to grip her desk. She chanced a peek at Dean, who nailed her with his full gaze. Caught, she returned his tepid lip-stretch smile from earlier that morning.

Dean picked up his desk and circled it around to Daisy and Julie. "Let's talk about how we want to break up the research."

Usually Daisy did all of the work on group projects. At least Dean was smart and worked hard. She didn't crush for nothing.

He continued, "Shall we read the introduction on pages 233 through 236 individually, then brainstorm creative ways to introduce our unit? I can cover the military."

"I want to study the royalty stuff," Julie offered.

Daisy stared at Julie, stunned, because Julie had never contributed to their group projects in the past.

"Daisy, you okay to cover art?" Dean asked.

Julie batted her big, brown eyes toward Dean. "We can meet at my house after school Friday to continue working together."

Dean's cheeks reddened. "Sounds great! I actually have been watching this cool Chinese drama online. It demonstrates the murderous competition for power in the upper echelons of their society. We could work hard, then reward ourselves with an episode for inspiration."

Huh. Dean watched Chinese dramas.

"Oh, wow. I'll make sure we're stocked up on popcorn and drinks. Maybe my mom will let us order pizza. Dean, you'll love our home theater. Dad built it himself."

Daisy hadn't contributed a single word. She simply watched in horror as her frenemy flirted with Dean hecking Whitley.

The bell released them.

She grabbed her books and stood. "Should I just meet you both tomorrow at Julie's?"

Julie raised an eyebrow in her direction. "Sure."

Dean didn't respond or shift his gaze.

If she could zoom outta class she would have, but her limp held every other step back like she'd stepped in glue.

"Why do you watch Chinese dramas?" Julie's voice lingered behind her, evoking memories of their preteen summer sleepovers.

Daisy submerged herself into the din of students slamming lockers and sighed. At least it was time to get out of there.

"I'M HOME!" Daisy expected her announcement to echo through an empty house.

Dad usually met with parishioners in the evening and

Mom . . . well, Daisy never actually figured out what it was Mom did throughout the day. Her gifts were social and she knew everyone in town. Maybe she organized events for the local junior college or something. She'd finally left the high school alone once she realized her daughter skipped all dances and pep rallies and fundraisers and plays and anything that involved being there.

"Hey, sweetie."

Daisy jumped.

Her dad chuckled. "Sorry. My appointments all canceled this evening, so I'm haunting the house."

Daisy released her breath and smiled. "All canceled at once?"

"An unusual situation."

Dad wouldn't say much more. Private matters and small-town gossip combined poorly, so he kept a tight lid on it. He didn't even share stuff with Mom—probably a wise decision.

"But looks like I get to hang out with my little buddy. We haven't made pancakes in a while. Whadya say?" He gave Daisy the familiar goofy smile that melted a little of the ice around her heart.

"You don't have to tell me twice." She limped past him into the kitchen and pulled down all of the pancake paraphernalia.

She and Dad didn't just plop batter onto a hot skillet. They had been practicing drawing pancakes for the last few years. The idea was to squirt batter from a bottle in shapes, then fill the shapes in with the rest of the batter. The batter that was on the skillet longer was darker. You kind of had to calculate backward, which was part of the acquired skill.

The smell of freshly baked pancakes filled the kitchen. Her dad tended to rush the process at this point, as his stomach growled.

"Dad, the tempting smell is part of the artistic challenge." She pointed at his creation. "These penguins are cute."

He scowled. "They're squirrels."

Daisy squinted. "So these blobs are acorns and not penguin poop?"

He flicked maple syrup on her nose. "If you draw another Mona Lisa, I'm done. You get to make all the pancakes."

"Don't hate me because I'm better than you." She wiped the syrup off her nose and licked her finger. "If it helps, you can show me up on reading Akkadian tablets next. I'm dying to know how Enkidu becomes civilized by copulating with a prostitute."

Her dad had picked up a love of ancient Near Eastern linguistics in seminary. That love had rubbed off on Daisy over the years.

He laughed. "And here I was so proud of keeping you from the filth on television."

"You did your best, Pastor Bloom, but it's hard to fight human nature. Here, I'll make you a pancake of that scene."

He peeled the batter bottle from her grasp. "I'd rather you didn't. Instead, I'll draw you struggling over cuneiform."

"That doesn't look like me . . . or even like a person."

"Shh. Just eat the squirrel and clean the mixing bowl."

Once they ate and finished cleaning the kitchen, Dad gave Daisy a piggyback ride into the library.

"Dad, duck extra low under the door frame. I don't need any more scars on my head."

He did as commanded and plopped her onto her desk chair. The leather seat spun with a squeak.

"Start with the Zukru Festival," he said. "I want you to compare it with the other Bronze-Age Semitic ceremonies."

She stared up at the poster displaying Cuneiform wedges. To be honest, trying to read old tablets made her eyes cross, but her father had taught her that all challenges ended with reward, if we fight through the difficulties. So far it had been true of learning, but she waited for the day it would be true of her daily rejection at school.

They were both deep in cuneiform when a melodic voice rang from the living room. "I'm home! Sweetie?"

Her mother's beautiful face, perfectly framed by deep auburn curls, peered around the library door. She smiled at her husband. "Hi, Dave." Her pouty lips pursed as she kissed the air toward him, and he blushed.

Her father's unabashed admiration of her mother never ceased to amaze Daisy. Maybe one day she could meet a man who looked at her with a fraction of that kind of love.

"What are you studying this week?" Daisy's mom glided over and perched on her husband's knee.

Maybe Daisy ought to give them some privacy. She was about to peace out when her mother said something interesting.

"Why on earth do you keep that painting around?"

The high pitch in her voice bespoke annoyance. Odd, considering the painting had been there for years and, before this house, it hung in the living room back in Denver.

Daisy focused her full attention on her parents.

"We've already discussed it, Phee. If we need to talk about it again, this isn't the right time." He shifted his eyes in Daisy's direction.

Daisy turned and stared again at the landscape's vivid hues and bold brushstrokes. Despite the audacity of the color, it maintained subtleties in a way hard to emulate as a painter. It was so masterfully rendered, she wished she could enter the field of flowers. When she was little, she had even dreamed she was there, smelling the deep, indescribable aromas such a place would emit in real life.

"Why don't you like it, Mom?"

As if noticing Daisy for the first time, her mother smiled. "That tacky old thing of your father's?" She hopped up and sauntered from the room.

The painting was *not* tacky.

"Dad, if she ever wants to throw it out, can I have it?"

"She's not throwing it out." He followed his wife from the room, probably to finish the conversation Daisy wanted to hear.

She stretched her arms overhead. Time for bed anyway. Perhaps she could hear important tidbits as she hobbled up the staircase. "Goodnight, parents!" she yelled as she passed the second floor.

Her dad opened their bedroom door. "Goodnight, sweetie. Mom says goodnight too."

Sure she does. Daisy kept the thought to herself, merely saying, "Okay. Sweet dreams to you both."

. . .

DAISY CONTINUED through her bedtime routine. The closer she came to falling asleep, the more her chest fluttered in excitement. She tried not to glance in the mirror, but the gashy scar over her left eye accosted her glance just as she turned off the bathroom light. She winced. The acne and her perpetual braces were a touch of evil genius. It would take forever to get the glance of her face out of her mind's eye.

She pulled the covers over her shoulders with a sigh. She had been training for weeks for tonight's mission, so she needed to calm down and let sleep pull her in.

Her attention lingered on the night sky outside her window—stars shone brighter out in the middle of nowhere. The harsh prairie wind blew dried cottonwood leaves around the yard.

Her eyes grew heavy with sleep, and then . . . she stood at attention in a round gymnasium, light pouring over her from above. A beautiful woman with white curls studied her.

Daisy knelt on one knee. "Greetings, my Parshant."

Her commander smiled. "Rise, Boshem. I'm glad you are in good form this week. You have new orders."

"Yes, Parshant." Daisy rose and planted her feet shoulder-width apart, her hands clasped behind her back.

"We've received word of a powerful, magical dagger stolen from the Houdar people." An image of a ruby-encrusted blade suddenly floated between them. "You can guess who took it, and you are being sent to retrieve it."

Easy. By now, navigating the castle's corridors and passageways felt like second nature to Daisy. The king responsible for stealing the dagger never seemed to learn—he often stole what did not belong to him—but he never hung on to the treasures, thanks to Daisy. The thought prompted a giggle from Daisy, which she quickly stifled. She drew herself to attention.

"At ease, Daisy. It's almost humorous to me too. Why does he keep taking what isn't his?"

"How should I access the castle this time? He's already discovered how to keep me from materializing inside the castle walls, so that's out."

"Yes. He may be testing you, trying to find your limits." The commander thought for a moment. "You scaled the walls last time, so I suspect he's smoothed the stones around the treasury."

"I haven't used cables yet. I can shoot one end into the wooden roof of the guard room and pull myself up."

"Why not? Boshem, I'm going to have you materialize a bit farther from the outer wall this time. There's a park half a mile from the gates." Her commander drew a map in the air using light as if it were a marker on a white board. Wherever her finger traced, a residual light remained in its path. "Here is where you will land. Pull your cloak over and you will be eighty percent transparent. At night, that should be sufficient. Are you ready?"

Daisy was more than ready. Her dream body felt limitless. And with the training she'd received from her Parshant over the past year, she could sneak past any guards.

Daisy smirked. "Yes, Parshant. Just waiting for the portal."

A black doorway materialized between them.

"Go with strength, Boshem."

Daisy nodded and ran through the door.

On the other side, trees surrounded her. She fought through a few scratchy shrubs to get to the road, which she followed to the castle. Then she climbed the outer wall as if she were rock climbing at a gym. Her cloak flapped more than expected, but she was quick enough that she doubted it attracted attention. Once on the top, she could climb a few rooftops and shoot her rope to the treasury tower.

She rarely encountered assailants, but it was no reason to drop her guard. The king's soldiers always stood a foot or more taller than she did, and she wasn't keen to know how well they fought. In fact, her ability to remain cloaked and darkened might have been the only reason she succeeded so often.

The arrow at the end of the cable whooshed overhead and lodged itself into the roof. From there, she could swing through the window. Using her gymnastics training, she pulled herself up by the power of her arms alone, avoiding the noise of her feet against the surface. Her biceps burned with fatigue, and she massaged them as soon as she found a ledge. Her dream body followed similar laws as her real body —the difference was that here her body wasn't broken. That, and the fact that Parshant had been upping the intensity at training. This body spent four or five hours a night in the gym.

She swung through the castle window into a darkened room, then pulled a cloth around her face that allowed her to see. On a table, next to an elaborate crown, lay the stolen dagger. Its deep, red ruby winked at her. She'd never touch the other jewels—she wasn't a thief. Just. Grab. That.

As she stretched her hand toward it, a light flashed. It blinded her for a second. When her vision cleared, she couldn't move her arm. She couldn't move anything. She was frozen.

A light grew in the tower, and someone tore the cloth from her face.

"Time to see you better, thief." The deep, calm voice came from behind her, and she could only make out the blur of a tall, strong figure from her frozen periphery.

He moved around her, as if viewing her from every angle. A swooshing sound indicated that he unsheathed a sword.

For the first time ever during one of her missions, she experienced a rush of fear. If she could have winced, she would have. Another swoosh followed, but the blade never made the contact she expected.

"You are not solid."

That was news to Daisy. She'd always thought she was really in this world, somehow.

The man snorted in disbelief. "Interesting magic, though my spell still holds you." He chanted something she didn't understand until a blinding pain filled her entire being.

. . .

Daisy bolted upright in bed, sheets sticking to her sweaty body. Her phone said it was 5:57 a.m.—three minutes before her alarm was set to go off.

What had just happened? She'd never been caught or even been mildly unsuccessful in her dream missions. Who was the man in her dream, and what spell had he used to stop her?

She reached for her phone and typed notes so she wouldn't forget the details. Her Parshant might know what went wrong. They would need to talk it out tonight.

She groaned. A whole day before she could talk to Parshant? She couldn't sleep again now. It was time to shower and get ready for school.

Daisy threw off her covers and clamored out of bed. Her knee gave way at her first step, and she whimpered. She had forgotten for a minute that she had a mess for a knee.

The day could not go fast enough. Daisy wanted to know what happened in her dream, but she knew by experience she wouldn't be able to sleep early, even if she could fake being sick at school. Might as well read about Ming Dynasty imperial kilns.

She groaned. She had to go to Julie's house after school. With Dean.

Fantastic day, this.

She threw herself into Ming art over lunch and made sure the volume of her research was overwhelming, even for Dean's standards. When study hall dragged on, she organized and theorized her research. What was the significance of the five-clawed dragon? Why did the king possess his own kiln? How much did European art affect Ming painting? The sweeping movement of their compositions reminded her of Rubens—sans the fat, naked ladies. Would a comparison be helpful?

Ming cloisonné enamel legitimately occupied her attention for an entire fifteen minutes, until an image of the Houdar dagger flashed in her memory. Its finely enameled and bejeweled handle held its own against anything she saw in the Ming treasures.

In art class, she sketched the dagger in color. Its finely detailed metalwork came back to her memory with each stroke. Then she remembered. The ruby *winked*. Why did her mind describe it as a *wink*? It's a magical object. Was it warning her of the trap?

A bright white light flashed in her eyes, breaking her concentration. She looked around at the now-empty art room and tore out her earbuds.

Mr. Wells laughed at her dramatic move. "School's been out for ten minutes, Daisy. I was about to tap on your shoulder, but a truck drove by and reflected the sun through the window." He approached her board and studied the dagger. "That's interesting. Your mind always manages to come up with unusual stuff."

She closed her notebook quickly. "Yeah. It's scary in here."

He smiled and shook his head. "Clean your mess and get out of here. You're late for the weekend."

"Yep." She *was* late for the group project meeting. She gathered her things and hobbled out to Maisie as quickly as she could.

DAISY BREATHED heavy as she rang the doorbell. It had taken some creative maneuvering to reach the door. Julie's parents were farmers, and their house sat on a quaint, fairytale-like hill in the country. Guest parking was at the bottom of a sweeping lawn. The dogs recognized Daisy and kept trying to jump on her as she tumbled up the walk.

Julie's mom, a spritely blond woman with an athletic posture, opened the door. "Daisy? It's been ages. Are you looking for your mom? She left an hour ago."

"Hi, Minni. Actually, a group of us are working on a project. Julie said we could meet here."

Minni lowered her voice and leaned forward. "Is that why that sweet kid is here? I was hoping Julie had finally chosen a classier boyfriend."

Daisy willed the grimace from her face. Few people knew about her quick romance with Dean back in middle school, and certainly none of the adults. "Sorry to disappoint you."

Minni wrinkled her nose and laughed in a loud, infectious way. "Darlin, if I get to see you, I can't be disappointed." She looked Daisy over with a genuine smile and giggled as she straightened Daisy's hair in a maternal gesture. "Did our dogs accost you? I can't believe how fast you girls are growing. Let me take your bag into the living room."

Minni grabbed the backpack off Daisy's shoulder. She had to hoist it up and shift her body under its significant weight. "Oh, girl, you're the top of the class for a reason, aren't you? Do you carry the whole library with you?"

"Minni, I can get that—"

"Nonsense. You just climbed Everest with this thing. Come on in."

Daisy's posture straightened and her limp eased without all the weight.

Minni called, "Julie, look who's here!" as they walked to the living room.

Julie managed to turn her head far enough to the side to recognize Daisy before she pivoted back into Dean's personal space.

Minni dropped the backpack on the table and tilted her head toward her daughter. "Offer your friend a soda or something . . . geez. What are we teaching you?"

Julie's cheeks reddened and she said, "Daisy, you want anything?"

Daisy kerplunked herself next to her bag. "It's okay."

"Get her water, at least. You had a lineup of options for Dean."

Julie ran into the kitchen and came back with bottled water, sparkling water, Coca-Cola, Sprite, and ginger ale.

"Here. Go crazy." Julie set them on the table next to Daisy, then moved her stuff to the other side of Dean.

"Thanks." A ginger ale *did* sound refreshing.

"So Dean, like I was saying, it would be really great to show that the aristocracy worked with the military."

"Doesn't that go without saying?" Daisy asked. "I mean, all monarchies depend on having total control of the military. It's the source of their power."

Julie glared at her.

"Yeah, I was just explaining it." Dean pulled out a chart. "It might make more sense for Julie to detail out the house of the emperor—namely his expansive network of wives and concubines."

Daisy's heart pattered at Dean's preparation.

"Oh." Julie looked confused. "So then the wives and concubines . . . what did they do?"

"They had babies, Julie," Daisy said, smiling at the horror on her former friend's face.

"But didn't they get to help with laws and ruling?"

To be fair, Daisy found the idea of an aristocratic baby farm abhorrent too. "Nope. They just kept the king happy."

Julie's voice rose as she squeaked, "That's terrible, Daisy!"

"But Daisy's right," Dean said. "Their job was to provide sons for the king and use that to ally their families to the throne. It wasn't a great life. They were rarely allowed to leave their palaces because they had to guard the claim that their children were rightful heirs. Talented women often grieved being wed to the emperor, even if their families had a lot to gain by it. The harem became a place of political maneuvering as the women vied for their own children's claim to power."

"Dean, I could never live like that. I'm so glad I'm not Chinese."

Dean smiled and patted Julie's shoulder. "You're glad you're not *Ming* Chinese. Modern China is . . . *modern*. And you should probably be glad you didn't live anywhere in that age. Women in European courts didn't fare much better."

Julie's eyes grew wide. "But I thought we were the free people."

Daisy didn't get to enjoy Julie's ignorance. Instead, her heart clinched as Dean rested his hand fully on Julie's shoulder and explained the whole of women's place in history. He then scratched her mid-back to sooth Julie's anxiety over the tragedy of women past.

Daisy *had* seen this Dean-Julie pairing coming, but the knowledge that her suspicions had been right didn't comfort her.

The rest of their "study time" dragged on with little production and a lot of flirting. The minutes ticked by slower than Walt Disney's cryogenic heartbeat.

They never even got to art. At six o'clock Daisy packed her things into her backpack. "I just emailed my part of the presentation to you both. Let me know if you see anything lacking."

"Mm-hmm . . . bye," was all she got from Julie.

"Thanks Daisy, I'm sure it's great." Dean turned and waved, his non-smile firmly in place.

IT DIDN'T TAKE LONG to get anywhere in Layton, and Daisy was soon at home in her bedroom. The TV blared from her parent's bedroom below. Her mother was watching an intense action thriller, the volume high enough to vibrate the walls. Daisy sighed. It was like her anxiety had a soundtrack.

She tried to read a story, but her concentration kept wandering to her dream from last night. She threw her book on the floor, put on soothing music, and turned out the lights. She couldn't wait to fall asleep.

But she awoke the next morning with nothing.

No dreams.

No Parshant to train her or even a dark dungeon in which to be held captive. Just one horrible day connected to the next by silence.

What had happened in that tower? Tears pressed hot against her eyes. She hadn't missed a dream in four years.

She hobbled to the bathroom, tears falling freely now. She washed her face, then looked in the mirror. A tall figure stood in the doorway behind her.

She screamed and spun around on her good leg, bracing herself.

But the doorway was empty.

She risked a step out into her room as heavy footsteps ran up her attic stairs. "Daisy!" Her door burst open and her dad's face rounded the corner.

"I'm fine. I'm sorry." She sniffed and willed herself to not cry. "Just spooked. I thought I saw something in the mirror behind me."

Dad released a deep breath and hugged her. "You scared me, punkin."

She fell into his embrace. As she sighed, her periphery vision caught movement again in the mirror.

Seriously. What had happened in her dream world?

CHAPTER FOUR

BACK IN NEW YORK, Brogan sat drawing at his desk. His phone exclaimed, "I'm a genius!" in an old man's voice—the sound bite he'd assigned as his dad's text tone.

He chuckled and perked up from the picture he had started hours ago. His pastels laid color so thick, he had lost himself in the joy of various layered hues on taupe paper. Drawing had been a good idea. So good, he'd done it every day this week.

Bright chalk now covered his hands, arms, and once-white shirt. He ran to the sink to scrub his fingers, but only enough so that they wouldn't discolor everything he touched, then picked up his phone. The text read: *Come to my office.*

Brogan darted downstairs. Dad's enormous office covered the second floor of their townhouse. Several workspaces and desks greeted Brogan at the door. These belonged to the various assistants who worked there during the day. Dad relaxed near the huge arched window facing Eighty-Second Street; his feet were lifted on the end of a reclining sofa.

Donna, the maid, waddled in with Brogan's favorite strawberry kombucha. She baulked at the sight of chalk thick over his shirt.

"My hands are clean." He held his palms open so she could approve.

She handed him the glass and tsked. "I'm never bringing that shirt back from the scrap heap, am I?" Her thick New York accent used to make him cringe, but Donna's colloquialisms had become endearing.

"Don't worry your pretty head about it, Donna." Brogan winked and kissed the air in her direction.

She guffawed. "You're trouble." She shook her head as she left the room.

His father's gaze followed the interaction, the lines around his eyes smiling.

Brogan plopped next to him. "Were you just wondering how your charming son could resemble you so much?"

His dad snorted. "You don't need any encouragement. I'm just proud of how much you pour yourself into things. You almost deserve all of the attention you get from those ridiculous gossip sites."

Brogan rolled his eyes. "I told you the paparazzi loves me, but it sounds like you already knew."

"How could I miss that horrible headline? 'Son of Technology King Is a Real Prince.' "

Brogan chuckled with him. "Don't remind me."

His dad put his arm around Brogan's shoulder. "Just don't let it get to your head, Lawrence."

He cringed. Only his dad insisted on using his first name, the ever-emasculating *Lawrence*. "How could I let anything that disgusting get to my head?" He put his feet up on the coffee table. A few papers shifted, revealing the corner of a small, brightly painted canvas. A rock formed in the pit of his stomach. His dad painted bright landscapes whenever his depression crept in. If it was really bad, he would take to writing in a strange, rune-type alphabet.

Brogan ventured to ask, "You're painting again?"

His dad folded the recliner, leaned toward the coffee table, grabbed the entire stack of papers and whatever they concealed, then dropped them on the floor.

He leaned back again and said, "I'm being transferred to the Seoul branch. My LCD patents were adopted in the Korean market, and they are struggling with implementation."

"So I'm finishing high school in Seoul?"

His father sighed and rubbed his temples. "No. You're staying with my parents."

"*Your* parents? Aren't they in Eastern Colorado? In the middle of nowhere?" Brogan knew from his father's stories that Eastern Colorado is very different from the rest of Colorado. There were no ski resorts or Front Range urban festivals. His father's hometown looked more like the old Dust Bowl photographs from the 1930s.

His dad took a drink and nodded his head.

This had to be a joke. He'd spent most of his life in Japan and missed it. Korea would be an easy shift culturally for him. "Don't they have international schools in Seoul?"

"That's beside the point." His father continued staring out the window. "I have decided that you should get to know your grandparents better."

"That doesn't make sense, Dad. I've never been away from you for a whole semester. You've always insisted I not be thrown into boarding schools because you're my parent. Can't we just visit Colorado over summer break?"

His father's face did not betray any emotion. "Layton High School doesn't have the kind of teachers you're used to, but I have already made arrangements with the principal. He has agreed to admit you as a part-time student while you learn from the excellent tutor I have hired. Your academics shouldn't be affected. You can replace whatever classes aren't challenging, and you will receive some of the more grounding benefits of a smaller community."

Brogan placed a hand over his mouth. His father had already hired a tutor. "You're serious, aren't you?" Bits of his soul began to whirl in a mess of confusion. "Since when?"

"Since Wednesday."

The whirl became anger. Years ago his father had actually *lectured him* on how, even though there was just the two of them, they were a family. And family stuck together.

Fury heated Brogan's head. "What about my future? What about Oxford?"

"The recruiter called me yesterday. I'd say you've got it in the bag."

"But Dad, I—"

"No arguing, Lawrence. It's done. You have a week to pack and say goodbye. You're on a plane next Saturday." His dad set down his drink and charged from the office.

And Brogan's heart broke.

BROGAN RAN up to his bedroom suite. Where did he put his phone? He tore through his pillows, throwing various items hard against the wall to work out his frustration.

He found it by the bathroom sink and dialed Emmy.

"Miss me already?" She yelled over loud music beating in the background.

"Em . . ." A rogue sob garbled his words.

Her background music died. "What's wrong? Where are you?"

"I-I'm home. Dad is sending me away . . ."

"Not possible, Brogan. Uncle Leo cried when you went to summer camp. He'd never be able to send you to boarding school."

"Not . . . boarding school." He took a deep breath. "He's going to Korea. I'm being sent to my grandparents in Colorado. He didn't say for how long, but knowing him I'll be there until I graduate."

"To the *hillbillies?* And excuse me, but I've seen pictures. You cannot call where they live *Colorado*. I'll be over in fifteen."

Ten minutes later Emmy fell breathlessly into his bedroom.

"You ran?" he asked, surprised. He'd never seen Emmy run outside of an air-conditioned gym.

"Yeah," she wheezed and crawled across the floor. "I almost

knocked over an old lady dawdling in our foyer. How are you doing? Tell me everything."

Brogan shook his head. "Dad barely spoke to me all week. Sunday through Friday afternoon all I got was 'good morning' or a few words on what I wanted for breakfast. I would look at him and he'd avert eye contact. Like, everything that happened over the weekend did something to him. Then he told me I'm going to his parents for *two years* while he works in Korea. And he's been painting those weird fauvist landscapes again."

"Ew. Leo's crazy streak is fierce for such a suave man."

"He freezes me out, Em. I have no idea why he makes some of his weirder decisions. Everything else is calculated, and then . . . *wham*. He throws me this bizarre, nonsensical stuff."

"So this is certain?"

"It's ironclad as far as I can tell. You know how he gets."

"Yep. I remember how you tried to drop equestrian camp last summer."

"He went ballistic, like I asked to punch babies for fun."

"It was his righteous indignation that tripped me out. He doesn't care about impressing anyone, so what's the big deal about dressage? It's almost like he wants you to be an old-timey king with swords and horses and stuff."

Brogan had wondered about that before. His dad was strict about martial arts. He even threw in Krav Maga last year because of its improvised weaponry training. Then the horses and the swimming and the gymnastics. His dad was training a killer ninja. "Maybe our family is schizophrenic."

Emmy merely sighed.

THE NEWS about Brogan's coming move spread through school like wildfire. He didn't realize so many people even knew who he was, but all week long well-wishers popped out of obscurity to say their goodbyes.

A cute girl stepped in front of Brogan Monday after lunch.

"Hi Brogan. I heard the news. We're all sad to see you go." Her pink lip gloss reflected the sunlight from the window behind him.

"Hi . . . Adrienne, right?" He recognized her from English Lit. He'd often stared at the blue tips in her hair, but this was the first time she'd spoken to him.

Her glossy lips spread into a smile. "Yeah. I wanted to tell you how impressed I was with your Byron presentation. I was working up the courage, but if I'd known you were leaving, I'd have asked you out or something sooner."

Her flirty smile twisted his gut. He breathed deep to keep his face and neck from lighting on fire. This move to nowhere disappointed him more and more. "Your Keats wasn't bad either. I'd never heard what he'd written for his epitaph. I thought about that for days."

Her eyes pulled him deeper, so he kept talking. "And who knows what the future holds. Hopefully I'll be back before senior year."

A masculine voice cleared its throat and said, "Mr. Lukes. Did you want to join our class today?" Dr. Self held the door to the science lab open. "And Miss Jonas, you're going to be late."

"See you, Brogan," Adrienne said before darting down the hallway. Her uniform skirt and ponytail swished from side to side with each step. Brogan marveled. Girls don't even have to try hard. Just the way they move makes boys crazy.

"Mr. Lukes." Dr. Self still held the door, smirking.

"Coming."

MARDELL MANEUVERED to be his lab partner and nodded with a compassionate half smile. "Hey, man, it's too bad you're moving. I was hoping to get to know you, now that . . . you know . . . Emmy and I are—"

Brogan laughed as he arranged the beakers and test tubes. "I didn't know you were. Sorry, I was a bit preoccupied last week."

"Makes sense. She said you're being sent to some post-apocalyptic dirt hole."

"She used the word *post-apocalyptic?*"

"Nah, but I can't repeat what she said. My mom doesn't want me to sound like I came from the gutter." He grinned and poured a blue solution from one of the beakers.

Brogan shrugged. "It's a small and isolated town. Spin doctor Emmy has impacted everyone's perception. People are looking at me like I've caught a fatal disease."

"As far as they're concerned, man, anything outside of Manhattan is for romps, vacations, or economic development. But small-town America isn't bad. I've spent a lot of time in rural Pennsylvania, and people there are fine. Just not used to the same stuff."

Brogan patted his friend's shoulder, appreciating that someone actually tried to relate to his situation. "I never believed New York was the center of the universe, but it's the first time I felt like I belonged somewhere. I worry my dad's hometown is a step in a very foreign direction."

The conversation paused as they watched how the control solution reacted to the blue variable.

"Just come back and visit often. Em will miss you, for sure."

Dr. Self hovered over their table. "Careful, boys. I know it's tempting to talk through lab, but you are handling chemicals." He studied their chart. "Looks good, but set an example."

Mardell lowered his voice. "It's bad enough my parents tell me my younger brother watches everything I do. Now I have to set an example for *you* kids."

Brogan shook his head. "Stop talking and focus on the dangerous chemicals, Mardell."

FRIDAY NIGHT, Brogan followed the directions Em had sent him. She wanted to hang out with him one last time before he left in the morning and had arranged some sort of weird goodbye rendezvous in true Emmy-style. The alleyway narrowed toward large, smelly trash bins. Rat squeaks permeated the garbage spilling around them. The experience at the club two weeks ago pressed irrational fears onto his chest. Each dark crevice might be large enough to cloak the creepy madman who could see in the dark.

He considered running back to the street until he recognized the symbol Emmy had described in her text—a lion silhouette painted on a heavy door. Still, he wasn't about to rush through another unknown doorway.

He peeled the door open, then used his foot to swing it outward. That freed his arms to tighten into fight mode as he peered in.

A hundred voices screamed, "Surprise!" just as a sick base started vibrating the walls inside.

Brogan nearly jumped out of his skin. *Emmy, you monster.* He patted his chest and let himself be pulled from the alley onto to the dance floor in the center of a large room. It seemed like all of his classmates were there. Em had even invited Davis.

After a few great songs with everyone dancing, the music quieted.

"Ahem." Emmy's official-sounding voice resounded through the sound system. "In honor of Brogan, tonight is all karaoke. Please keep dancing, but this weirdo is barely American, so we can't send him on his way without appealing to his Asian roots."

Brogan cringed at the stereotype, but then again, he *did* love karaoke.

"I'ma start us off with 'Yo My Frin' by Buff and the Autos."

Brogan watched Emmy belt out the popular tune with an awesome beat. As always, she owned the room. No one danced; instead, they watched her entire quirky performance. Mardell's gaze followed her like an obedient puppy. He may even have had his tongue out, drooling a little.

As soon as her song ended, the DJ played more dance music until another kid got up to sing. Then another and another.

Who's the real MVP, huh, Em? He smiled over at his cousin and thanked whatever god was out there for making the last two years so great.

It was the best night he'd ever had—despite never once using the bathroom.

As the party wound down, he felt the reality of his morning flight. Maybe it would have been easier had no one come or if Em hadn't been such an awesome best friend. Now the unknown, possibly empty landscape of his future threatened to swallow all hope. No, not a threat. Its teeth already drew blood.

A tipsy Emmy sat down hard next to him, her arm around his shoulder. "I'ma walk you home, Bro Bro."

"Uh . . . not likely. I think I should walk you home."

"Tomato tomahto."

"I don't expect you'll be awake at six in the morning to say goodbye either. So I'll relish your drunken blather the whole walk. Dang it, Em, your mom is not cool with you drinking. I'll be guilty by association."

"Oh Mahhm. Watchshe gonna do? Send you to Siberia?" she said, slurring as she screwed up her face while appearing to think deeply about her words. "It might be better than Leo's parents."

"You make a good point, Delinquent One. Promise me you won't keep doing this. I don't want my favorite family member to need a liver transplant before we're forty."

"Talk your buzz-kill talk when I'm sober, kay?" She leaned in close enough for him to get a terrible whiff of her breath.

He turned his head in disgust just as the last song ended.

Mardell sat on the other side of him. "I can take her home."

"Let me do it. Her mom won't murder me, but a boyfriend—"

Mardell's nodded with furrowed brows. "Good point. Hey, I'm going to talk with her about this. I'm not into frequent intoxication anyway."

Mardell's clear and sober eyes brought relief, and Brogan nodded his thanks.

Several kids hugged him or patted him on the back as they left. He hoisted Em's arm over his shoulder and waved his last goodbye to Mardell.

CHAPTER FIVE

A GRAYING YET STILL SPRITELY couple waited for Brogan outside the terminal of the small Colorado Springs airport. Aside from an occasional video chat, he hadn't seen them since they visited Japan back in the sixth grade. Their mannerisms would have been completely foreign had they not resembled his dad's so much.

"Lawrence? You might have been your father!" His grandmother's eyes glowed with love. "Joe, doesn't he look just like Leo?"

The older man nodded and grabbed Brogans suitcase. "Welcome, son." Without further greeting, he trudged toward the door.

He and his grandmother followed. She leaned in and said, "He's a man of few words. I talked to myself the whole way here."

"I suppose I was eavesdropping then?" His grandfather glanced sideways but kept walking. In the parking lot he chucked Brogan's suitcase onto the bed of a large pickup truck between bales of hay.

Brogan cringed. That suitcase was a work of art he'd purchased directly from the designer. Emmy had been so impressed with it that she made him pick out one for her, followed by a pair of shoes, then a coat, then a haircut. "I think you have a gift, Brog," she'd said.

Now his treasure sat on the bed of an old farm truck, surrounded by hay and dirt and who knows what else. He scanned the cab. It was too small to squeeze three people *and* his luggage. Brushing off the salty feeling, he told himself he could buy the suitcase again if he had to, and he didn't want to start his time here with a meltdown. His emotions had been tweaked enough.

As his grandfather drove down the highway, the city diminished behind them. They drove straight into a great expanse of nothingness.

Brogan sighed.

"I felt the same way when my parents moved here from South Carolina." His grandmother patted his head. "It grew on me. Over time."

He stiffened at her touch, unable to imagine enough time passing for this place to grow on him. A gust of wind picked up, throwing dozens of tumbleweeds across the highway. The bleak scenery stretched on despite their drama.

Mile marker after mile marker swished by. Three hours and 165 miles later, he extracted himself from the polyester seat. He stretched his back and took in the situation around him.

They stood on a spacious driveway behind a small farmhouse. Spacious was the appropriate word. There was little else on this foreign terrain but space. Two trees stood, missing large tufts of branches, as if they fought the desert for the few leafy bits remaining. Tractors and combines sat neatly in a row next to a large garage. Various machinery lay around an otherwise well-kept and tidy yard.

"How does anything even grow out here?"

He asked himself the question, but his grandfather answered, "Irrigation. We're in a river valley. Otherwise, nothing but yukka would live through a summer."

The bone-dry air confirmed his grandfather's report. Brogan searched his backpack. His dad had handed him chapstick at the airport without explanation. Now he knew why. "Thanks, Dad," he growled under his breath.

A herd of cats came out of nowhere and rushed his grandmother like a crazy pack of pop-idol fans. They mewed and stood on their hind feet, hailing their queen. She smiled at Brogan, delight in her eyes as if showing off her children. "They're missing lunch, I suppose." She hustled in through the back door of the house and returned with scraps of food.

His grandfather grabbed Brogan's suitcase from among the stacks of hay on his truck. The well-defined muscles on his large forearms shifted around with the movements. At sixty years old, his body exuded surprising strength.

"Do you still do the farming?" Brogan nodded toward the tractors.

"Yup. I could retire, but I'd be bored. I don't see the point of watching TV or moving into the fancy house your dad wanted to buy for us." His sturdy frame didn't even struggle as he hauled the large suitcase into the house. Brogan followed him up narrow wooden stairs and into a small bedroom that had been decorated with a masculine bedspread and matching curtains. "I talked Peg into taking down the flowery stuff."

"Thanks."

His grandfather placed his large, weathered hand on Brogan's shoulder. Green eyes, like his fathers, like his, peered down at him. "Make yourself at home, son."

The gesture almost softened him, but as Brogan sat on the twin bed and took in the room, despair flooded into the cavern where joy had only hinted its bloom. He collapsed backward and pulled out his phone. There was no signal and no available Wi-Fi.

He sat up and slammed his phone on the bedside table. He stood and paced exactly three steps before turning to pace back. The tiny room had a large window with a window seat but a closet too small for half the clothes he had shipped.

At least the fabrics wouldn't smell like this house—like forty years of fried bacon absorbed into every porous surface and cross-stitched pillow. He threw the window open, lit one of the candles on the desk, and sprayed scent neutralizer around the bed. He wrote Emmy a long email that he couldn't send due to the lack of internet access.

A phone rang throughout the house. He heard a loud bell from downstairs and a chirp from a small American football on his desk.

"Brogan!" his grandmother yelled from downstairs at a surprising decibel, adding to the chaos of Brogan's mind. "Your father is on the phone."

He picked up the strange football, which fell open as if it were a melon sliced in half. Inside were phone buttons and holes for sound. Perplexed, he held it to his ear.

"Hello?" he asked, wondering if he were the most gullible idiot on planet earth.

To his surprise, however, his dad's voice rang through. "Just checking to make sure you made it. Dad says there's no reception out there, which is why they only have the landline. How was the flight?"

"Better than the drive."

"Next time I'll charter a small plane to Layton. Sorry I didn't think of it."

Brogan didn't trust himself to respond to an apology. He didn't want Dad to call him petulant. "I'm talking through a football."

"They still have that thing? Oh, gotta go. I'm getting another call, " he said, rapidly shifting gears. "Love you, son."

The line clicked and disconnected.

Love?

"Dinner's ready!" his grandmother's voice called up to him.

He pressed his temples and made his way toward the stairs, which opened up to the dining and living room.

As he walked toward the table, three bright canvases caught his attention, each a landscape in the same vivid colors his father painted at home. Only, instead of creepy jungles, unattainable and twisty, these paintings invited the viewer into lush scenery. The first depicted a thick forest where strange animals sat on a branch above a rope swing. An auburn-haired girl kicked her feet off the ground, laughing. Another depicted a magnificent waterfall, flowing into a clear, blue pool. Vined flowers climbed up the cliffs on both sides. The third scene opened up into a desert with strange beehive structures in the distance. Runes like the ones he often found around the house surrounded the periphery of the canvas.

His grandfather sat himself at the table.

Brogan pointed at the paintings. "These are Dad's?"

His grandfather grunted an affirmative.

"What does this say?" His finger trailed along the runes.

The old man shrugged. "No idea. Leo's imagination, you know."

"Yeah, he still writes this stuff, but he won't talk about it."

His grandmother swept into the room and set a steaming hot casserole on the table and seated herself with great ceremony.

"It looks good, Peg." His grandfather tucked a napkin into his collar.

Brogan stared at the yellow, gelatinous square as he sat down. It smelled alright, but it certainly didn't adhere to keto.

"I can't get over how much you look like our Leo," his grandmother said with glistening eyes. "I hope you don't have the problems that plagued him. Girls were always driving by the property or calling our line and hanging up. I'm his mother, so of course I think he's handsome. But it was a *bit* much."

Brogan's grandfather guffawed. "Don't know what they were trying to accomplish. He only had eyes for the one. That boy would not be nearly so successful had she not jilted him. Drove him to conquer the world."

"Jilted? As in, my dad was rejected by a girl?" It seemed unlikely.

His grandmother patted his hand. "Of course, he met your mother at sports camp, and everything worked out for the better. The other married a local boy."

Brogan's dad did not talk about his past. When Brogan asked him about his school years, he firmly directed conversation elsewhere. Brogan never had a clear image of what growing up in America had been like for his dad.

Yet, here he was, stuck staring at shelves displaying porcelain dancing poodles, Celtic crosses, and calligraphic Bible verses. He couldn't have pictured this, so why try picturing relationships?

Brogan afforded a half glance at his grandfather. "So, what should I call you?"

His grandparents stopped serving the dinner and stared at him with raised eyebrows.

"I feel strange calling you Grandpa and Grandma. I barely know you." He knew he was being a brat, but something would blow if he didn't relieve some of the steam.

The old couple shared a glance with each other, then peered back at Brogan, but he would not give in to guilt.

His grandfather cleared his throat. "Call me Joe. I don't care."

His grandmother's eyes softened and she smiled. "I suppose you can call me Peggy. This is quite a shock for you, isn't it?"

Brogan shrugged. "Don't you think it's weird? Dad wasn't concerned about me connecting with his past before, so why now? And why to this degree?"

Joe nodded. "He left under hard circumstances and never wanted to come back. But I couldn't venture to guess what he's thinking by sending you here. Peg and I are just as intrigued by it as you are. We're just happy to have you, Lawrence."

"He goes by Brogan, remember?" His grandmother patted his grandfather's hand.

Brogan moved cheesy chunks of gluten around on his plate through a lull in conversation. "If you don't have Wi-Fi, is there some other way for me to use my phone?"

"I've heard you can get a cell signal on the back porch or anywhere in the backyard," Peggy said, pointing. "But we've never had the internet. We're a little behind the times out here."

Joe halted his fork. "Your dad said you need it for school, so I called the cable company yesterday."

Peggy lifted her eyebrows. "You did?"

"Why not, if he needs it? They'll be out to set up a satellite Wednesday."

Brogan thanked the satellite gods and counted out four days until Wednesday. The rest of dinner was quiet, with the occasional witty observation from his grandmother met with a harrumph from his grandfather.

Joe stood and began clearing dishes. "It's time for bed."

Brogan stood to help. As soon as the dishes were washed, he ran to the back porch.

No. Signal.

He went outside where a frigid blast of air pelted him. Still no signal. It wasn't this cold when they'd rolled in.

Joe leaned out the back door. "The signal is spotty. You might as well come in."

"The temperature—"

"It changes fast around here. A cold front followed us home."

Brogan trudged up the stairs to his new bedroom. He'd left the window open and now frozen wind blasted through it. He slammed the window closed. Little good it did; the cold seeped right through it. He threw on a puffy coat and curled onto his bed. Without the internet, he had nothing to do, except turn off his lamp and hope for sleep.

A HEAVY KNOCK woke Brogan the next morning.

"We're leaving at 7:30, so be ready," Joe's deep voice announced from behind the closed door. "And dress warm."

"Leaving?" Brogan rubbed his eyes and picked up his phone. It was only 6:30, and it was the weekend.

He stumbled downstairs to the kitchen. "What's for breakfast and where are we going?"

Joe handed him a plate with bacon and scrambled eggs. "Orange juice in the fridge. We're going to church."

"Church?"

"Yes, dear." Peggy strolled into the kitchen wearing subdued designer jewelry over a navy cotton dress.

"Is that necklace David York?"

She shrugged. "Your father bought it for me, and I've always thought it was quite nice."

Yeah, eighty-thousand-dollars nice. Did she know each ruby could go for an easy ten grand? He chuckled to himself.

Whelp, if Peggy was throwing down David York, he might as well toss on his Italian-cut, double-breasted navy pinstripes . . . for church.

Normally he'd have refused to go at all, but it had just become an occasion, like a gallery opening. Besides, he had yet to understand how his grandparents worked. They hadn't *asked*, they *told* him he was going. If they were anything like Dad, he needed to pinpoint their Achilles heel for getting out of such things.

He grabbed his food and ran upstairs to prepare.

CHAPTER SIX

DAISY WATCHED each breath escape her mouth in a white puff. The crisp air inside the worn pickup truck wouldn't be warm by the time they arrived because the drive only took five minutes. She stared at old, brick houses. Yellow lights warmed them from the inside while the frost turned everything a shade of light gray on the outside. Soon snow would cover it all with a blanket of white.

She wondered if her imagination might be overactive, but imagination didn't explain the consistent and vivid dreams she started having four years ago. Nor did it explain why they stopped suddenly after her botched mission. Or why she kept seeing things from the corners of her eyes.

"—wouldn't you say so, Daisy?" Her dad's direct address forced her to relinquish her train of thought.

"Hmm? About what?" She looked over at her father in the driver's seat, her mother in between them.

Her mother rolled her eyes. "Sweetie, I wish you wouldn't disappear like that."

Daisy stiffened and stared back out the passenger side window. "I was only thinking."

"About what?"

Her mother wasn't interested in her thoughts. She would use them to point out idleness or some other deficiency.

"Calm down, Phee. She doesn't need to listen to everything I say. I wasn't technically speaking to her anyway."

"She needs to come down from the clouds she swims around in all the time. It's ridiculous. She's almost seventeen."

Daisy turned her head enough to see her dad mouth the words, "She's fine" as he parked the truck. He hopped out and ran around to help Daisy step down from the cab. It wasn't necessary, but it did make it easier on her knee. He squeezed her shoulders and kissed her head before turning to help her beautiful mother make an entrance.

Ophelia Bloom was a knockout. Ten out of ten. Daisy had even heard the boys in her class joke that she was an eleven.

The same classmates would shift their eyes away from Daisy. Revolted expressions took in her scars, her twice-broken nose, the mangled teeth that her braces couldn't seem to straighten, and her perpetual limp.

She tried to recite 1 Peter 3:3–4 to herself again: *Your beauty should not come from outward adornment . . . Rather, it should be that of your inner self, the unfading beauty of a gentle and quiet spirit, which is of great worth in God's sight.* Saint Peter didn't understand the twenty-first century at all.

To make it worse, Daisy's mom had a thousand deluded ideas of how to fix her. "Try this haircut. Eat this antioxidant. Use these cosmetics."

All Daisy heard was, "You're so unattractive, even your mother thinks so." She resisted the urge to mock her mother's incredulity. The woman just couldn't accept that Daisy, *her own daughter,* could be—*gasp*— unattractive.

Daisy wiped a self-pitying tear before stopping in her tracks. Joe and Peggy Lukes sat on the bench outside of the church with an attractive young man tucked snuggly between them. And what was Mr. Handsome wearing? She'd never seen such a suave getup on the boys from Layton. It was the type of thing Hollywood actors wore for their premiers. Judging by the boy's scowl, he knew he didn't belong there too.

A chuckle escaped her throat. "It's a pretty cold morning to come early to pray for the service."

Peggy tittered. "We may have thought better had we known it was *this* cold. Daisy, let me introduce you to our grandso—"

A firm shoulder shoved Daisy to the side as her mother brushed passed. Daisy's knee gave way and her backpack nearly threw her off balance. She caught herself, but by the time she had straightened, her parents were already sentences deep in the conversation.

"This must be the grandson you've been talking about. You go by Brogan, right? I'm Ophelia. This is my daughter, Daisy, and my husband, David Bloom." Her mother didn't gesture or turn toward Daisy.

Daisy stared at the adults' backs. Brogan's frown didn't disappear as her mother talked with him, which made Daisy like him a little. Not *like-him* like him, because he was way out of her league. Dark hair, bright green eyes, thick eyelashes, carved lips, flawless skin. This kid was *princely*. But she appreciated anyone who could see through her mother's . . . arresting charms.

Daisy shivered. "Dad, can I have the keys? It's cold."

Her mother turned and glared at her.

Her father's eyes widened. "Oh, sweetie, of course." He tossed the keys, which she caught, and opened the doors in a flash. She limped into the sanctuary and threw her coat on the front pew. She needed to play something. Fast.

She wouldn't have a lot of time before people streamed in, so she pounded out her favorite Buff and the Autos song. She chose one of their ballads, so it might be confused for processional music. "I kissed my mother before we left for war," she sang to herself. Movement from the doorway signaled the end of her little vent sesh. She locked eyes on Brogan as he followed Joe and Peggy to the front of the sanctuary. He raised his eyebrows in a not-exactly-friendly way.

Whatever, Mr. Scowly-Face. She moved on to the hymnal.

She couldn't help feeling sorry for this Brogan kid. Early service was droll. It remained contemplative and old-fashioned even after the church moved to more modern music. Mostly old people attended, along with a handful of early risers. And *them*.

There was a strange clan of younger adults who took a more mystic approach to their faith. Something about the quiet style of first service drew them from every church in town. They swayed around in their seats with their eyes closed, barely singing. She would see their lips moving throughout the service as they whispered prayers.

From time to time, they approached Daisy and said unsettling things. "I see that you are a powerful warrior. The Lord showed me how you led twenty against a stronghold."

Daisy shivered just thinking about that one. It had transpired in her dream the night before. She had stormed a distant castle and retrieved two prisoners, and she *had* taken the twenty extra *praidas*—a type of martial artist.

After the sermon she plunked out the last hymn. Time to slip out and hobble home. There was no way she'd go to youth church today, as she was ninety-nine percent sure Julie would invite Dean along as arm candy.

A small commotion in the pews caught her attention. A line of Brogan's grandparents' friends snaked around him, introducing themselves. The expression on his face was taut with forced patience, and his eyes worked themselves into slits.

She labored down the stairs from the piano. Her backpack threw her balance off, but she managed not to fall on her face. The goal was to reach the door unnoticed and beeline home.

"Daisy!" Her mother's voice rose from among the hive of Brogan's admirers.

"Good heavens, woman, leave the kid alone," Daisy whispered under her breath. But her mother motioned with her hand that Daisy should come join the throng. There would be no peace if she ignored her.

Thunk-step-thunk-step. The sound of her limp opened passage into the circle like she was Moses. Gazes shifted in her direction. Even Brogan's angry eyes landed on her now-hot cheeks.

"Daisy, escort Brogan to youth church."

Youth church was the youth pastor's way to build community for teenagers on Sunday mornings.

Her mother was not reading this situation well. This kid wasn't ready to stay longer.

But she forced a smile at Brogan, who stared her down. Heat expanded from Daisy's cheeks to all over her head. She motioned for him to follow, and he broke out of the throng.

* * *

BROGAN HAD JUST SUFFERED through the weirdest series of pop songs, cold hymns, and chanting hippies, with a guilt-inducing sermon on top. Now he had to go to more church? Even pinstriped Italian suits couldn't fix this new low. His found his biggest frustration, though, in having a cell signal without a place to hide and call Em.

He scrolled through a long line of her texts demanding a photo of himself next to the latest newspaper as proof he still lived. She watched too many police shows.

Meanwhile, Quasimodo stopped in the church corridor and squeezed her thumb and middle finger around her temples. It was the same gesture his father used when an unpleasant task awaited him.

"What's wrong?" he asked.

"Nothing. I was going to go home early and skip youth church. But my mom will have kittens if I leave now." She looked him straight in the eyes. There was something familiar about her expression, if you ignored all the scars.

"Let's skip then," he said. "No one needs to know." Convenient, since he didn't want to go in the first place.

"I know you're new, Italian suit man, but in Layton no one gets to live anonymous, private lives. Everyone in this building knows what we do before we even do it."

Interesting. This was a situation Brogan had never encountered. Even in cities where he was the only kid of European descent for miles, people were too busy to care what he did. "Blame it on me."

"What?"

"Blame me. If we sneak away, you can say I wanted to call home. I'm about to test my boundaries anyway."

"But my mom—"

"I can be very persuasive. And you saw her. She already wants to adopt me."

Daisy scowled. "Probably right about that," she mumbled.

"Why talk to yourself when I'm right here?"

She crossed her arms and narrowed her eyes. "He thinks he's so suave with his suit and his plans," she said.

"Times a tickin' and I'm promisin' to take the blame. You don't have to trust me, but it's better than going where even you seem loathe to go."

Daisy's demeanor softened in resignation. "Fine. But if you think I'm going to pass the blame, you don't know me at all."

"I don't know you at all."

"Exactly."

This girl amused him. "Rhetoric isn't your strength, is it?"

She grunted and pointed to a door.

* * *

DAISY PLODDED THROUGH THE ALLEYWAY, hoping no one would notice the limping pastor's daughter fleeing with the most attractive man-child to ever grace the streets of Layton. She nearly cackled at the impossibility of their going unnoticed. Her mom's anger was a done deal, yet possibly less stressful than seeing Julie and Dean together in youth church.

Bringing boyfriends to church was Julie's modus operandi. As soon as she snagged one, they trailed on her arm to all youth group activities. Thinking about it only set her resolve in following Brogan.

"Wait a second." Daisy stopped walking. "Do you know where you're going?"

"Nope. It's too cold to stay outside though. We should find a cafe or something."

"No cafe near here. Our house is just a few blocks that way," she said, pointing ahead. "It's warm and it's got cookies."

Brogan walked the direction she pointed, but he slowed down and waited for her to keep up. "Actually, I have another objective. I really need to make a phone call. My grandparents have no cell reception and no internet, and right now there's a girl in New York wondering if I was murdered out here." He held up his phone and displayed an endless stream of texts from someone named Emmy.

"Your girlfriend?"

"Ew, no. My cousin."

Daisy pulled the phone screen closer so she could read: *Bro! Do I need to call the police? Are you ok? Please say you're alive.*

"Does she think we're savages?"

"That's what I told her." He winked. "I'd have texted her in church, but then she would have called nonstop until I answered."

"Here's my house. Call her now."

As she unlocked the door, she could hear the girl's frantic voice through Brogan's phone.

"Sorry, Em. My grandparents don't have cell reception or the internet."

Daisy could make out a high-pitched, "No internet?"

"Yeah, not yet anyway. I had to sneak to this girl's house so I could call you . . . Just a girl from church . . . Yes, my grandparents took me to church. Hey, can I call you back on FaceTime? Okay, give me a minute . . . Daisy, do you have Wi-Fi? The signal isn't consistent."

Daisy held out her hand for the phone. "It's easier for me to just type in the password. It's in ancient Urdu." She handed it back to Brogan's eager fingers.

A few seconds later a cute blond girl with big doe eyes stared through Brogan's phone. "Where are you again?"

"At Daisy's house. See." He turned in a circle with the phone facing outward. He stopped and pointed it at Daisy as she pulled the milk from the fridge. The girl in the picture flinched.

"Hi, I'm Daisy." She lifted the milk as a greeting. "I was in a car accident, thus the scar face." She pointed to her nose and the scars across her eye.

The girl nodded, her eyes wide. Brogan turned the phone back to him. "I have a hundred things to tell you, but I won't be able to until tomorrow—Wednesday at the latest."

Daisy had to tell him. "You know, the Lukes *do* have a land-line. You can look up their number in the phone book. It's old fashioned, but it still allows talking."

Brogan's jaw dropped. "You're a genius, Daisy!"

"Yeah, a genius." She handed Brogan the phonebook, then poured milk for their cookies. When she turned back, he was flipping through the yellow pages.

"The people are in the white section." She flipped it to Joe and Peg Lukes and pointed.

Brogan read the number to Emmy. "Call me this afternoon or something. I should be at the grandparents' by three o'clock New York time."

"I'll call at three. Bye, Brogan. Bye, Daisy."

Daisy warmed that Emmy would include her. "Bye, Emmy."

He set his phone down and his frame decompressed. "Thank you. It didn't occur to me to use the landline. I've never known someone without a cell phone."

"Joe and Peg don't have one because there's no signal at their place. Once you have your internet connection, you can boost your cell signal too."

Daisy set Brogan's cookies and milk on the far side of the table for him and sat in her usual chair. She loved dipping chocolate chip cookies in milk.

He curled his lip. "What are you doing?"

"Dipping cookies."

"It looks gross."

She laughed. "Are you even American?"

"Depends on who you ask. I've lived mostly overseas."

"Oh." Her comment now sounded more like a jerk thing to say. She held up her cookie. "You have to at least try this. Break the cookie in half so it's bite-sized, then dip it only long enough to soften the cookie. Don't dissolve it."

Brogan followed her instructions with a grimace before putting the saturated cookie into his mouth. "Iff okay, but too fugary." He swallowed and passed the small plate of cookies back to her. "I'm still not used to American sweets. Our cook always makes stuff in a Japanese or European style for me."

Daisy made a mental note: *Italian suit doesn't like sugar.*

* * *

BROGAN STARED over at this strange girl. Her blue eyes mimicked the ones that peered out from her mother's face that morning. That's where the similarities ended.

What must it be like to be a small-town beauty's daughter? He'd seen plenty of fashionable women groom their daughters to be as attractive as possible, but Daisy showed no signs of cosmetic care. Her straggly hair hid scars on the left side of her face, but she wasn't hopeless. A good surgeon could fix her nose. A dermatologist might clear her acne. The scars were gnarly.

"Mind if I ask what happened?" He waved his hand over his face.

"My mom flipped our car when I was thirteen. It was only a couple of months after we moved here from Denver. Being the new kid is tough enough in a small town. I don't advise facial trauma as a way to fit in."

He chuckled. "What about hallucinations?"

"Definitely sexier." She studied him with squinted eyes. "Why? You crazy?"

"Maybe."

"Some girls love drama. Man friends might be a harder sell though."

He laughed and said, "I've never had problems making *man friends*."

Daisy dipped her last cookie. "Maybe we're all a little crazy. Have you ever wondered how a person knows they're only hallucinating? What if they see things that no one else sees but are really there?"

"Like a superpower?"

"Yes. A lame superpower."

"The question is getting weirdly specific." This girl cracked him up.

She shrugged. "I have a strong imagination. It's probably time to head back to the church. Mind if I run upstairs for my gloves?"

He didn't, so Daisy hobbled upstairs, leaving him to wander through the house. The living room welcomed him with plenty of light, warm colors, and zero knickknacks. No television. Two short bookshelves with biblical reference materials flanked a fireplace. Only a family photo sat on the mantle. The library off the main room housed floor-to-ceiling bookshelves. Two desks sat inside the door, a little cluttered but with space to work. One book, *A Linguistic History of South-Eastern Europe*, lay on the smaller desk. On the other sat *Stories From the Ming Dynasty*. Multiple sticky notes hung from the edges of both books. It hadn't occurred to him that out here, in Forsakenville, there might be someone equal to his intellectual curiosity.

He smiled to himself and turned to exit the library. Something hanging on the wall knocked the breath from his lungs, and his body chilled. A bright painting, thick with oils, hung to the right of the doorway. The scene depicted a field of flowers, fierce in its multiplicity of colors. Not only was it his dad's style, but he had seen this field in his paintings before—just not quite as beautiful or brilliant as this. Instead of sorrow and heaviness, this one exuded joy and hope. Like the landscapes in his grandparents' house.

Anger churned deep in Brogan's chest. His dad had dragged him all over the world, from city to city, never allowing him to have a real home. No lasting friends. The man himself had been Brogan's connection to everything for his first fourteen years of life. Now, looking at this painting, the reality screamed at him. He didn't know his father at all. He certainly knew nothing about his past here in this small town. Dad had given this painting to someone. And it wasn't one of his weird, trippy landscapes but a lovely, sound-minded work of art.

Why? Who were these people?

This wasn't the place for him to deal with his emotions. He'd only recently learned to trust Emmy with things, and that was a big first for him. His MMA trainers had taught him to channel anger, so he sat down, breathed deep, and counted. *One, two . . . thirty-eight, thirty-nine, forty.*

Daisy's clopping limp announced her return.

"Do you like art?" She gestured to the painting and sat on top of the smaller desk.

"I do, but this one looks familiar. Do you know who painted it?"

"My dad's best friend from high school. I guess they were big nerds together or something, but neither of my parents will talk about him. To be honest, they sometimes fight over the painting. I've always wondered who he is. Like, do I see him at the grocery store, ignorant that a man I'm standing next to painted this thing in my house?"

Her gaze swept over his face as she asked, "Are you okay? You look pale."

Brogan let out a long breath. "Yeah. Let's head back, shall we?" He wanted nothing more than to be alone, but he could keep up pleasantries for the walk back.

"So . . . you were banished to Layton?" Daisy's question broke the rhythm of her gimpy walk.

Seriously, she didn't know how close she was to the target. "My father loves me so much that he felt a good dose of old-fashioned living was better for my character than enjoying life. It's only two of the best years of my youth I need to squander."

Daisy rolled her eyes. "Wow. It's so sad being you. But I guess Layton isn't much compared to—?"

"At this point, I would even take Miami."

"Ooh, Miami doesn't measure up to your discerning urban tastes?"

Brogan straightened his back. Maybe playing her game would get his mind off the painting and whatever it was doing in her house. "I used to joke that bad people died and went to Miami. Who knew I'd find somewhere even worse? Hey, I heard I could become a cowboy while I'm here."

"Ranching cattle looks like hard work. Then again, my dad says hard work is a blessing from God. It gives men a sense of worth."

"My dad says something like that. 'You won't be happy until you've conquered the world.'"

She huffed a laugh. "How is that even close to the same thing? Are you Caesar or Napoleon?"

The tightness in his chest loosened. "Maybe Genghis Khan?"

"Whatever. You might make a convincing Alexander."

"Thank you."

She raised an eyebrow and smiled. "Not a compliment." Then she pointed to the door and sighed. "Time for me to face the music."

For a second, Brogan saw both pain and joy in her scarred blue eyes. It seemed he wasn't the only person imprisoned by their parents' unresolved issues.

* * *

DAISY'S STOMACH tightened as they slipped back into the church. She hated sneaking around, especially when it wasn't going to work. Mom was going to find out; it was just a matter of who she'd hear it from.

She and Brogan were about to pass the high school room just as the students filed out, and she cursed their unfortunate timing. *Avoidance tactic ruined.*

"Hello, Daisy." Julie's voice reflected a sweet smile that faded when she noticed Brogan. She stared between Brogan and Daisy, her eyebrows raised.

Daisy had to admit, Brogan made Dean look like a monkey in an outfit by comparison—not that she took any joy from the fact. She had liked everything about Dean since she moved to Layton, back when her admiration didn't affront boys. But now she stood mute, her face probably turning some awful shade of puce.

"Daisy, it looks like you've met someone interesting." Julie eyes narrowed, even though her smile stayed cemented.

Daisy shook her head, but she couldn't get any words out.

"I guess we'll talk later." Julie grabbed Dean's arm and sauntered toward the exit.

"Ew. What a mess." Brogan stepped closer. He tilted his head in Julie's direction. "She doesn't seem worth whatever is going on in there." He pointed at Daisy's head.

"Yeah. Things are a little tense in there lately."

"I never liked playing these games back in Manhattan, but it feels totally pointless here. Less money. Less power. But just as much self-importance."

"It's childish." She sighed.

"And . . . what else do you want to say about it?" Brogan crossed his arms and peered down at her.

Daisy wasn't sure she should say any more, but she kind of wanted to get it off her chest. "Last summer Julie sort of tricked me into sharing something embarrassing."

He raised an incredulous eyebrow. "You don't seem trickable."

"I agreed to play truth or dare when our moms were having a barbecue. She thought I had a crush on that kid, Dean, but she forced me to say it. Strangely enough, the whole town knew within the week. I'm not even retaliating. So why is she so awful to me?"

"Maybe she wasn't hugged enough as a little girl."

Daisy chuckled. His simple joke lightened a weight from her chest. "I would like to take a minute to appreciate your twisted sense of humor."

He shrugged. "Emmy has taught me well. It gets me through the tough times."

"Hey Daisy, who's your friend?"

Daisy twisted toward the classroom, heart racing. A tall man stood in the doorway of the youth room.

She needed to calm down already. "Hi, Dexter. This is a new student. I'm supposed to introduce you." She turned to Brogan. "Dexter teaches the high school crew Sunday mornings."

Brogan nodded his head, though Dexter grabbed his hand and shook it. "You look so much like Leo. He was a year ahead of me in school, and we both played basketball. Did he tell you about the state championships? He was a sight on the court."

Brogan's eyes narrowed. While controlled, the tension around him could have been plucked like a harp.

Daisy wanted to help somehow. "Brogan was talking about history earlier. Maybe he'd like to hear about your '56 Plymouth. Dexter is restoring an old car." No one could shut him up about that old car, and it should take his focus from whatever Brogan found so unpleasant.

"Of course you can see it any time, Brogan. She's a classic. I spent two years restoring everything. Just put in a new stereo last week." He was telling them all about how hard it was to get just the right shade of aqua on the hood when the two of them finally met reprieve in the form of Daisy's mother.

Dexter simpered. "Ophelia, isn't Brogan a great kid? He was just asking about the Belvedere—"

"How fascinating. Brogan, your grandparents are waiting in their car outside."

Brogan practically sprinted to the door.

Then it occurred to her—they totally got away with sneaking out. No one noticed they were gone. Dang. That kid had some awesome luck.

CHAPTER SEVEN

BROGAN STOOD in the school commons studying his schedule just after the first bell rang. The school secretary had given him a quizzical stare-down as she handed over his class list. Now he understood why.

He shook his head. He had gym, art, one English class, and a lot of library time. His tutor had to defend his thesis at Columbia and wouldn't begin teaching him for another three weeks, which explained the back-to-back study halls.

Every student who filed past the office eyed him. It was a larger student body than he had expected, but small enough that a new kid stood out.

"Excuse me," he said to a short girl whose hazel eyes bugged out at his address. "Where would I find the library?"

She didn't speak but pointed in the direction from where she'd just come. Her eyes remained enormous.

"Thanks."

She nodded her head with vigor and continued staring after him as he walked in the appointed direction. She wasn't the only one staring either.

He took his phone out so he could pretend to not notice everyone's rapt attention.

Emmy had sent rattlesnake and tornado emojis followed by question marks.

He texted her a photo he'd taken of a sign outside the school. It said "Rattlesnake Warning."

Just thought I'd feed your fears, Em.

How can you tease me when I'm sincerely worried about your miserable living conditions and bleak social life?

Because it entertains me?

More dramatic emojis followed. Poor girl.

After sitting a few hours in the library filled with silent gawkers, he strolled into an art class. Simply seeing art supplies made his hands twitch. He grabbed some charcoal and paper. The teacher—a short, plump man with shaggy gray hair—raised an eyebrow at him. "And what am I supposed to do with a new student midsemester? This is a *progressive* drawing class."

Brogan pointed at the still life that had been set up in the middle of the room. "Don't worry. I know what to do."

He didn't wait to hear no; instead, he set up an easel with the paper and began sketching out what he knew to be an impressive composition.

The art teacher calmed once Brogan demonstrated his abilities. "I see. That's very nice. Brogan, is it?" He went back to organizing something at a big table outside of the still life circle.

A few of the students whispered and glanced in his direction, but most kept their focus on their work.

"Did you guys hear about the party out at the lake Saturday night?"

Brogan looked up to locate the speaker.

A girl on the other side of the circle said, "Gavin threw Abby's backpack into the lake. He likes her or something, but he really doesn't get how to impress the ladies."

A different voice said, "To be fair, he'd had quite a few."

"Before or after Sarah threw up? That's when we left."

Classy. Brogan looked back at the teacher. The man stood twenty feet from them, but no one filtered their stories.

"Don't worry, new boy, we aren't all barbaric," a plump brunette girl with rosy cheeks and a button nose whispered to Brogan's right. "I'm Cassidy."

"Brogan," he replied as he shook the girl's charcoal-stained hand. They both chuckled at the cloud of black dust that poofed around their handshake.

"Where are you from, cutie?" Cassidy tilted her head.

Brogan looked in her eyes and flashed the smile that he knew charmed girls. "I just moved here from New York."

"Wow. The big city? What's it like?"

"It's great. My school is . . . was nice. I miss everything, even the homeless guy who loudly predicted my death each day by envisioning me 'lanced by a golden spear.' He's really special."

Cassidy giggled. "I hope I don't get stuck here after graduation. I want to see places like that. Maybe you'll have to take me."

Brogan blinked a few times at her frank and ridiculous invitation. "You should definitely see it."

"Give me your number and I'll make sure you know where the party is this weekend."

"I'm sorry, I lost my phone a few days ago." He learned his lesson long ago about giving his number to enthusiastic girls.

"Okay, well we're here every day, right?"

"I think so." He put his mind back into drawing, while Cassidy kept looking in his direction, commenting on his work. Brogan ignored her, but she continued to talk to him. Pretty soon a tall, athletic boy approached his easel.

"Hey, man. I'm Chad. You should come check out the angle from that side of the room."

Brogan stood and followed Chad to the farthest point from Cassidy.

"Dude, you looked uncomfortable. Cassidy's okay, but she does get a little excited when she crushes. She'll calm down and be normal if you don't give her extra attention."

Brogan exhaled. "Thanks. I'm Brogan." He stuck out his chalky hand, which Chad grabbed.

"My buddy Dean and I are going off campus for lunch. I live across the street and my mom left some enchiladas. Wanna come?"

"Yeah, okay."

As soon as the lunch bell rang, Brogan followed Chad outside to where Dean waited. "Hey, man, this is Brogan. He's coming too."

"We met yesterday, right? You were with Daisy?" Dean asked as the three started walking toward Chad's house.

"I wasn't *with* Daisy," Brogan corrected. "My grandparents really wanted me to go to church, then second church. Why is that a thing?" He earnestly wanted an answer, but they both shrugged. "Anyway, Daisy helped me sneak out and call my cousin back in New York."

"That's cool." Chad laughed. "Daisy is Dean's first love, so we don't talk to her at all."

Dean rolled his eyes. "Stop it, Chad. I feel bad enough about it."

"What do you mean?" asked Brogan.

Dean groaned. "When she first moved here, we sat next to each other in math. We ate lunch together a few times. She was my first, you know, 'girlfriend,' and then her accident was pretty bad." He scowled as if struggling for the right words.

Chad put a hand on Dean's shoulder. "She spent a few months in the hospital in the city. When she came back, she was in a wheelchair."

Dean shrugged. "I didn't know how to talk to her after that."

"He's *really* sensitive about it." Chad fake whispered, to which Dean pulled him into a friendly neck hold.

Brogan chuckled. "You're seeing her friend. Julie?"

"She's not exactly Daisy's friend, but yes," said Dean.

Chad laughed while Dean maintained the neck hold. With a throaty voice, Chad said, "Julie was pushing him around yesterday and being weird."

Dean released Chad from his grip. "Nothing I can't handle," said Dean. "She's so . . . pretty."

"We all must decide." Brogan took on a philosophical tone. "Can a pretty face make up for the trouble it brings? At first it does, but then one day you're asking yourself, 'Why am I miserable?' The misery sneaks up on you."

Dean laughed. "Are you saying I should avoid the misery?"

"No!" replied Brogan, emphasizing his shock at the suggestion. "This is just my seventeen-year-old experience. Women are like a loaded gun. Find one you can trust not to pull the trigger. But she should still be sexy."

"Have you found someone like that?" asked Chad. He had a smile on his face and seemed to be enjoying Brogan's theatrics.

"Nope." Brogan sighed. "The hot ones love the trigger."

They all laughed.

At Chad's house, the enchiladas blew Brogan's mind. "Who made these?"

"Welcome to authentic Mexican food, my friend." Chad grinned. "My abuela taught my mom, who's white as that lamp there, how to keep the tradition alive."

"*This* might be the first thing I love about Layton." Brogan wiped fake tears from his eyes.

"Yeah, Mamá Jimenez was famous for her cooking. Even the immigrants envy Chad's mom for this recipe." Dean further boasted over Chad's mom by dancing as he shoved a forkful of food into his mouth.

"*Vato*, how could they not? It's like crack for your taste buds." Chad's Hispanic accent peaked out for the first time.

Brogan smiled to himself. "Thank your mother for me. I'm going to dream about these enchiladas tonight."

Once they finished eating, they made their way back to school.

"Hey, Brogan," said Dean. "A few of us guys are camping in my parents' barn next Friday night. You in?"

"In a barn? I really am in the sticks."

Dean put a hand on Brogan's shoulder. "Sorry we aren't more sophisticated, Mr. City Man."

He liked this kid. "Yeah, okay." Brogan waved and headed to gym.

* * *

THAT EVENING, Daisy finished her homework early. She sat in their cozy library, staring absently.

"I found a great lecture," her father said, breaking into her malaise. "Do you want to listen and help me map out language families by historical era and geography?"

Daisy turned her glassy stare toward him and nodded, which made him chuck an eraser at her. "Wake up, space cadet." He kept his voice low so her mother wouldn't hear. "I don't know what's churning up there, but I think ancient Near Eastern linguistics is your key to freedom."

He said it with a twinkle in his eyes, but Dad was serious about the linguistics. He had a high view of children's intellectual potential and often took opportunities to instruct Daisy in theology, history, philosophy, and as many languages as possible—and that didn't stop with living languages. Daisy had all kinds of ancient texts in her repertoire: Homer, the Code of Hammurabi, the Akkadian collection from Mari and Ebla, to name a few. She might as well snag a PhD in linguistic anthropology on her way out of high school. Not that she complained. Some of her favorite memories involved reading and learning from her father.

It's not like sports were getting in her way.

After two hours of comparing the Hittite language with classical Greek and Sanskrit, Daisy's brain rejected any further input. Her thoughts wandered to Julie and Dean.

"Why did we leave Denver again?" she asked her dad.

"Your mother wanted to be near her mother before she died. And since there are plenty of sinners in Layton, I found a job here."

But Layton doesn't have room for a weirdo like me.

Her father looked up. "What's wrong, Daisy?"

She didn't want her dad to know how lonely she was or that

she was dwelling, yet again, on her unfortunate appearance. She felt childish enough without voicing it.

But her father never echoed those inner voices of disapproval. "There's a reason you struggle with this, Daisy. I don't know what the reason is, and I don't agree with your self-assessment. I do know that God often allows intense pressure on his children, especially as he prepares us for important work. Now, while you are young, it's good to learn how to trust him in your pain and seek truth. Don't just accept these thoughts—they might be lies."

She tried to hide her tears, but her dad had honed his perceptive abilities to an annoying degree. He stood and walked over to her and gave her a bear hug. With his large frame, he picked her up out of her chair. She giggled into his neck, her feet dangling several inches off the ground.

"I love you, Dad."

"I love you, too, flower poo."

"Dad!"

"But you've always been my flower poo!"

"Stop calling me that!" But she couldn't keep the laughter from spilling out. And she wondered if, maybe, real life rewarded such stubborn optimism.

CHAPTER EIGHT

BROGAN AWOKE A FEW DAYS LATER, dying for a fresh bagel—not a bagel out of a bag, but one straight out of the ovens of a New York bakery. Back home, a maid would have already set one on his breakfast stand next to an exotic blend of fruit and vegetable juices. Not to mention freshly roasted coffee waiting for him, steaming in a French press.

The memories pained him.

His grandmother tapped on the door. "Breakfast is on the table, dear."

Those days will be gone for a while.

He picked up his phone. Emmy texted a few photos of herself frowning and holding a fresh bagel on the steps of the Met. *Miss you, Bro.* The time stamp indicated 8:35 a.m. New York time.

Me too, Em. Now go to school, you delinquent.

She replied with devil emojis.

He trudged downstairs to pick at the now-familiar burnt toast, scrambled eggs, bacon, and canned coffee. It unsettled his stomach almost as much as the trio of porcelain poodle figurines peering down at him from an aluminum shelf.

His gaze shifted to the three bright canvases. Their beauty gave his soul a break from the overwhelming kitch, but they also reminded him of a question he had for his grandparents. "I saw one of Dad's paintings over at the Bloom's house. Does he know the Blooms?"

His grandfather cleared his throat but didn't answer. His grandmother walked to one of her knickknack shrines and opened a drawer. After shifting through a short stack of photos, she handed one to Brogan.

It appeared to be an old prom photo in which a young Ophelia Bloom wore a simple but flattering formal gown. She stared into the eyes of a teenaged Leo Lukes, who stared back with wonder. He had never seen his father look at any woman like that. The longing. The sheer joy.

Brogan tossed the photo on the table.

His grandfather cleared his throat again. "What were you doing over at the Blooms?"

"Just . . . hanging out." He cleared his breakfast setting before more questions could be asked, then grabbed his backpack and the keys to the old Toyota Corolla and headed out the door. He never had to drive in New York, and now that a car proved necessary, he wished he'd made arrangements for a better one. It somehow sputtered into action and got him to school.

He sat in the parking lot and texted while other kids pulled in around him.

Hey Dad . . . I think this Corolla wants to retire. Hint hint.

It only took a few seconds to get a response.

Loud and clear, son.

They still driving that old thing?

I love you.

And that was all his dad responded. Brogan's heart panged. His dad could reply in an instant, but he hadn't initiated contact since Brogan left. Hot tears stung his eyes, but he wouldn't allow himself to cry over something so stupid. He opened the car door and let the cold air chase his emotion away.

His phone vibrated again. Emmy had texted back.

Seriously, are you visiting over a weekend anytime soon? Tell Uncle Leo to send a jet or something. What's all his money good for anyway?

Good question.

Fortunately, school relieved him. His tutor, Rolf, had sent instructions to read *The Idiot* by Dostoevski. Brogan enjoyed the spectacular classic while the other kids stressed over midterms.

"Hey, new kid," someone whispered. He turned to see a pretty redhead smiling big enough to exhibit her straight, white teeth. "You don't, by any chance, know which island Napoleon died on?"

"Saint Helena," Brogan whispered back, happy to show off as he took in her subtle freckles and the flirty way she wrinkled her nose.

"Thanks. How do you know?"

He shrugged. "I just know." He had vacationed there with his dad when he was eleven. How could he forget the long, painful days the yacht had traversed across the Atlantic, only to arrive at the most boring place on earth?

"You're right. I just googled it."

"Why are you asking me then?" Brogan flashed a flirty smile.

The redheaded girl blushed. "Brogan, right?"

He'd already checked the name on one of her papers. "Yes, Paula."

Paula's cheeks reddened and she scooted closer. "Brogan, do you know the name of the English general who defeated him?"

As a matter of fact, Brogan's old tutor made him memorize details of the Napoleonic Wars as they made their way toward the island. Both he and his tutor loathed the long days at sea. Out of boredom they dangled a bloody ham from a large hook. Their infamous "shark trap" had prematurely ended the young tutor's employment, but only because it had worked. His dad might still be angry over that one.

"Arthur Wellesley, Duke of Wellington. But the British weren't alone. The Prussian Army joined them. Why aren't you googling?"

"Because I want to see how smart you are."

Fine by him.

"You might know as much as Daisy. Will you knock her grade average out of first place, please?"

"Daisy Bloom? If you are so adamant, why don't you do it?"

She scowled. "She knows everything before we even cover it."

Brogan recollected the Bloom's healthy library and cocked a half smile. "I think she reads. You might try it."

Paula threw a wad of paper in retaliation. "Whatever. Are you going on the class field trip this weekend?"

"What field trip?" He would pack bags this instant if it meant leaving Layton.

"There's a Van Gogh exhibit in Denver. It's supposed to show the progression of his work or something. You should come. There's still a few seats left on the bus."

"Thanks for the info, Red." As soon as he could, he signed up.

THE BUS WAS SCHEDULED to leave at six o'clock on Friday morning. Unaccustomed to Layton High bus rides, Brogan did not bring a pillow like the other students. He didn't realize how far they had to drive.

Four hours? For a school outing? He trudged into the bright yellow tube with wheels. Dean and Chad sat together near the back. Obviously popular, they were surrounded by other students. "Sorry, man." Dean looked around for a vacant seat, but there weren't any.

"No sweat. I'll see you in four freaking hours." The boys chuckled as Brogan returned back toward the entrance. Paula shoved another girl across the aisle to open a spot next to her. Brogan almost sat in the newly vacated seat when he noticed Daisy sitting alone a few rows farther up. Compelled by God knows what, he sat with her instead. She took out one of her earbuds and studied him. Recognition registered on her sleepy face. She nodded, placed the earbud back in her ear, and stared out the window again.

"It's alright. I'll just talk to myself." Her lack of social charm amused him.

"I can hear you. My music isn't on." Daisy took her earbuds out altogether. "It's just early."

"It is," Brogan agreed. "What are you reading?"

She held up her book. "I grabbed it from my dad's study. It covers modern debates in metaphysics. I started this chapter last night. The writer is trying to argue whose identity would remain on two bodies if their heads were switched."

"Fascinating. The old head-switching debate."

The two shared a glance and laughed, drawing the attention of a few nearby students. He looked back and saw Paula's tight face, her eyes steely. Brogan ignored her. "We dialogued this topic in philosophy last year. Who knew I'd ever get the pleasure of discussing it again? What are your thoughts?"

"We may actually find out one day soon, because some scientist in China is attempting to switch people's heads. But I don't think identity is as fragmented as they suppose. Our bodies are not our only substance. They ignore the concept of souls. I guess one cannot prove souls philosophically. But there are more things in heaven and earth, Horatio, than are dreamt of in your philosophy."

"And then she quotes Hamlet."

"God, in his mercy, let my first language be English so I could love Shakespeare."

He shook his head. "*Romeo and Juliet* just wasn't the same in Japanese."

Daisy laughed again. "Exactly."

The bus rolled along, lulling to sleep everyone on board. Daisy set her pillow against the window and fell into dreamland. Brogan, having nothing else to lean on, though without fully intending to, fell asleep against Daisy.

* * *

DAISY STOOD on one end of an elongated, grand flower garden, a tall masculine figure haunted the other end. The figure did not attempt to walk toward her. He spoke from a distance, as if eager to calm her. "This is important. Be diligent to walk through the doorway given to you."

"Doorway? Is my Parshant here?"

An abrupt motion jostled Daisy awake, much to her frustration. She needed information, and she hadn't dreamt in weeks. The bus had stopped at a traffic light on the outskirts of a Denver suburb. The bright light from her dream translated into a fierce ray of sunlight pelting her face through the window.

Brogan's unconscious body weighed against her. She gently pushed him back to his side of the bus seat. He awoke and blinked a greeting in her direction. Immediately she noticed a line from her jacket had etched itself onto his cheek.

That early morning silence permeated the bus while students rustled through backpacks, pulling out their smartphones. Daisy typed in her passcode. No email. She flipped to Instagram out of habit. Someone had posted a photo of Brogan sleeping against her on the bus, but it looked less like leaning and more like snuggling. Her face heated, and she quickly handed Brogan her phone.

"What is this?" she whispered.

He took her phone and turned it over in his palm. "A dinosaur. How do you keep this thing working?"

Her temper flared, but she held it back by spitting out, "The picture. Look at the picture." The dream had tenderized her emotions, and she knew it. But knowing and controlling are two different things.

"Huh. That was fast. Looks like Paula posted a photo of us."

"No kidding? Somehow your arm is across me and we're sleeping. What do you think people are going to say about this?"

"Geez, Daisy. I fell asleep against you. Sorry."

She noticed Paula leaning toward them, trying to listen in, so she dropped her voice to a whisper. "It looks inappropriate, Brogan."

"No one will care, if you don't make a big deal of it. I'll squash any gossip that comes my way."

The flippant shrug of Brogan's shoulders pressed her anger

button again. "That's beside the point. Even my parents are going to see it. Small town, Brogan."

Brogan looked like he was about to counter attack, but he didn't follow through. "Why are you blaming me? It's not like I told her to take the picture."

Daisy saw the logic in what he said. It hurt to find herself the subject of a callous social media post, but she shouldn't take it out on him.

Brogan leaned closer and kept his voice low. "She only did it because I sat with you instead of her."

"Paula?"

"Girls get mean when they're ignored."

"You ignored Paula to sit with me?" It was kind of hard to believe.

He put his hands up. "Don't read into it. She is too eager. You're just . . . you."

"Me?"

"Yep. You're as good as one of the guys."

Daisy relaxed. She could accept those terms. "Maybe I'm over-reacting."

He faced her with a half smile. "Yeah, but I also haven't figured out the small-town thing you keep mentioning."

In an effort to move to a more civil conversation, she changed the subject. "Brogan, what do you like about Van Gogh?"

Brogan's expression grew dreamy. "His work looks as if someone was captive to a gray world, then suddenly set free to experience color for a few fleeting moments before death. It's fierce, beautiful, and brief. Before I discovered the Frank Lloyd Wright room at the MET, I used to trek to the MOMA to stare at *Starry Night* after a bad day at school."

Daisy's jaw dropped. "*Starry Night*? I . . . I'm so jealous."

"Have you seen it?"

"Only on the internet and on my mom's beach towel. I haven't seen much in person. Our family has never traveled outside of Colorado."

He shook his head. "Your existence is weird."

Did he just call her *existence* weird? "As if you're the standard for normal," she muttered.

He snickered.

Enough small talk with this one. She snatched her book from her backpack and continued reading until they arrived at the museum.

* * *

ONCE INSIDE THE ART MUSEUM, Paula, Cassidy, and a pack of girls walked closely behind Brogan and Dean at the exhibit.

"Can we pretend they aren't with us?" asked Dean.

Brogan gave him a commiserating nod, though he noticed the girls less and less as he meandered throughout the rooms to study paintings. He also began to watch Daisy as she studied each frame. She was adorably studious. Her smile would widen as she looked over each canvas. On a few occasions she sketched on a small drawing pad, her tongue peaking out. Brogan even noticed Dean noticing Daisy, though the other boy played it cool and walked on as soon as he suspected an audience. *I bet you'd like to know what I just saw, Daisy Bloom.* Brogan grinned.

Near the end of the maze, Daisy looked at a particular painting of the French countryside. Her face lit up as she studied the varied themes on the canvas. Brush strokes conveyed movement in the grassy foreground. Thick, Japanese-styled lines contoured the mountains. Clouds containing every color blended into a perfectly stormy sky. She didn't move. Her eyes affixed to the scene as something new began to happen. A sudden airflow lifted Daisy's hair from the direction of the painting, as if the picture were a window open to a breeze.

The breeze grew stronger. Daisy's face brightened as sunlight poured onto her. Brogan did a double take. *That can't be real.* Plus, the Daisy that had just been walking around awkward in her cheap dress, face full of blemishes and scars, suddenly had smooth skin. Her tacky dress was caught by a wind gust and pressed against her body. Her hair, usually stringy, flowed beautifully behind her back.

And then the painting moved. It didn't just convey motion by the skill of Van Gogh's brush; it actually swirled. Windy brushstrokes stretched outward, caressing Daisy's forearm. Painted sky wrapped around her wrist and pulled her forward. Brogan stepped up to her and touched her shoulder.

As quickly as the wind began, it stopped. Daisy returned to her blemished and scarred self. She turned her head and smiled, flashing braces. "I felt for a minute as if I were there, in the painting."

"Yeah. I guess these paintings have that effect." Did he really just see that?

Daisy hobbled away to study the next frame, and Brogan turned to stare down the canvas.

Nothing. Just a painting.

CHAPTER NINE

"Okay, class," Mr. Wells broadcasted in the museum's foyer. "We have three hours before the bus leaves. There is still a permanent exhibit to walk through. There is also a cafe where you may buy lunch. This gives you plenty of time to do homework if you wish. Do not leave the museum."

Daisy had already seen the permanent collection and prepared to study for her precalculus midterm. Alone, she limped toward the cafe when, to her left, Dean, Chad, and Brogan slipped out a side door toward downtown Denver. She grabbed the door. "You guys can't! You could get in so much trouble if you go running through the city."

"Well then, Daisy, it looks like we'll have to kidnap the only witness to our crime." Brogan grabbed Daisy's arm and pulled her toward Civic Center Park.

Chad scowled when he noticed her.

"Sorry, guys, but you don't need to worry about Daisy. She's a pro at sneaking around." Brogan had the nerve to wink at her.

Dean and Chad both looked uncomfortable for a moment. Daisy wilted as Chad sized her up. Then he shrugged. "Yeah, okay. Just keep up."

Brogan snapped her out of her trance by hissing under his breath. "Relax. Just be yourself."

"Yeah. Because that's always worked before," she hissed back.

He pressed her forward, limping and all. "Just talk to me and point your face at all three of us."

Daisy groaned, then quickened her half-hopping gait to keep up. As she trudged along, she looked up at the new buildings, amazed at how quickly everything had changed since she had lived there. "Where are we going?"

"We don't know." Dean shrugged. "Just anywhere."

Brogan took a deep breath of what could only be bus exhaust and exclaimed, "This isn't *my* city, but it's *a* city. I need this stretch of filthy concrete like a diabetic needs insulin."

Daisy couldn't help but laugh at his analogy.

As Brogan studied the skyline above him, a few girls stared and pointed their camera phones in his direction. Daisy looked to Dean, who shrugged and shook his head like he didn't know either.

Brogan pulled his hoodie up and said, "I'm hungry."

Chad must have been focused on food because he remained blissfully oblivious to the scene of girls gathering. He pointed toward some shops. "Let's grab food at one of these places."

"I could eat," Daisy said. She knew something about the area and suggested they continue exploring after lunch. "There's a cool bookshop at the end of the mall. Also, there's an old hotel on Seventeenth Street that was around during the prohibition. Their lounge is a rare art deco treasure." The boys stared at Daisy and she doubted herself. "So I've heard." *Limp. Limp.*

"That settles it then. Food followed by a rare art deco treasure," Brogan commanded.

While in line at Build-A-Burrito, people in the restaurant stared at them. A few took their phones out to take Brogan's picture. He didn't even seem to notice.

"Dude, people know about you in Layton, but I thought that's just because your dad was from there and infamous for being successful. I didn't realize you were like famous-famous." Dean nodded his head sideways toward transfixed patrons of the restaurant.

Brogan pulled a ball cap out of his backpack and pulled the bill down low over his brow. "This isn't normal."

When they sat at their table, Chad maneuvered his large frame to block Brogan from the restaurant's view. "You say this isn't normal, but these strangers aren't taking our picture." He dug some sunglasses from his bag and handed them to Brogan.

The sunglasses and cap disguised him pretty well, but a tall, flashy brunette approached them with a coy smile. "Hi, Brogan. Can I get a photo with you?" Another girl, several feet back, held up her phone.

Daisy interjected. "Actually, we're sneaking away from an event, and we'll get in a lot of trouble if photos of Brogan in Denver show up online."

The girl eyed Daisy with a scowl, but walked away.

Brogan flashed a broad smile. "I should hire you as a manager, Daisy! Thanks for protecting me."

"I'm not protecting you. I don't want to get in trouble." She shoved in her last bite of burrito.

Chad laughed through his nose. Dean also grinned.

Brogan's smirk didn't decrease. "Whatever you say. Finish up and show us this art deco business."

They followed Daisy to the Oxford Hotel.

Daisy turned into a tour guide with a litany of facts. "It's a luxury hotel, originally built in the 1890s within walking distance of the main train station. The man who built it was the biggest alcohol producer in the Rocky Mountains during the prohibition. His name was Zang, I think. Adolph Zang. I've always wanted to see the Cruise Room. It was modeled in the 1930s after a lounge on the Queen Mary."

Dean raised his eyebrows. "Where are you getting this information?"

"A friend of my father's told us about it. The intrigue made the details stay with me."

"What's *intrigue?*" asked Chad.

"That just means it's interesting. The hotel is supposed to be haunted, and I'm not a fan of ghost stuff."

"What's your opinion on the paranormal?" Before the incident at Mardell's party and the painting today, this topic wouldn't have interested him. Now that he had reasons to investigate, this was a inconspicuous opportunity to ask questions.

"It's dangerous to play around with spirits."

Daisy dropped the word *spirits* like a bomb that made Brogan's hair stand on end. "What do you mean by spirits? Like ghosts or something solid?"

"Maybe things pretending to be ghosts that can manifest themselves as solid."

He recalled the thing that caressed his fingers. "How do you know what they are?"

Chad huffed. "You guys watch too many horror movies."

Daisy gave Brogan a kind smile and shrugged. They would have to discuss it without Chad and Dean around.

"Here it is: The Oxford Hotel." Daisy gestured to a quaint brick building.

Brogan removed his sunglasses as they entered through the revolving door.

"Are you guests?" A trim, young bellman stared them down until his gaze locked on Brogan. Then his eyes widened. "Mr. Lukes! I didn't realize you were staying with us."

Brogan held up his hands. "I'm actually not a guest here."

The bellman drew close. "I'm a huge fan. I just moved from New York over the summer. I follow you on Instagram, but you haven't posted in a while. Why are you in Denver?"

Brogan felt his cheeks warm as Daisy, Dean, and Chad stared at the exchange. "My aunt runs that account to advertise her line. She's going to have to hire a real model, I guess."

"So you didn't really go to Niagara Falls with Tony Edge and Tara Mock?"

"No, I did. Those are her real models." The memory alone bored him. How many conversations could he have about facial lighting and diet tips? "What's your name?"

The eager bellman grabbed his hand and shook it. "I'm Andrew. How can I help you today?"

"Andrew, we wanted to see the . . ." He looked to Daisy.

"Cruise Room," she finished for him.

"It's off limits during the day and only for guests, but I can get you in. Let me grab a key." Andrew sprinted to a door nearby.

Chad whispered. "He might wet his pants with all this excitement."

Brogan rolled his eyes. "Shut up. He's coming back."

"This way." Andrew bounced toward an intricately designed door with *The Cruise Room* engraved on a plaque. He held the door open. "I have to get back to the main door, but here's my card if you are looking for a photographer in the area."

Brogan took the card and nodded at Andrew's eager face. "Sure thing." If this guy's work was any good, he'd pass the name to his aunt. His dad had taught him to appreciate favors.

He followed his friends into the now-unlocked room and stepped back in time. The decor appeared to be original to the 1930s. Panels lined the long, narrow chamber, each displaying a different cultural scene from around the world.

Chad studied the scenes. "Are these . . . racist?"

Daisy shook her head. "They're just from an older point of view. Before globalization, cultural differences were physical and noticeable."

Brogan thought about it. "Now every culture wears the same clothes, drives the same cars, and listens to the same music."

Dean sidled up to Daisy and held out his phone. "Brogan, will you take a picture of us?"

Daisy froze.

"Sure." As Brogan framed the shot, Dean scooched shoulder to shoulder with her on the nautically themed bar. He smiled and asked Daisy if he could buy her a whiskey.

Her smile softened. "I never drink only one," she answered in a rough, Western accent. Dean rewarded her with a chuckle. Daisy clipped his gaze short and bounced from the bar.

Dean's cheeks reddened.

Interesting.

Brogan took out his phone. "Let's head back to the museum in ten minutes."

"Should we check out the rest of the hotel?" Dean motioned them to the hallway. They all followed him to some stairs.

Dean and Chad darted upward. Daisy held her arm out to stop Brogan from following. "Can we go down instead?"

"Enough Dean for you?"

She let out a breath. "You could tell?"

"Yeah. Let's see what's in the basement." They took what looked like a servant's staircase downward and opened a door at the bottom. He expected a kitchen on the other side but found a narrow hallway where he and Daisy could barely stand side by side. It was paneled with old wood and had obviously never been decorated for guests.

Daisy stopped short. Her face drained of color as she pointed at a wall at the end of the hallway. "Brogan. What is that symbol? There, carved in the wood?"

"It looks like a figure eight with a knife through it."

At that moment the hallway twisted sideways, throwing them between the walls and eventually to the ground. The doors behind them slammed and the lights extinguished.

A familiar breathy giggle put Brogan's hair on edge. "There you are, Brogan," the darkness hissed. "So glad I could find you again."

Brogan reached for Daisy and found her wrist. "Stay behind me."

A damp finger or tentacle slid around his other forearm and yanked him forward, breaking his hold. "Why would I let you have her, the better of the two prizes? Conceived by magic, that one."

Daisy's clipped scream pierced the darkness. Brogan reached around, trying to find her again.

Her voice registered in the darkness, this time more calm. She wasn't calling for help or anything, only chanting in some other language. As she chanted, the atmosphere calmed.

The creature hissed a curse and released him. A dim light grew from the cracks around the door at the end of the hallway.

"Brogan, we have to get back to the staircase," she said, in between her chants.

He could see her vague outline now. He grabbed her arm and barreled through the door. The twisted ground leveled so quickly, they toppled over onto the stairs. Everything was suddenly at peace.

"What's going on, Daisy?" He wheezed the words through short breaths. "This isn't the only strange thing I've seen with you today."

She worked to stand on the stairs and climbed upward. "Let's get out of here first." She hobbled toward the lobby, ignoring Brogan's attempts to help her.

Dean and Chad waited by the exit. "Where did you guys go?" Dean asked.

Daisy hobbled past them and rushed into the sunlight.

* * *

DAISY PLAYED IT COOL. Rattled as she was, no one needed to know she and Brogan had just fallen into some vortex of terror. She'd been in plenty of stickier situations—granted, that was in her dream life.

She used her pronounced limp to breathe deeper with each clunk. Brogan touched her elbow as if wanting to help. She shook him off. "Act normal."

Dean rushed up beside them. "Did something happen?"

Daisy's face heated.

Brogan shook his head. "No big deal. Some guy ran us out of the basement."

Chad's voice boomed behind them. "Why? Were you guys doing something you shouldn't be doing?"

Daisy, Brogan, and Dean all turned to Chad at once. He winked. "What? Too close to the truth?"

"Nothing like that." Daisy resisted the urge to roll her eyes.

Dean shook his head. "Sorry, Daisy. Chad isn't trying to be a jerk. He thinks he's funny."

Chad confidently affirmed, "I am funny."

Daisy forced herself to laugh. "Chad's right. I'm overreacting to a weirdo, but I'm calm now. Let's head back to the museum and take a minute to appreciate this amazing day."

Dean laughed nervously and changed the subject. "What do you guys think of this downtown area?"

Brogan jumped on the topic, prattling on about architecture and culture. Something about how Denver was such a new city.

Watching Brogan ramble effortlessly, Daisy thought, *Geez, he must have nerves of steel.* By the time they crossed the square in front of the museum, the panic sweat had evaporated from her neck and forehead.

They were readmitted into the museum because of their exhibit pins. No one, not even Brogan's fan club, spied their entrance. Daisy marveled over his good luck for sneaking around as she plunked her backpack down on a table.

"Oh, there you are." Mr. Wells's nervous energy demonstrated his hurry. "We're loading the bus now. I must have missed you when I swept through the permanent collection."

She grimaced at Brogan and threw her backpack back over her shoulder. "Yes. We must have *just* missed you."

Once on the bus, Brogan shifted and sighed in the seat next to her. She ignored him at first, but he kept making his nonverbal cues more obvious.

She drew a deep breath to prepare for what she was about to do. "Some strange things have happened to me lately."

He sat up and straightened his back, then asked, "Do you remember earlier today, looking at the Van Gogh painting with the stormy sky in the countryside?"

She thought back to that painting. "Interesting that you should ask. I felt an affinity with it. It reminded me of the painting in my dad's study. Not the colors, but the feeling around it." If Brogan hadn't mentioned it, she might not have stopped to put words to it. Now that she did, the connection didn't make any sense. The painting in the study resembled Henri Rousseau's work more than anything from Van Gogh.

Brogan's jaw flexed and he closed his eyes. "Were you aware that the Van Gogh painting . . . reached out to you?"

"What do you mean, *reached out*?"

"Just what I said. I saw the colors leave the painting and reach out for you."

Her dream from the morning suddenly flashed in her memory. *Be diligent to walk through the doorway given to you.* Was the man in her dream trying to prepare her for some supernatural doorway? "But I didn't see the painting reach for me." She was talking more to herself than to Brogan.

"I believe you. You skipped along like it was normal."

His answer startled her back to the conversation, back to Brogan's pooling green eyes.

His voice cracked a little when he asked, "What else? You said strange things were happening."

Most of her encounters were in her dreams, and only recently did she have waking glimpses. "Sometimes I see things. They're there, and then they aren't."

Brogan's face turned a disconcerting white color.

"Are you okay, Brogan?"

His voice came out gravelly. "This is the second time I've met the whispering thing in the dark. The first time was in a club in Manhattan."

Daisy shivered. Did everyone have these crazy experiences? Should she share the fuller extent of hers? "It did say you'd met before, didn't it? But then, it also said I was conceived by magic, which is nonsense."

If she was going to spill, she should spill now. "But . . . I've been having dreams for years now. Dreams about another world."

Brogan cocked an eyebrow. "Dreams?"

"Yes. Every night, I live an entirely separate life apart from this one. A place where my body isn't broken."

His forehead creased with thought lines.

"I've never told anyone because it's kind of crazy. But my

dreams stopped suddenly just before you came to Layton. All my connections from there have been cut off. I had friends and adventures there. I used to even get love notes from a secret admirer. I suppose it could all be my imagination, but it felt real."

He nodded. "How soon before I came to Layton?"

"Maybe two, three days before?"

Brogan leaned closer. "Daisy, it's not just the supernatural stuff. The landscape in your library—it's my dad's painting."

Not what she expected. Maybe it wasn't an amateur painting but instead some master's work. It had a way of drawing her in and holding her. Brogan's dad had made a lot of money and could easily buy something like that. "He owns our painting?"

"He *painted* it. It's like his other paintings in both style and content. I think my dad knows your parents as more than just kids who went to school together. My grandma has a prom photo of your mom and my dad together."

He turned slightly at some movement across the aisle. Paula and her seatmate stared at them, probably misunderstanding their body language for intimacy rather than engrossing conversation. He blocked them out with his back and rolled his eyes.

Daisy gestured and encouraged him to continue. "My mom, your dad . . ."

"They looked a little starstruck with each other."

"If your dad painted the landscape, that might explain why my parents fight over it. Except my dad's the one who insists on keeping it."

"I think our dads were friends."

"Do you think my mom came between them?"

He shrugged. "I don't want to be a jerk, but—"

"She seems the type?" Daisy didn't want him to have to finish that out loud.

Based on his apologetic expression, that's exactly what he meant to say.

"Brogan, my mom hasn't always been like that. When we lived in the city, our family was happy and peaceful. I think living in Layton reminds her of things in the past."

"And my dad refuses to come near the place, even to see his own parents."

"Let's do some more snooping this week, see what we can find out. I'll meddle at my house. You meddle at your grandparents' house. Let's swap numbers. Text me if anything else weird happens."

"Agreed."

* * *

THE BUS ROLLED into town around 9:30 in the evening. When Daisy stepped on the sidewalk next to the school, she saw her dad waiting in the old truck. She fumbled with her backpack, trying to keep her balance as she hobbled toward him.

Brogan maneuvered beside her and took her pack. "I got this. You didn't drive?"

"Thanks. No, my dad likes to pick me up from trips. I think he misses me when I'm gone."

"That's cool." He opened the passenger door and leaned down. "Hi, Pastor Bloom."

"Well hello, Mr. Lukes."

Brogan set the backpack on the front floorboard.

Daisy flopped onto the seat. "Bye, Brogan."

He closed the door and waved as he turned toward the student parking lot.

"I missed you, punkin." Dad quickly shifted gears, suddenly curious about her personal life. "What's going on with you and the Lukes boy?"

"Nothing. Just friends."

Daisy couldn't see his expression in the darkness, but he paused as if trying to frame what to say next.

"It's a good idea that you not encourage a different kind of relationship. Do you know what I mean?"

She let the comment register and calculate. Her face grew warm with a wave of embarrassment. "No, I don't understand at all." She crossed her arms. "Maybe you can be more specific."

He waited until a red light to continue. "It's not really for me to explain."

"For who, then? Is it top secret? Is he a robot sent from the future to kill me?"

Dad sighed. "Daisy, you can trust me."

"Brogan and I are just friends, Dad. But you really need to give reasons for this kind of random, extreme caution."

Dad nodded. "Fair enough." But he offered nothing, and they finished the ride home in silence. He parked in the driveway, and Daisy darted up to her room as fast as her gimpy leg allowed.

What was going on? Why would her dad say something so out of character? Did he assume Brogan was too far out of her league to be safe and chose an evasive way of saying it?

The idea that even her dad, her last holdout for dignity, thought she was ugly cut her open. She leaned backward against her window and began to shake just before sobs burst out.

It would be better for the alternate universe to take her already.

Even as she formulated the thought, the glass from the window burst around her. Large, strong arms wrenched around her torso, pulling her backward into the night.

CHAPTER TEN

EARLY THE NEXT morning a knock on Brogan's door drew him from heavy sleep. His grandparents weren't going wake him before eight o'clock every Saturday, were they? He stumbled out of bed and opened the door.

His grandfather filled the doorframe with a travel mug of coffee and a key fob.

"This just arrived. I don't think you need anything this fancy, but I'm not your dad." Joe Lukes placed a fob with a Maserati symbol into Brogan's left hand and the coffee into his right.

He smiled up into his grandfather's weather-beaten face. "To be fair, I didn't ask for a Mazz." But he wouldn't say no to it either.

"Just be careful. It's tempting to go racing on the backroads out here, but kids die doing that."

Backroads? He'd ask Dean and Chad to show him.

He ran outside. Sure enough, a dark gray SUV sat in the drive, its beauty accentuated by the night's fresh snowfall. Brogan swore he could hear it say in an Italian accent, "Salve! Let'sa go for a ridah, shall we?"

He hopped in, sank into the leather, and grinned at the mere three hundred miles on the odometer. He pressed the ignition button and the motor purred.

His grandmother tapped on the window, his black coat in her hand. He rolled down the glass. "Take this in case you have to get out," she urged.

"Thanks." He threw it on the passenger seat. "I'm going for a drive."

She stepped back and waved as he pressed the gas.

After an hour or so of putzing through the town's six stop-lights, he realized he'd forgotten to bring his phone. He drove by Chad's place, but there were only tire marks in the snow from their driveway. No lights were on either. He didn't know where Dean lived.

He drove to the church and followed the path he and Daisy had walked to her house. As he pulled up, two local police cars, one state trooper, and a black SUV were outside of the Bloom's house. A yellow police line had been set around its perimeter.

He parked and approached the line. Daisy's parents were talking with an officer on the front lawn. Her dad looked up, his eyes swollen and red, and held Brogan's gaze.

Brogan gulped as Pastor Bloom made his way toward him.

"Brogan. What are you doing here?"

"I was going to see if Daisy wanted to go for a ride." He held up the key fob.

Pastor Bloom moved his hands to cover a sob. "She's not here. I hoped maybe you kids knew something."

A cold fear stole over Brogan. Yes, in fact, he knew some things about supernatural creatures hissing at them in the dark-ness. "I'm sorry. I don't have any information."

"All we have is broken glass from her third-story window and a lot of blood in the snow below. No footprints. Just blood and glass. You were with her all day yesterday. Could you tell the police if you noticed anything odd?"

Brogan couldn't tell them any of that. He'd be taken to a psych ward and perhaps arrested for murdering Daisy. "I didn't notice anything." If he kept his breathing regular, he could control his erratic heartbeat and ease his facial expressions. "Was it her blood on the ground?"

Pastor Bloom exhaled as he nodded, his face red. "But she couldn't have gone anywhere. Phee and I ran up when we heard the glass break. It was dark, but the snow below her window was undisturbed, aside from the blood."

A policeman joined them. "Is he a witness? Colorado law requires we talk to his parents before we can ask minors any questions."

"He's not a witness, but he was with Daisy yesterday."

"I would text my dad, but I left my phone back at the house. I was so excited about the car." He pointed to the Mazz.

The policeman let out a slow whistle. "Who wouldn't be? Do you know your dad's number?"

"I don't have the Korean number memorized. I know his secretary's number. She can forward you to him." He recited the digits as the officer noted them.

Ophelia sidled up to her husband and asked, "Why are they calling Leo? He doesn't need to know about Daisy."

Brogan stared at Daisy's mother, curious why she acted indignant about it. If it helped locate her daughter, why the resistance? This woman had issues.

Pastor Bloom nodded and said to the policeman, "Maybe it's not necessary just yet. Brogan simply pulled up this morning to show Daisy his new wheels."

The officer raised his eyebrows. "Mr. Lukes, you're free to go. We may call your dad later, but it doesn't seem likely."

Brogan said something about hoping they find Daisy soon and hopped into the Mazz. He started the engine and drove, his thoughts sprinting through the last month's odd events.

Daisy had been seeing people out of the corners of her eyes. The painting tried to pull her into itself. The creeper in the darkness expressed interest in her too. Her touches with the crazy were beyond what he'd experienced. There was no doubt she'd been taken by one of those beings—a malevolent one, based on the blood and shattered glass. But what could *he* do about it?

Brogan stopped. He'd managed to drive himself out to the middle of nowhere. He saw only unpaved roads, fields, and a single barn. He couldn't remember which direction had taken him here, so the compass on the rearview mirror did little to help.

He turned on the navigation system. A pleasant voice greeted him. "Hello. To set up your navigation, choose a network. You have zero networks available." He groaned, realizing he'd never stopped to get his phone either.

If he chose a direction to drive, he'd come across a farmhouse eventually, right? Or maybe there was some sort of information in the barn.

He pulled up and parked. Something about the weathered old structure invited him in.

Brogan shook his head at the notion. It's just an old barn. Yet as he walked in, it enveloped him like a hug. A warm, golden light spilled around fresh bales of hay. Then he noticed a puddle of water glimmering, unfrozen, in the middle of the floor, despite freezing temperatures.

It reminded him of when he jumped into puddles as a young child. Mom would scold him for getting soaked through. Dad would only laugh. Once, his dad even joined him, laughing as he ruined his clothes with mud. Mom scowled and said it was on Dad to clean them up when they got home.

Those few moments when Dad laughed so hard his sides hurt were magic to Brogan. Maybe it was time to relive one.

He ran and jumped with both feet into the puddle, fully expecting the same kind of furious splash he'd loved so much as a kid. Instead, he fell through the surface of the water, deep into a cavernous pool.

To his utter horror, hands grabbed him and pulled him down into the depths of the water. He gasped, choking as he was sucked into murky darkness.

Instead of growing darker, however, a warm light glowed in the water below him. Or was it above him? The hands flipped his body around in several directions until they brought his head up into warm air. He heaved the grateful breath of a man who, for a brief moment, had expected to drown.

Two of the hands maintained a firm grip on his upper arms and held him chest high above the water. He coughed violently as they moved him forward, as if he were a ship's masthead with a spasm.

"Let go!" he finally managed to yell, kicking at no one.

The hands let go. He descended under the water again, not having been prepared for immediate compliance.

Surfacing, he bobbed around to look for the nearest shore, reminded how difficult it is to tread water with shoes and pants on. When he finally reached shallow water, his panic had dissipated a little. He stood and coughed out a pleasantly sweet-tasting liquid. "Is this even water?"

"Yes, but it's from a unique spring."

Brogan stiffened at the words.

"I do apologize, Lawrence. If I had known of a less jarring doorway, I would have used it."

Brogan located a man approaching the bank of the water and eyed him. Was he a man? His complexion was so light, he was almost *bright*. Blue beads fastened onto a strand of his long, silver hair—silver not gray or even white. He had a young, well-cut face, and his trim body strode forward with hands clasped behind his back. His frame was lithe to the point of weightlessness.

Brogan couldn't speak. He had no context from which to draw appropriate behavior. Had the man seemed less angelic, his anger for having been nearly drowned might have dictated a response. Instead, he was stuck trying to make sense of mismatched puzzle pieces.

To make matters more confusing, dense foliage surrounded the small body of water where he stood. Multiple flowers perfumed the warm breeze, and lush, mossy grass carpeted the ground—not the barren, snow-covered wasteland from which he'd come.

The landscape spun, forcing him to take a knee in the water.

"Breathe deep. The altitude here is high enough to make you lightheaded. Other than that, you are quite safe." As the man drew near, his pale gray eyes shifted into an intensity entirely directed at Brogan. "My name is Orya. I am king of the light realms. Follow me. We have much to discuss."

He pivoted and strode away, leaving Brogan trying to steady himself in knee-deep water. The man turned back and tilted his head. "Are you coming?"

Brogan might have said something snide, but he needed to sit down. He trudged to the shore and plopped himself on the mossy grass. "Who are you?"

"Did I not explain? I am King Orya—"

"I heard you." Brogan breathed deep to control his temper. "*What* are you? Where am I? And what is going on? I was just in a barn in the middle of a snowy field."

The man's countenance softened, and he strolled back to Brogan, his hands still clasped behind his back. He stopped a few feet from where Brogan sat.

"Lawrence, you are now in a universe that is different from your own, but it is real. We have been instructed to treat you as an honored guest. I am a man, though not quite like the men of your world. I understand that you have no reason to trust me, but you should know that this pond will not take you back to your world. That door has closed. You have little choice but to come with me"—he touched his chest with a closed fist—"or try to run away and live off our lands without any knowledge of them." He gestured outward with an open hand, away from the pond. "That would not bode well for you, so my advice is to let me treat you as my friend."

He reached his hand toward Brogan in a gesture of help.

It took a minute for Brogan to calm down, but the man steadily held his hand out. Brogan pushed himself to stand and marched past him. He couldn't be friendly at that moment, but he would at least head in the direction the king had started.

The king maneuvered himself and resumed the feather-light steps he'd started earlier.

Brogan followed, the water in his shoes sloshing. His jacket also dripped. He peeled it off; the warm air didn't require a coat anyway.

He stared at the clothing of the king. He'd never seen anything like it. The king wore dark gray leather pants made from some reptilian beast; his coat, a lighter shade of gray, was also made from reptile skin. Small lapis beads clasped a strand of his long, silver hair on one side.

The king met Brogan's gaze. "Ah yes, Lawrence, it's dragon skin. I wasn't particularly pleased to put the beast down, but he had become feral. A pity, as he was once a friend of mine."

"My name is . . . I go by Brogan. Isn't it callous to wear the skin of your friend?"

"If he were a man, then yes. But dragons are vain creatures and want their skins to live on, which is wonderful for us. There is nothing else like them. My sister has a particular coat made from rainbow scales. The ailing creature came to her and bequeathed her own hide. I suppose it's one of those things we've become accustomed to." The king laughed to himself. "You must think it barbaric."

Brogan could only shake his head. *Dragons?* He must have lost his mind.

The walk through the grounds calmed his agitation. Soothing scents wafted through the air. Peppermints, honey-sweet florals, and an undertone of some bitter herb perfumed the warm, humid air. His senses couldn't ignore it, and despite all his travels, he'd never smelled anything like it before.

King what's-his-face stopped in front of a beautiful stone structure. The ivy-strewn doorway set off a bright yellow door.

"Here is your villa. It's one of a few on the castle grounds. My servants will show you how to use the bathing apparatus and will give you new clothes. I will see you again this afternoon, once you've settled in. Meet me in my drawing room at red. This vine marks the path that will lead you there." He gestured toward a green vine with pink, swirly patterns on the leaves. "Of course, if you aren't prompt, we are forgiving. It has been quite a morning."

"Will you give me poor marks if I don't come at all?"

The king raised an eyebrow at Brogan, indicating confusion.

"Fine. What does it mean to meet you at red?"

"The time. You will see flashes of color throughout the day. That's my mother's legacy. Red would mean something like three o'clock in the afternoon for you. My servants will remind you. Oh, and mind that they gossip, so try to remain dignified in their presence."

Brogan sighed in disbelief. "Red. Gossip. Dignity."

The king moved to leave but stopped. "Brogan, you are a remarkable young man. I am pleased to have you here."

With that, he bowed and glided away like a ninja. Not a leaf shook at his feet. Brogan studied the mechanics of each footfall. Could he replicate it?

He thought again about his conversations with Daisy. Another realm? A world that snatched her from her room? Then it snatched him through a puddle that pushed him out of a pond, after which a king greeted him. By the king's behavior, this was all totally normal, like pulling up to a Ritz Carlton. *Let me show you to your room. Sorry about the water.*

He opened the door of the villa and gazed at an enchanting foyer within. The walls were white, but gold trim lined the entire structure. He followed a subtle pattern woven in the floor's gray tiles. The farther he stepped, the more appealing each detail became. In the center of the house, a tall, golden-domed ceiling floated above a row of windows.

"Who slipped me acid?" he said out loud. Beautiful, wide-eyed servants peaked around corners to stare. Brogan jumped because they were so silent he'd not known they were there.

A man with honey-colored hair and amber eyes opened a door. "This is your bedroom and dressing chamber." The winsome servant led him into a washroom and showed him how the faucets worked and where to put his wet garments. After he left, Brogan threw his wet clothes on the ground instead. It felt good to retaliate against his abduction, no matter how benevolent it had been.

A hot bath awaited him, and he did everything he could not to enjoy it nor the fantastic scents in the water. His skin even tingled as it soaked up minerals and oils. Brogan hopped out and wrapped a towel around his waist. He pointed at the bath. "I am not in a good mood, you sneaky unicorn broth." He slammed the bathroom door open and found clothing set out for him in the bedroom.

Leather pants. Leather jacket. Silk shirt. He picked up the pants and opened the bedroom door to find the servant. He held the pants toward the man. "Leather?"

That man averted his gaze from Brogan's bare chest. "It's dragon skin. You will like it."

It's not like he was naked. He huffed again. "Of course it's *dragon* skin."

Brogan slammed the door and dropped his towel. The first garment was a type of underwear, similar to boxer briefs but so soft he shivered as he put them on. Then he fought to pull his damp legs through the fitted leather pants. His anger abated in awe when he fastened them.

They fit perfectly—more than perfectly, in fact. They were like an extension of his own skin. They flexed through his every movement as he pushed the limits of his flexibility to test them out. *High kick. Low kick. Front splits.* A dull pain reminded him he should warm up before the splits.

He wobbled back to his feet and grabbed the silk shirt. It also had its unique qualities. Heavier than silk as he'd known it, the fabric accentuated everything manly about his chest.

He looked for a mirror and found a full-length one inside the door of the wardrobe. "There's nothing like leather pants to make you look like a member of an '80's hair-band." He stared at his ridiculous reflection, then drew a breath. The unfamiliar clothing made something else about him look familiar. His father. The same light-green eyes, straight eyebrows, dark brown hair, and sturdy frame stared back at him. "Hey, Dad, do you like your dragon skin in dark green?" His chest warmed.

Brogan put on a pair of velvety slippers and strutted out of his room and around the villa, snatching exquisite foods each time he passed through the kitchen. Most of the servants had left or avoided him. He wandered through double doors onto a terrace and looked out at a view that couldn't be real. The house rested on a stark cliff at such a great altitude, clouds below him blocked the earth underneath. He could see a distant mountain range and only bits of land in between.

"One thing is certain, this beats that dump in Eastern Colorado any day."

A loud screech over his right shoulder split the air, startling him enough to roll to his side and position himself for a fight. An eagle, at least four feet tall, stared him down from a rail post. The bird fully deserved the term "raptor." Its terrifying talons gripped the remains of a carcass. A large one. Maybe a sheep?

It didn't help calm Brogan that the whole world turned red at just that moment.

And then everything casually turned back to its normal color. A servant stepped out on the terrace, which broke the death stare the eagle had fixed on Brogan. "Sir, it is time to meet with the ki . . . ahhh!" The servant jumped once he saw the eagle and hastily backed into the villa.

That was enough indication for Brogan. If the locals were afraid, he should be afraid. He bowed to the eagle and backed inside. The eagle stared after him, tilted its head, then tore a leg off of the sheep.

CHAPTER ELEVEN

BROGAN FOLLOWED a path through the gardens to the main house—more aptly called a palace. A servant motioned to a door that opened into a large, warm drawing room. Brogan found the king inside, relaxed in an armchair, legs crossed and reading a letter. He lifted his eyes to greet Brogan. "Have a seat, friend." He motioned to a chair near him.

Brogan blanched at the word *friend* and chose not to take a seat. Instead, he wandered the great room while the king finished reading. Afternoon light poured in through the many windows. He could see the pond he had been pulled from. He must have been too distracted at the time to notice the awe-inspiring beauty surrounding it. Trees and bushes twisted wildly around each other. Flowers of every color grew in effusive clumps around them. Light poured over and through the arrangements, casting colorful hues toward the drawing room.

"My mother and father used to argue over it," the king said.

"Over what?" Brogan flopped into the chair.

"Over the garden. He liked shaped gardens; she liked wild ones. In the end, she did what she liked. Her work in the garden probably kept her sane through the wars."

"Is war common here?"

"Not at all."

"Did your parents just happen to live through a rough time? You said wars."

"I did. At least four they talked about. Each of those was devastating. My mother would have fought, too, if she didn't have to stay and do the politics."

"Four is a lot."

"Yes, well, they were centuries apart. My father didn't neglect his kingdom. It is rare for the distant wilds to organize for battle."

Centuries? "How old are you?"

"That's a personal question, Brogan, but since I am the king, you could ask anyone and they will tell you. I am one hundred twenty-six years old. My sister is one hundred forty-four. Many of our people consider us children."

"And your parents?"

"They each died about twenty years ago. I don't know how many years they lived prior. They weren't counting. My mother would tell the elders she was born during the Moss Plague, and they would nod their heads as if that were a perfectly acceptable answer." His eyes twinkled as he pointed to a painting of a beautiful elf-like woman. "Supposedly, that was why her hair was green. Her mother had no choice but to eat moss her whole pregnancy."

Brogan stood to study the painting. The woman in the painting bore the same angelic qualities of her son, while the painting itself demonstrated masterful techniques in capturing her impish yet regal expression. Flawless skin glistened in the painter's light. Had he met her, he'd never have assumed she was human. "Green hair."

Orya chuckled. "She said she put herself on a strictly 'white' diet when my sister and I were conceived. That is why my hair is silver."

"What about your father? Did he also—"

"His hair was a normal coppery color. Her family passed down the hair-coloring trait. It's quite rare."

"What happened to him?"

"He was executed by our enemy after a particularly brutal battle. I inherited the crown from him. My father was a man I will love and respect until I leave this world." The king choked up a bit. "I miss them both dearly. What great wisdom and joy we lost the day he died."

Brogan found that, in spite of the uncomfortable sharing, he was able to empathize. "I'm sorry. My father only moved to a different country, and I feel cheated. I don't know what I'd do if he died."

The king smiled. "How fortunate that we both we respect and admire our fathers. You said he moved far away from you?"

A little clamp rested on Brogan's throat. "It's a little raw."

"You are welcome to keep it to yourself," Orya said without any sort of unpleasant tone or reaction.

Brogan stared at the gardens, then around the room to the man sitting next to him, looking impressive and otherworldly. He sank back into the chair, resigning himself to the bizarre circumstances. "This can't be real. If it is, my problems are suddenly stupid in comparison."

"Isn't that always the case when you travel? One leaves problems behind only to pick up new ones. It can happen in a single day. When you return, you can have your old problems back." Orya's eyes twinkled, but the impish smirk was gone.

"Do you really want to know?" Brogan asked in a low, toneless voice. "I mean, about my situation."

The king's eyes softened. "Of course. You are with friends and welcome to tell me why your heart is heavy."

Brogan nodded. He could try it. "I feel like I don't belong anywhere. I've lived all over the world with my dad, which has been great, but it also means saying goodbye over and over. No one can relate to my past. New York *started* to feel like home, and my cousin, Emmy, was a good friend. Then my dad sent me away to live with my grandparents. They don't know me either. But what's worse is that I don't know anything about them or that town where my dad became who he is. I'm a foreigner, even though they know all about me."

Orya waited until Brogan had finished. He leaned forward and placed his elbows on his knees, breaking his perfect posture for the first time. "You are a prince in your world. It's lonely being a child of opportunity and power. No one will understand because of shared experience. But if you are patient, those who are dear to you might understand because you let them. Good people rise to the challenge of loving a friend. You might find that you aren't such a cat in the water."

"What?"

"I think he means *fish out of water*," laughed a pleasant voice behind Brogan. He turned to see a lady who might be described as the female version of King Orya. Her eyes sparkled in the same striking gray-blue. She had shapely pink lips, and her flawless skin was on the pale side. She wore a cobalt blue velvet dress, fastened in front with large diamonds. "He has worked hard to learn your idioms, but he confuses them."

The king laughed and stood to greet the lady. "Brogan, this is my sister Choral, who has never struggled for the right thing to say."

Choral curtsied and bowed her head before standing again with her chin high. Her skin practically glowed with life. "What a pleasure to meet you," she said.

"My pleasure too." But instead of his words being their typical caramel, he delivered them on a rusty gurney.

Her eyes danced. "I am only here to tell you that Cook is ready for us. Dinner will be served as soon as you enter the dining room." Choral turned and floated back through the double doors, her dress flowing in perfect femininity.

The king interrupted Brogan's entrancement. "I wish our meeting could be only pleasant, but we need to get to the business of rescuing Daisy."

"This is about Daisy?" A pang of guilt twisted his chest. In all of this otherworld business, he'd forgotten about her. "Where has she gone?"

Worry etched itself onto the king's brow. He led the way into a dining room. Natural light poured from large floor-to-ceiling windows flanking two sides of the room. He sat down at the head of a modest table and motioned for Brogan to take the seat on his left while Choral sat on his right.

"Daisy is in danger. Scouts in every known territory are seeking her whereabouts, and I received word that she may have been brought in through the swamps of Psoih, which terrifies me. A portal there isn't likely to be stable. Even if I knew for certain, I would be foolish to take men in there after her. It's the only reason my enemies chose it. The swamps are a vast, unchartered labyrinth, and the pathways keep shifting. I am concerned she will attempt to escape and even more frightened that she will not. I'm not sure which is more deadly—the swamps or the final destination of her captors."

"Which is?"

"The Castle Sfioused in the ancient language. In their tongue, it is called Ahl. It is the heart of our enemy and a source of evil and suffering. Your father did make sure you learned how to fight with a sword and ride horses? This was his promise to us."

Did he hear that correctly? "*My* father?"

"Leo? Yes. He promised to prepare you when you were a child —in case you were needed. I was specific that you should learn the skills of combat and weaponry."

Brogan cursed under his breath, remembering Emmy's words. *It's almost like he wants you to be an old-timey king with swords and horses and stuff.*

His face must have been contorting, because Orya said, "I'm sorry, Brogan. You may need to lean into your wells of patience while you are here. I promise it won't be the strangest detail you will encounter, and we have a lot of work to do."

* * *

As Orya, Choral, and Brogan ate, Brogan's mind filtered through recent conversations, trying to understand his degree of trust, or mistrust, in the people he had recently met or had known his whole life. It seemed as if Daisy was a shining star of vulnerability among them.

"May I ask . . ." Brogan cleared his throat and glanced at the King, "what is your relationship with Daisy?"

The king met Brogan's eyes and answered without hesitation. "She is my betrothed."

Brogan choked down his spoonful of soup. "Does *she* know?"

"She doesn't know, though she should suspect some connection to our world by now. But betrothal is rarely the choice of the betrothed. Our parents agreed in our infancy. Or should I say my parents and her great-great-grandparents up the line. Magic never keeps things clean and tidy. It is always messy business."

Choral chimed in, "Yes. Poor brother. He keeps losing out where the maidens of that family are concerned. They are all beautiful, and by the time they come here, they've been spoken for. Because of our parents' promise, he cannot marry except from among their offspring. It has become somewhat of a joke."

"Good thing I only get better looking." Orya smirked.

Choral chuckled. "After losing out last time, he had a spell cast. Poor Daisy is doomed to be . . . unappealing to men until she first sets foot on the altar stone in our castle."

Brogan stared at Orya in disbelief. Did he realize that Daisy's *lack of appeal* had everything to do with a gnarly car wreck? "Is that what you mean when you say magic is a messy business?"

Orya stopped eating and sighed. "Brogan, magic is wild. We might have dominion over a small part of it, that which was determined from before, but even then it always obeys a bigger master." Remorse stole over his face. "I was rather tipsy when that satrap convinced me I should do it. I shouldn't have invited him to the solstice in the first place. And I regret the pain it has put the girl through. I tried to have the spell reversed. It wasn't until I saw what a remarkable woman she is becoming under that pain that I felt like my sin was somehow redeemed."

Choral patted her brother on the shoulder, "For all of our bumbling, the Eternal One manages the details. His promised care is what we must lean into while we search for her."

Brogan could hardly call it *bumbling*. Coral and Orya were attempting to make a heavy offense look innocent.

The king finished. "I meant to call her to our court on her seventeenth birthday. I, of course, would not expect to wed her right away. I want her to know and love me first. The way I have come to care for her."

Brogan shook his head. *Seventeen?* This isn't the nineteenth century. Which was weirder: The age of marriage? Or that this otherworldly monarch expected to marry Daisy Bloom?

CHAPTER TWELVE

GLASS from the broken window had gashed the inside of Daisy's left bicep. Blood soaked her pajama top from her armpit to her stomach. She sat on wet dirt as the world wavered around her and her vision blurred. Darkness pulled her head backward, but she fought for consciousness.

A man had flickered in and out of reflections in her window that morning before she left for Denver, but nothing could have prepared her for what happened that evening.

Now the man, her abductor, hovered over her. She stared at him.

Deep, long scars covered his large, powerful body. His exposed chest, neck, face—everything she could see of him—was mangled and distorted. Two other figures pulled the scarred man away from her and threw him on the ground.

She peered through her haze at a swampy landscape. A canopy of trees stretched high overhead. Warm, wet air suffocated her each breath.

"Why is the girl bleeding?" a smooth, deep voice demanded. "Surely you understand the difference between kidnap and murder?"

Daisy tried to see the speaker, but her view continued to worsen. She saw only a blurry figure in green clothes.

"Somebody bind her dripping wound."

Men clambered over each other to obey. A smaller figure fell at her and whispered an incantation. The two edges of her split skin fused back together and the burning pain subsided.

"Try not to move it, and drink this," the deep voice said as a cup was forced into her hand. "It will keep your wound from infecting. If you haven't noticed, we are in a swamp. Plenty of creatures live the mist. Drink the concoction, or we will leave you for their feast."

Hadn't he just said they needed her for ransom? She called his bluff and tossed the drink on the ground before her world went black.

* * *

DAISY AWOKE IN A WARM, humid tent. A thick, net covered the space around her bed, and she couldn't see beyond it.

"Can we move her tonight?" asked the same deep voice from before.

"Master, she is not accustomed to our air, and she has lost a lot of blood. She can't travel on horseback. We will need a stable gurney, which is impossible in this swamp. If her health is important, give her two days."

The voice cursed.

The servant said, "She is lucky Plank didn't kill her."

His master scoffed. "*Plank* is lucky he didn't kill her. I will guard her. I can't risk being outwitted by Ellesian *praidas*. Tell the men to set up camp for two days. We march at the second yellow from now."

Daisy struggled to keep listening, but darkness pulled on her again.

After several hours in and out of a feverish sleep, she awoke with a clearer head. A man paced back and forth outside the net, talking to himself. Daisy couldn't place his accent. Its effects on the

English language would be musical and lovely if his words weren't so off-putting.

"What kind of a prize are you? Your looks aren't appealing."

He didn't sound like the creature that had whispered to Brogan and her in the darkness. Where had she heard his accent before?

The man stopped pacing. "Can you hear me?"

Suddenly the netting flew open and a young man strode inside. He had piercing black eyes and an unearthly beauty. His auburn hair had been tied back from a uniquely sculpted face, with large, angular eyes and full lips.

She forced herself to hold his gaze. She wouldn't be afraid of him, his beauty, or of the magic that had just pulled her from her bedroom into a netherswamp.

Clad in taut green leather, his muscled arms tightened over his chest. He sat down and stared at her from a chair. "You are not the warrior I expected. And yet it is you, the waif whose soul I tracked from the tower." He chuckled slightly as if pleased with himself. "If I hadn't thought to bring the magic bindings that night, you'd still be pilfering our treasury. But how brilliant of Choral to use a *praida* from another world."

Praida. It had been weeks since she'd heard a word from her dreams.

Then this was the man who tried to slice her with his sword. She doubted he felt any conviction in doing it again. Fear pressed its gnarly hands against her chest, forcing her to take deep, even breaths.

"And now you are weak." He poked her upper arm. "Not a muscle. Your only hope is for the light fairy to rescue you."

Of course he'd been looking for the warrior, the girl who existed in Daisy's dreams while Daisy herself awoke every morning to a body that could barely walk. Then she wondered aloud, "Light fairy?"

The man shifted forward. "She can talk after all," he said to no one, a self-satisfied smirk oozing across his face. "The light fairy is Orya, king of the lightpeople."

"Orya?" Daisy whispered. Why did that name sound familiar?

The man tilted his head. "Are you playing games? Are you going to pretend he is not tearing up the hills looking for you? Are you not his beloved?"

"I-I'm not anyone's beloved," Daisy answered in all honesty. Her face warmed. She wished the beautiful, horrible man would stop staring at her.

"You aren't the flower?" he asked, his brows knit together. "What is your name?"

"What on earth are you going on about?"

"We are not on Earth, and I'm talking about the flower on Orya's crest."

She stared up at the deep red fabric that made up the roof of her tent. "Where am I?"

"No answers without your name."

"My name is Daisy Lorrian Bloom," She exploded with sass.

"I will call you Weed."

"And I will call you Jerk Face."

The man-boy cocked a half smile and chuckled. "You will?" In other circumstances, his mirthful face would have been charming.

"Yes, Jerk Face. I think so."

He pulled out a knife, leaned toward her, and touched her cheek with the flat edge. "Some have died for less."

She slapped his forearm to get the blade out of her face. The movement felt slow and heavy without her awesomely talented ninja body that engaged in parkour and knife fights. Now her weakness was apparent because her slap did not even cause his hand to sway.

His smirk remained.

She would have to use her wits. She pressed fear from the periphery of her mind; she could freak out later. "Jerk Face, I happen to know you need me alive for ransom."

He rolled his eyes, sheathed his knife, and resumed his crossed-arm sitting position. "It's my decision how alive I deliver you, brave Weed. I suppose you haven't seen enough to be afraid."

She tilted her head. "I was pulled from my bedroom window into *another world*. What more can you do to intimidate me?"

He didn't answer her question. Instead, he asked, "Why would your mother name you Daisy?"

She shrugged and studied her nails. "She never told me, but lots of people are named after flowers."

"You didn't think to ask her?"

"Nope. She's quirky."

"Those who visit our realm often are." He clasped his hands behind his head.

Now he had her attention.

"You didn't know? Phee is not a stranger to us."

"You know my mom?"

"Not personally. She is rumored to be beautiful." At the word *beautiful*, he exaggerated a rolling gesture with his hand before pointing back at her. "So how did you come from her?"

If he was trying to rattle her, he chose the wrong topic. This was familiar territory. She flopped back onto the bed. "I guess it's *is* a good question." She imitated his rolling hand gesture.

He puffed out a small laugh. "My king will be disappointed."

"Who is your king? And who are you?"

"I was beginning to wonder at your lack of curiosity. You may call me *My Lord*."

Suddenly the tent faded, and Daisy found herself in a dark inner chamber lit with lamps. A woman with long hair held a newborn child as her chest rocked with sobs. "My precious boy, you are Zerek Sivha Kindleheart, beloved of your mother and of her Eternal One." Her deep, agonizing moan filled the chamber. As it faded, Daisy again faced the man under the net coverings of the swamp tent.

"Your name is Zerek Sivha Kindleheart."

His eyes widened, then seared.

"Am I right?"

"How do you know this?" he asked in a whisper.

She shrugged and made her response sound as casual and unperturbed as she could. She'd been in dangerous situations before. She could do this. "I just now saw a woman holding a baby and naming him."

He stood, his frame tense. "It's no wonder he sent me. I felt he was overreacting. You are only a waif. But you are something more, are you not, Weed?"

She rolled her eyes, but he had already disappeared into his own thoughts, too preoccupied to see her open rebellion.

He flashed her one last hateful glance and strode from the tent. "Let her rest," he yelled to the guards outside. "She is not to leave the tent."

* * *

THE EXTRA DAY IN BED, along with some very interesting fruit, gave Daisy newfound energy. She couldn't be sure if her senses were heightened by the adrenaline that never seemed to stop or if the world around her buzzed more than Earth or in a different frequency or something. Little noises dropped, snapped, and howled from various distances and at different volumes. Lights fought their way through holes and cracks in the tent walls, and the heavy humidity swirled in occasional eddies around her sweaty body.

This strange swamp carried rich, often putrid, smells. She especially smelled her own body odor. Her skin had only ever known the typical thirty-percent humidity of Colorado, and it must be confused right now.

Two young women, one with red hair and the other with dark brown, brought a wash basin into her tent and set it on a folding chair. They also draped clean clothes on the back of the chair— strange black leather pants and a burgundy leather coat.

"You're to wash yourself. Soap and a cloth are here." She set both in the water and turned with her fellow maid to face outward from the tent, like guards. "We'll make sure you aren't interrupted."

Daisy, assured by the two women guarding her door, peeled off her grimy pajama pants and bloody T-shirt. She picked up the wet cloth and soap and began working out the smell. She was shocked to see all the blood flake off without a single cut left behind.

The unusual leather pants were paired with a black shirt, which went on easy enough, but pulling the tight pants over her hips could have been a new form of working out. Once she'd worked them up to her waist, they fit in a startling way. The entire suit breathed when Daisy needed it to breathe. It constricted against the cold whenever a chill passed through.

Somehow the female attendants sensed she'd dressed, and they came back inside. They washed and braided her long hair in an intricate coiffure.

"How do we remove these things from your teeth?" The redheaded woman tugged on her braces.

"Remove? I don't think you can. It's cement or something."

"Healer!" the woman bellowed.

A small man ran into the tent.

"Can you remove these?"

The healer grabbed Daisy's chin and studied her teeth. "Barbarism," he muttered, then chanted some incantation. Daisy startled as little pops when off in her mouth, accompanied by a release from the tugging metal. In awe, she pulled out the remaining contraption.

"You might as well straighten her teeth too," the woman said with irritation. "You'd think a healer would think of these things."

The man death stared at the sassy redhead and chanted again. Daisy's gums suddenly felt a fierce, fiery pain and a pressure worse than any of her braces. She went to scream, but he clamped his hand over her mouth. "I'm not getting a beating for you, miss, so hush for a minute until we're through."

It was a long minute, but the burning, agonizing pain ceased instantly. He released her, shaking her tears from his hand. She fell to the ground, panting for breath, then felt with her tongue to discover that her teeth had all moved.

She stood and snatched a mirror one of the women had brought and pulled it to her face, smiling. Her teeth aligned perfectly, though her face was now sweaty and beet red from the ordeal. Her hair looked disheveled, with strands popping from the intricate braids.

Daisy's laughter mixed with sobs and tears as the perplexed women tried to fix the frizzy strands. "I guess you can't fix everything."

They released her once they admitted defeat.

"Is this tight suit necessary?" Daisy asked. It clung to her body like plastic wrap.

The servants nodded. "We were told to have you ready to ride. These clothes are the safest. You won't get caught on branches or be easily tracked."

"And your butt won't chafe," added another. "It's dragon skin."

Of course it is.

She limped out of the tent and saw Zerek holding the reigns of an enormous, black unicorn. Daisy had to do a double take because the unicorn didn't have hooves; instead it had paws and carnivorous teeth. And the horn was not for decoration. It looked more like a blade for killing things. She wondered what twisted maniac pulled this creature from the bowels of hell.

One of the men guffawed, "She's afraid of the shadow beast."

Zerek eyed him and asked, "Are you not?"

The soldier said no more and melted away from them.

The beast nuzzled Zerek, but no one else approached it.

"Your ride is there," Zerek said to her, pointing at a spotted, gray horse.

Daisy limped toward it, but Zerek interrupted her. "Healer, can you take care of the leg?"

The healer looked confused.

"Do you not see her limping? When did this happen?"

"It didn't happen here or in the window," the man insisted.

Hoping to save the man from a beating, Daisy piped up. "I've been limping for years. An accident crushed my kneecap. It's technically healed, but the ligament damage makes it painful to walk."

Again, the general scowled at the healer.

"Right away, master!" the healer cowered, grabbing Daisy's arm and pulling her into a tent.

She wasn't keen to fix another thing on her body after the teeth incident, but she hadn't been the one to call any shots lately. That, and the last thing worked, so . . .

The healer pointed to a linen-covered chair. "Sit down there and take off your pants. After you've taken them off, put these on." He tossed her a pair of white shorts. "I'll count to ten."

Daisy panicked. "Wait, what? I'm not taking my pants off—"

The man raised an eyebrow, interrupting her. "We can force them off. Or you can just put on the shorts while I step outside." He exited the tent and began counting. "One. Two . . ."

Daisy worked the tight dragon skins off as quickly as she could, but with her lack of flexibility and the tightness of the leather, this was not happening in ten seconds. "Count to 30 . . . or 40!" she cried through the tent canvas, ignoring her keeper's impatient groan as she pulled the shorts on.

The man came back in and jerked her leg up onto a bench. He put a salve over her kneecap. It soaked through her skin and made its way *into* her knee, burning like fire. Daisy gripped the arms of the chair. Tears stung her eyes and she grit her teeth. The man's quick hands reached over and pulled her kneecap so hard it dislocated. Daisy screamed as the pain tore through her knee.

Zerek dashed into the tent, looking ready to beat the healer, but the healer didn't stop the torture. He yanked her kneecap yet again, tendons twanging. The searing pain subsided to a dull bite after the fourth jerk. Finally, a fifth, then a sixth tug, followed by pouring oil over her knee.

The oil penetrated her skin the same way the salve had, only this time a cool sensation calmed the burning pain left by the first salve. Her tears stopped and the ringing in her head cleared. Her knee didn't hurt anymore, though the skin around it had turned a deep purple.

The healer stood. "As long as she stays off of it for two days, she'll be fine."

Daisy looked up to see Zerek grimacing at her bright-purple knee. She covered it with the healer's cloth and watched his eyes shift to her tear-streaked face. She wiped her eyes with the back of her hands.

"Get dressed and we'll be on our way," he said, then followed the healer from the tent.

Daisy had to squeeze into the leather pants again, but her knee had swelled enough to make the process of stretching the leather over her legs even more laborious than the first time. She wanted to throw medical paraphernalia from the healer's tent when she heard Zerek's huffs of impatience.

"As if *I'm* the one making any decisions here," she muttered.

Once the pants were fastened, she limped toward the door.

Only, limping wasn't necessary. Her knee didn't give out and the old pain had gone. She stopped and gaped down at the swollen lump around her knee. She lifted it toward her chest. It moved smoothly, like water. She took a natural step and bumped into Zerek just outside the tent. She looked up into his eyes as her tears cascaded over an awkward smile. "Did that man just *heal* my knee?"

He sighed and looked around before his face hardened. "Just stop walking for a couple of days. The tendons haven't finished setting." He carried so much command and authority that it made her feel small. He reached down, picked her up, then handed her off to a nearby soldier with the words, "Link, finish this."

Apparently "this" was the act of tossing her onto a horse. Link caught Daisy and hoisted her onto a saddle.

Daisy didn't ride horses. She grabbed the saddle horn and put her feet in the stirrups, but that's all she could think to do.

Zerek rode up beside her on the shadowbeast, shook his head, and placed the reigns in her hands. "Weed, you will only ride with my most trusted men. You will be locked up at night. I will sleep outside of your cage. Be on your guard."

CHAPTER THIRTEEN

ZEREK'S TRUSTED men were hardly men and hardly seemed trust-worthy. Twelve enormous warriors, each no less than two hundred pounds of pure muscle, all dwarfed their master. Scars covered their exposed flesh. Their faces looked as if they were torn open and sewn back together on a regular basis.

"Tim Burton would be proud to feature such gruesome crea-tures," Daisy said aloud with a sigh. She shouldn't be surprised, since this is her own personal nightmare, sans the unexpected healings.

Everyone ignored her comment, except for the shadowbeast. It eyed her and licked its teeth.

Zerek turned its head away from her. "She's not food, Shadow."

He called three men out. The warriors rode their mounts up to his, and he divulged plans to them that she couldn't overhear. Their scowls probably indicated the degree to which they took their mission seriously.

One broke off from the huddle and moved his horse to hers. "I am not to allow more than four paces between us at any time," he said. "If you try to move beyond that, I'll knock you off your saddle."

"Where would I possibly go?" Daisy quipped, peering at the stark drops from the road into the swamps. There was nothing but gloop on both sides. Still, each man scanned every direction as they walked as if some marauder might swoop in at any time.

After the first day riding, Daisy's entire body hurt. *At least my butt isn't chaffed,* she glowered. They had stopped at a wide, dry clearing to set up camp, and she got to see firsthand how challenging it was. They all had tasks that involved putting up tents, making food, caring for horses—in a swamp. Everyone was busy, so Daisy thought she would help with something.

Someone tugged at her collar. She turned and found herself face to face with Zerek.

"Just rest. Your knee, remember?"

"I can at least clean stuff."

"Not without moving your knee."

Was she really that precious? She rolled her eyes and looked for her tent.

He grabbed her arm and led her firmly through the narrow maze of tents. "You're in my tent this time. Don't worry; I don't like it either. I don't trust most of these men." He opened a tent flap and waved her inside before guiding her into a cage large enough for her to sleep comfortably.

She didn't question it. She was exhausted and grateful to eat and sleep right away. She must have been out for a while when Zerek's voice woke her.

He wasn't talking to her. Rather, he seemed to be talking in his sleep. "I won't disappoint you, Father." He whimpered like a child in some strange language.

She gasped when she realized she understood the language. It wasn't English, nor was it one she had studied. Had he been speaking this language the whole time?

She shook her head, unable to think about it while his cries for mercy continued.

When the whimpering didn't stop, she escaped to a memory

of snuggling with her own father and reading the Bible in front of the fire. Her father often interrupted her to ask if she understood particularly complicated points of theology—like the atonement. She once confessed to him that it didn't make any sense that Jesus' sacrifice could mean anything if He was only going to rise up a few days later. "Is that really sacrifice, knowing it would be reversed?" She had given him a pointed, skeptical look.

"It's like a rich man paying a poor man's debt. The rich man could easily pay the debt and still be rich. Likewise, Jesus' spiritual capital is endless. He could pay our debt because that much payment wouldn't impoverish him. That doesn't mean that it wasn't a terrible price. But his infinite life swallowed up death the same way one light bulb can illuminate an entire room full of darkness."

With Zerek still muttering in his sleep in his nearby cot, Daisy prayed. "God, Zerek didn't have a father to teach him about you. Have mercy. Let him know a father's love. And be with my parents right now. They're probably scared or confused." Was God limited by worlds? Would he hear her in this black and hopeless place? She kept praying. She prayed she would get out of this horrible and weird kidnapping. She prayed for the miserable soldiers and the attendants who were around her. She prayed for a sign that God was with her.

Sleep had just pulled her into its warm embrace when Zerek shot straight up. The sudden movement made her jump and bang her head against on one of the bars.

"Ow. What's wrong?" She rubbed her head, disappointed to be awake again.

He turned to her with intensity. "What were you doing?"

"What do you mean? What can I be doing *in a cage?*"

"I dreamed that you were moving things. Large things. Things as large as this kingdom."

"Maybe you were dreaming," she mumbled, willing herself back to sleep.

"Not just a dream. My enemies are not my dream pawns, nor I

127

theirs. Something else put them before me, and their directives were coming from you in that cage."

"I don't know what you're talking about, Psycho."

The warrior didn't lie back down, but she ignored him. It was her turn to sleep.

* * *

DAISY WOKE EARLY the next morning, and her knee felt amazing. She couldn't help her elation and took opportunities to skip and run around, helping people pack up their camp and take care of animals.

That evening, after they marched through the swamp all day, she came across several foot soldiers making fun of one of the archers who had fallen in to the swamp. His clothes reeked with a putrid smell.

"I can't wash my clothes without stripping down," the man whined.

She stepped close enough to get a whiff of the stink. His clothes definitely needed washed. "Stay in your tent and hand your clothes to me. I'll clean them."

All of the men stopped and stared at each other. A few whispered.

"It's no big deal. I've got soap and there's a washbasin over there. Even if I'm terrible at it, they'll be cleaner than they are now."

The man shrugged and walked into his tent. A minute later he dropped the soiled clothes outside.

She nearly gagged when she picked them up, but she managed to drop them into the wash barrel that the servants had been using. She wondered if all swamps carried this kind of stench or if this one was special.

One of the men scowled at her and mumbled something about ruining an entire barrel of water. When Daisy caught his gaze, his scowl softened and he bowed his head.

"I'm sorry," Daisy offered. "You probably have a system for the resources you carried in here."

"It can't be helped now."

Daisy thought she caught a glimmer of a smile as the man strode away.

She rung out the soldier's uniform and then stood, holding the clean clothes outside the flap to the man's tent. The light was quickly fading. Zerek would come scowling after her if she didn't hurry.

"Excuse me," she called through the canvas. "Your clothes are wet, but clean . . . well, cleaner."

A man who didn't bear the countenance of a soldier ran up to Daisy and chanted something. The clothes dried instantly in her hands. She stared at the smaller man, remembering the healer who straightened her teeth and strengthened her knee.

A single arm shot out from the opening of the tent and took the now dry clothes. She released them, startled.

When she turned back toward the enchanter, a dozen sets of eyes greeted her, most with a soft expression she didn't understand.

She raised one hand in a slight wave and made her way toward Zerek's tent, feeling stares bearing down upon her back.

* * *

THE NEXT MORNING Daisy received cheerful greetings from the soldiers and maids she'd met the night before.

The man whose clothes she'd washed smiled at her. He'd washed the swamp scum from his face and hair, so now she could see he had curly, black hair and stood a head taller than most. He handed her a bowl of rice and vegetables. "Sit with us."

Why not? she thought as she took the portable chair he'd vacated for her.

A young redheaded soldier asked, "Why aren't you more afraid? You're a captive."

The question bewildered Daisy. "I am afraid."

"You don't act like it," he insisted.

Daisy wasn't sure what they expected. Disappointment and fear had so normalized in her existence that it simply didn't require extreme expression. Her father had counseled her through all of the events since their move to Layton. Maybe she'd come to expect trauma.

"Where did you come from?" the soldier continued. "There's no one living in these swamps, so you had to have been brought here by magic, right?"

She studied his curious green eyes and shrugged. "I was sitting in my room one moment and found myself here the next. We don't have magic where I'm from, so I don't know how."

One of the two maids in their company gasped. "Oh, I wish there was no magic here either. Only the worst people have it."

The tall, dark-haired soldier shushed her. "This ain't the place, Adina. Master don't police our words none, but he ain't the only scary one with ears."

Adina's suntanned face paled. "You think Taph can hear us out here?"

"Good Zorlock, Adina," the redhead joined in the scorn. "Just stop!" He turned to Daisy. "Maybe you can just tell us about where you came from."

"Not sure what you want to know. I'm a pastor's kid, and I drive a junker."

Nothing but blank stares met her.

"I go to school every day and read books no one else is interested in."

"You can read?" The redhead's eyes widened with longing. "My pa wanted to learn, but he wasn't of age yet before the schools were burned."

"That sounds tragic," Daisy said. "Do you all live in a swamp like this one?"

"Gads, no!" The tall man laughed. "Yeh, just was unfortunate to come into Ahl through this death pit. There's a reason there's so many of us trekkin in here. Mighty dangerous this is, so we needed the safety of numbers."

"Why is it so dangerous?"

A collective gasp stole over their circle.

"Master?" The tall one stuttered out the word.

Daisy shifted herself around to see Zerek standing ten feet on the other side of her.

"Weed, if I see you talking to any more of my men, I will beat them senseless." His tone, as always, remained even and unaffected.

He turned to face the rest of his soldiers and servants. "Do you all hear me? You *and your families* will regret speaking to the weed!"

The crowd that had been building around her melted away. Each of her new friends finished their meals quietly, then found work to do elsewhere. These were not empty threats.

Dread and heavy sorrow returned to her chest. She glared at Zerek and thought, *Do I really have to pray for my enemies?*

She packed her saddle and rode the day in silence, after which she handed her horse to a groom. He took its reigns with only a nod.

Adina handed her a serving of rations, but no one made space for her to sit as they all chatted in a circle. The only space for her to eat was near the shadowbeast, where no one else wanted to sit.

Daisy loathed the idea but found a rock about ten feet from the creature. She'd finished eating when the circle of soldiers peered at her, mouth agape.

"What?" she asked, annoyed that they couldn't respond.

One of them pointed behind her. She turned to see the beast's head mere inches from her own. It didn't bare its long fangs, making it seem a little like a regular a horse. It sniffed at her, then nuzzled the bottom of its head against the top of hers and exhaled a long breath.

The soldiers gasped.

Daisy ducked down and stood to face the beast. It studied her and tilted its head. She backed away and hastened to Zerek's tent.

She stopped at the door. "Excuse me. Commander?"

The flap swung open and Zerek glared at her. "That's *general*."

She took in his youthful face. "Aren't you young to be a general? Where I'm from, only seasoned military men lead armies."

He shrugged. "It's a blessing of my birthright." His voice didn't waver, so he must be confident in his position.

He took her in for a moment before moving to the side and allowing her passage.

She crawled inside her sleeping cage and under the blankets to escape into her thoughts. She'd been praying the whole day, wondering if God could even hear her. "Maybe I'm just talking to myself," she whispered. "Maybe I'm going crazy."

"What's that?" Zerek asked.

"Nothing," she said with a small sigh.

He locked the cage and continued whatever he was doing.

She'd have to reach for whatever hope she could. So she prayed for Zerek. She prayed for his health in the swamp. She prayed for the softening of his heart—the kind of stuff she'd always heard Dad pray for when he didn't like someone.

She fell asleep, finally, and dreamed she was sitting above the army, safely on a cloud, while thorns and barbed wire ensnared everyone else. They were bleeding and no one could stop the outflow of their lives. Chains gripped Zerek, pulling him toward a dark cavern. No matter how he resisted, the chains dug deeper into his flesh, and his feet slipped closer toward the mouth of the chasm. He fought until the inevitable end, taking all of the soldiers with him.

In her dream Daisy edged toward the dark chasm and peered into it. The darkness inside screamed its agony, filled with thousands of voices begging for mercy. It was a thousand times more terrifying than being pulled through her window. A stench of decay and sulfur rose up to her nostrils, and she awoke nearly vomiting.

Daisy sat up. The door to her cage lay open, and three floating lights, one blue and two yellow, beckoned her forward toward the opening of the tent. She instinctively followed them. Slightly fresher air indicated that she had stepped outside, but darkness still veiled her eyes from any detail. Without the little floating lights, she might have lost her equilibrium altogether.

The two yellow lights floated in front of her feet and the blue light hovered at eye level, still beckoning her forward. They brightened enough that she could see the ground, but they moved faster than her feet would allow and kept circling back, waiting for her. She followed the lights deeper into the black night, alone.

She must have walked for hours because her feet hurt. She crouched to rest, and her stomach rumbled. This was no dream.

The world brightened around her until a yellow light filled the sky, stayed a moment, then receded. It was the sign for the troops to awake—but there were no sleeping troops. She had wandered too far from camp to see anyone. She stood alone, surrounded by blue tree trunks rising from a boggy floor, arching over her head in a canopy of yellow leaves. Her feet rested on a twisted, raised path. She blinked. The lights had guided her safely on thin strips of solid ground between patches of swamp and bog.

As the day grew brighter, amphibians chirped and little wings whirred around her.

She scanned the horizon for any sign of her captors, but there were none. She chuckled in disbelief that she was free, and the sound echoed in the voices of little creatures mimicking her laughter. They passed the sound from tree to tree.

She cleared her throat and the little voices returned throaty sounds, causing her to peal into real laughter. The returned laugher from every direction made her imagine herself as a stand-up comedian, surrounded by an adoring audience.

She sang a chorus, and the animals shifted to carry her tune.

"I'm so hungry," she said aloud. As the word *hungry* echoed in the animals' small voices, a strange fruit dropped onto the path in front of her. She looked up. Where had it had come from? A fruit tree canopied above her. Several, in fact. She picked up the fruit and bit into it. A refreshing and sweet juice tingled in her mouth.

All joy halted when someone grabbed her from behind.

"Where do you think you are going, Weed?" Zerek hissed into her ear.

CHAPTER FOURTEEN

DAISY STRUGGLED to breathe as Zerek's grip on her neck tightened.

He threw her onto the trail. "Start walking back." He approached her as she lay stunned on the ground, his face tense and lethal. Just as he reached for her, a large reptilian creature jumped out of the bog and pinned him to the ground. The quick reversal meant that the young warrior suddenly fought for his own life, his chest clamped between the large creature's jaws.

Daisy knew that this would be an ideal time to run, but she couldn't leave the man to the terrible fate that seemed to have leapt straight from her nightmare. She picked up a heavy branch and swung it at the reptile's head as hard as she could, hitting her mark. The creature turned on her, but rather than attacking, it hissed and scurried into the nearest gloop.

Zerek rolled on the ground, coughing up droplets of blood. His leather suit had protected his skin from tearing, but she knew he must have broken ribs, accompanied by some internal bleeding.

She knelt next to him. "Can you stand? The creature is likely stunned, but I doubt I wounded him."

Zerek nodded and leaned into her as he stood. She was glad he wasn't one of the two-hundred-pound warriors, yet his solid and strong frame nearly buckled her. The little blue light bounced farther ahead on the trail, then swerved a few feet from the path to reveal a ladder. Daisy felt a surge of hope as her gaze followed the ladder up to a platform perched high above the swamp's gelatinous depths.

"Can you climb a ladder? I think we should rest up there." She pointed into the canopy.

Zerek nodded, and when they managed to reach the ladder, he heaved himself upward one rung at a time. Daisy followed, pushing his rear up with her shoulders. At the top, he collapsed onto the platform.

She fell alongside him, catching great breaths. "I am so out of shape."

He didn't respond—he had passed out. His chest moved in short, methodical spasms.

"Hang in there," she said, watching him breathe. Not that she could do much for him. If he really had spit up blood, he may be dying . . . and that was extent of her medical knowledge.

She studied their surroundings. They had stumbled onto what appeared to be a commonly used platform hideaway. Clean water collected upon large, open leaves. A stash of clay jars revealed treasures of granola. The tree itself offered the same fruit Daisy had encountered on the path earlier.

Zerek groaned.

She rested her hand on his shoulder. His breathing deepened and calmed.

He didn't wake for hours. When he did, Daisy gave him water, which he took without speaking. He stared at her, his expression blank.

Daisy drew her knees up her to chest and looked out over the swamp floor. She sang, and again the creatures mimicked her song. As soon as she had them all mimicking the melody, she switched to harmony. Her success made her laugh, forgetting Zerek until she heard a faint chuckle.

She turned to the warrior. He rolled his eyes and lay back.

"It isn't a fair fight," he said wheezing with each breath.

"Who is fighting?"

"Exactly. *You* aren't. So who is on your side? How came you into these powers?"

"I don't have powers."

"You are ignorant." He scoffed, laying an arm over his eyes. "You could have had the whole company turn against me had you tried. I had to threaten their kin so they would stop adoring you. I've never seen anything like it. Do you know that the light people will not go near them?"

"The light people?"

"The stewards of the daylight. Isn't that why you escaped? To go to them?"

"I didn't know where I was going. I was following . . ." her voice grew soft with realization, "the lights."

"You escaped the cage, which was sealed with two locks and a spell. You managed to leave my tent without *me* waking. *That* is impossible. You found the only trail through the swamp in the dark, and not one beast attacked you. I had to use dark magic just to track you, and now I am completely at your mercy. What kind of witch holds that power?" His arm dropped again to his side. "You should leave me here, weed-witch. You may not have another opportunity. Were I you, I would slit my throat."

"Were I you, I wouldn't put the suggestion in my head."

"I am not one to think death could be worse than the life I live now. You might actually be doing me a favor."

Not true. She had seen what awaited him after death. But she merely said, "I thought about running, but you might die."

"So, you're going to keep me alive?"

"I don't know if I can. You're bleeding from the inside."

He studied her for a second. "Do you see that vine?" He pointed to a vine growing around one of the supporting trees. "Pull three leaves for me. They will help."

She reached for the vine, tore three large leaves from it, and handed them to him. He ate the first one, set one inside his shirt, and rolled the other into a straw that he put in his mouth. "It's basic medicine and painkiller. That's why it's up here. Now, take the amulet tied around my neck. It is my seal. You must break it. If you don't, my master will send his monsters to find and kill us both: me for showing weakness, you . . . for being you."

Daisy huffed. "What's so bad about being me?"

He groaned. "Just take the amulet."

As Daisy approached the warrior, she smelled a pleasant aroma, like leather and sandalwood. Even though he had been living in the swamp for days, maybe weeks, she couldn't smell any body odor. She pinched her elbows to her sides, aware that her pits emanated an unpleasant grapefruit odor.

She grabbed the leather cord from his neck and pulled it until the cord snapped. He didn't resist. She backed away, then climbed down the ladder. Two large rocks lay on the path. As she situated the amulet on the bottom rock, it caught the daylight perfectly, stopping her heart cold. She had seen the sign before many times—the eternity sign with a knife through it. She read aloud the name above the seal. "Zerek Sivha Kindleheart."

The air around her shook. In a panic she brought the rock down several times to crush the seal, which shattered into a powder.

Daisy assessed the food stashed on the platform. She could stuff enough granola and dried fruit in the pockets on her dragon skin jacket to feed her for a few days on the trail. If fruit fell from trees throughout the entire swamp, starving wouldn't be necessary. The little lights waited for her, frolicking like kittens around the tree. *These little guys might lead me out of the swamp,* she thought to herself. *I could drink from moistened leaves and eat fruit and this granola.*

A low moan interrupted her plans. She sighed, wondering if she could, in good conscience, leave Zerek in his condition.

No, she would wait for him to be out of danger, like an idiot.

She peered over at him, muttering beneath her breath, "How long will that take, you big, horrible man?"

As she sat in the silence, she distracted herself by mentally sifting through past assignments from her dreams, grasping for details she might remember. There was something in Zerek's third name, Kindleheart, that rang familiar. She'd heard it before. Or had she read it?

Kindleheart.

Her thoughts wandered to the anonymous letters she had been receiving for some time. She'd received the first one on her sixteenth birthday, which had felt odd but not unpleasant. She had continued to receive them until her dreams stopped.

She thought about the writer's tone and his admiration for her, then compared them to what little she knew about the young man on the platform. She couldn't correlate the two together. The writer of the love letters seemed to know Daisy, a quality that made him both appealing and a little creepy. Also, whoever had been writing to her had been vulnerable and warm. Zerek wasn't even chatty, let alone the type to spill his guts.

She turned toward him again and startled at his fixed gaze. She let out a silent breath before asking, "Are you thirsty? I've been collecting water in this jar."

He nodded. Daisy took the small jar in one hand, then struggled with her other arm to prop Zerek upright so he could drink.

After he drank, she set him back down with a thud.

She didn't mean to drop him, but he was heavy. "I have no muscle," she explained.

He nodded.

She looked away to set aside the jar, and when she looked at Zerek again the blue and yellow light beads circled his head. He stared at them with a slight smile playing on his lips. The blue one booped his nose. He chuckled and shooed it away.

As Daisy watched, something inside of her lurched—a sleeping kitten twisting in her chest. She turned away and determined not to look in his direction again. "Eyes straight, head down," she said out loud.

"What was that?"

"Nothing. Talking to myself."

"You probably want to start running down the path again, and you are right to do so. If my master catches you, he will think of new and creative ways of destroying your sweet little heart."

Daisy shuttered, and the kitten fell again into sleep, anesthetized by morbidity. How could she have let her mind wander there? "No, it isn't that. I mean, I do want to start moving, but I'm glad to wait."

"Glad to?"

"Yes, I would rather you were safe first. It would be good if you heal."

"Good for whom?" Zerek's voice remained calm, almost lazy. "I just tried to recapture you, and it wouldn't have gone well for you if I had."

"Yeah, well, that's you and this is me," Daisy insisted, refusing to give in to his attempts to frighten her.

"There is an evil that seeks to destroy you, and it will use me and any of my men to do so. You have no sense of self-preservation. I can't see you lasting long in this world."

Evil. Daisy wondered at his easy use of the word to describe his own people. "Your master must be frightening," Daisy assented. "I will meet pain when it comes, but should I always be panicked by the threat of it?"

The warrior did not respond for several minutes, but when he did, he surprised her. "Daisy, have you read *Jane Eyre*?"

Daisy had to sort through internal reactions to his question. For one, he used her first name, forgetting his disrespectful moniker. Secondly, he had asked about an earthly book, which happened to be one of her favorites.

"Have *you* read *Jane Eyre*?"

"I have. It came into my hands once. One of my servants took it from a traveler, then presented it to me as booty. Had he any idea of the content, he would have burned it immediately. I hid it from my master so I could keep it."

"You read it? And liked it?"

"I can't describe . . . I didn't know . . ." and he finished his sentence in a beautiful, melodic language Daisy had never heard before.

She breathed out a laugh. "You lost me at 'I didn't know.' "

He laughed too. "It is my heart language. Whenever something is hard to describe, I find myself rambling off in Ellesse."

"Ellesse? It's beautiful."

"There is a legend. Our founder was always heavy with sorrow. He could only muster up the strength to communicate by singing. As he raised his children, they also spoke through song, and the language was passed down through his family that way."

"Why was he sad?"

Zerek looked thoughtful, then after a pause answered, "Remorse. He was hopeless in the knowledge of his own brokenness. He was given a revelation of great beauty and realized he could only taint it."

Daisy sensed themes that were familiar to her.

Suddenly a thought occurred to her. "Does everyone here speak English?"

Zerek laughed. "Of course not. Most of the people here are speaking with you in Ahlfang. Part of the magic you are given is the ability to understand the first language you encounter."

"But it sounds like English."

"It won't for much longer. As you jump between English and Ahlfang, you will realize the difference."

"Are we speaking Ahlfang now?"

Zerek smiled. "No. I happen to know English because of a strange past."

"Is that a story worth sharing?" Daisy asked.

"Of course."

"And so . . . ?"

"And so you must suffer your curiosity."

Daisy scowled. "And *Jane Eyre*?"

His eyes sparkled with mischief. "I am continually reminded of a particular line because of you."

"Let me guess. I am Helen Burns, and it has something to do with me dying by my own pathetic meekness?"

Zerek laughed harder, then pressed his hands against his chest and winced.

Daisy moved toward him. "Is there something I can do to help you?"

"Try not to amuse me." This made him laugh again at his own joke until he turned toward her in his pain.

Daisy felt helpless. "I'm so sorry. You need to rest. I will stop talking with you now."

"Please don't." His eyes closed tight enough to wrinkle at the sides. "Please don't stop."

"Oh, okay. I won't." Except now she could not muster a thing to say.

"Tell me about your childhood," he commanded, though his voice weakened.

"*My* childhood?"

Zerek nodded.

"If I tell you about my childhood, will you tell me about yours?"

"I'm too weak to talk."

"How do I know my childhood won't give you some new insight into how you might control and torture me?"

"You don't. It's part of my game." He threw a little stick at her. "Your caution is encouraging though. It tells me you are starting to take your mortal peril seriously. If you can't tell me about your childhood, then tell me your favorite story."

"I don't have a favorite."

"Just choose one," he said with a huff, as if Daisy were the most tedious creature he had ever encountered. She almost got angry except that he was smiling. His eyes were closed with pain, but he was smiling.

She sighed. "There was a woman named Hannah. She had a husband, but she was not able to bear children. The man married a second woman as a result, so he had two wives. The man didn't love the second wife the way he loved Hannah, but the second wife bore him many children. Out of jealousy, the second wife would mistreat Hannah, constantly reminding her of her failure as a woman.

"The family visited the tabernacle to pay homage to their God. As often happens when sad, lonely, hurt people encounter God, Hannah was overcome by her sorrow. She promised to dedicate her first son to God if he opened her womb. She cried until the priest came out and chastised her for being drunk. She insisted she wasn't drunk but was instead praying out of anguish. When the priest recognized her as a pious woman, he blessed her and told her to go in peace."

Daisy's voice wavered. "She did give birth to a son, and once she had weaned him, she brought him back to the temple to live there and serve God. The boy grew up to be a great prophet, a good man who spoke to the people on God's behalf. He even anointed the king whose lineage was destined to rule forever.

"But had Hannah never been in such destitution, she might never have devoted her first child to God. Her pain brought faith, which brought blessing to everyone. I doubt Hannah dreamed she had a lofty part to play in God's redemptive story. And we, likewise, never imagine that our sorrows may be preparing us for God's greatest purpose for our lives."

Tears fell from her eyes. She looked over at Zerek, who had turned away from her. Daisy suddenly felt very lonely, so she lay down on her mat and fell asleep.

DAISY HAD to help Zerek do everything. It took a few days for him to feel strong enough to move about, and even then he only made slow, deliberate movements. Most of the time they sat on the platform talking. Daisy asked a lot of questions about the swamp and about the world she had been pulled into.

Zerek likewise asked no end of questions brought up by the book *Jane Eyre*. He mentioned Jane's overly high standards, which sent Daisy into an explosion of counterarguments of Jane's character.

"I still get goosebumps," she argued, "from when Jane said, 'We shall work hard and be content,' as a reply to the question, 'Shall we be very happy?' It was the first time I realized that pleasure is beyond our control, but self-respect and accomplishment are not. Call it 'overly high standards' if you insist, but she did not rely on any luxury or comfort. Jane is one character who finds a way to be dignified in the midst of turmoil. She never wavers in who she is. She is inspiring."

Zerek's mouth twitched. "That deluded girl Jane couldn't accept her own feelings."

Daisy realized he was baiting her and met his eyes with a glare. He released a wry chuckle.

The more they talked, the more he let his guard down. He told her stories about people he knew. His descriptions were so astute and detailed, Daisy felt like she knew them herself. She laughed at most of his stories because he had an eye for the ridiculous. Daisy wondered if, given a different upbringing, his sensitivity would have led him to the arts.

One morning, a rustling on the platform woke her. A soft glow declared the morning, and as her vision cleared, Zerek's curious black eyes peered at her only six inches from her face.

"Good morning."

Startled, Daisy pushed herself away from him. She had been sleeping at the edge of the platform, and the motion would have sent her off the edge had it not been for Zerek's lightning-fast reflexes. He caught her torso and pulled her back onto the shelter and against himself.

His laughter vibrated from his chest to hers. "I'm not used to suicide as a response to my flirtation, but you are unusual."

Daisy pulled herself up out of his arms and glared down at him. His playful demeanor instantly cooled. He sat up and grabbed a bowl. "I made breakfast, but I take it you don't want these?" He moved to toss the warm, porridge-like substance out into the swamp.

"No! I'm hungry." She held out her hand.

His shoulders relaxed, and he handed her the bowl.

"That was the last of the provisions, so you need to start walking toward Elleson today. As for me"—he gestured to the ground—"my horse has found me, and I am still too weak to force you back to my camp. I can guarantee my master had someone following the shadowbeast, so my advice would be to walk quickly."

That was no horse, but she wasn't going to argue that point. "You are going back to your army?"

"I am not sharing my strategies with you, Weed." He worked his way down the ladder, still weak. Daisy followed him. "Next time we meet, we will be enemies. I may even be the one to drive a knife through your heart." He did not laugh, and Daisy felt his words were meant to warn rather than frighten her.

"I don't know what pain makes you this way, but I am grateful for your friendship these last few days."

"Generals and nobles of Ahl don't have friends. Our friends are the first to die in our political games." He said it almost to himself as he prepared his horse-thing for riding.

"Then let me thank you for being a pleasant and honorable enemy."

A slight smile lingered on the side of his mouth, but he didn't stop preparing his tack. "For that, you are welcome. It is the kindest payment I've ever given for a life debt."

"A what?"

"You saved my life, which binds me to you to some degree. Let's just say, for a time, I was free to neglect one master for the other. But a slave has to return eventually to his real master or pay the penalty. Even he will understand why I let you go—this time."

Horror clenched Daisy's heart. "You are a slave?"

He snorted. "We all are. Anyone who believes otherwise is a fool."

"This is not the first time I've heard that, but my father told me that slavery to righteousness brings freedom."

Zerek turned his full attention to her. "Your father sounds like a wise man. Is he good too?"

"He is wise, good, and kind."

His face softened and his gaze moved across her face. "I am glad. Farewell, Daisy Lorrian Bloom. I hope you beat me to Elleson." Then he climbed his mount and rode back the way he had come.

CHAPTER FIFTEEN

THE MORNING after Brogan arrived in Ells, a great, rumbling song woke him. He thought for a minute it might be an earthquake.

Instead, ten thousand voices in harmony told the light to grow bright and awaken the day. As he lay in his bed, little twinkling beads of light shot through his room, refusing to be rounded up with the rest of the daylight. Some of them hid behind doors until they grew bored and thought it might be more exciting just to do as they were told. A few of them were particularly impish and slapped themselves as hard as they could against Brogan's face.

"Ow! You little punks. Get out of here!"

He swore he heard tiny, toneless giggles as they backed out through his window.

Brogan got out of bed and stretched into his dragon skin, shaking his head again at his reflection in the mirror. Something about his new look still reminded him of his dad.

A servant knocked.

"Come in." Brogan fumbled with the unusual clasp of the belt and noticed the servant hiding a smirk. "Fine. You fasten it." He raised his arms and turned the buckle toward the servant. He controlled his temper, but he didn't need to be nice about it.

The servant buckled the clasp without losing his serene expression. "Breakfast is served in the king's drawing room."

Brogan brushed past the man and made his way outside. Perfumed air set a stage for the remaining voices still singing the morning song, as if it were too joyful a tune to release. A reluctant smile crept onto his face when he smelled the perfumed flowers.

He ambled into the sitting room, again awed by the wall of windows that offered a view of the gardens. Had he ever seen anything so beautiful as this castle courtyard? He backed toward the dining room in order to enjoy the view a little longer.

From the other side of the door, he heard Choral's muffled voice, saying, "There is darkness around him."

Orya mumbled something in return, followed by, "This wasn't the case with our other visitors, but we must trust the Eternal One."

Brogan didn't want to eaves drop, but it sounded like information that wouldn't be shared with him otherwise.

"Like we trusted for the prince?"

"Choral, you know that was different."

The temptation to keep listening clenched Brogan, but he forced himself to press through the door. The conversation halted as he stepped into the dining room.

Neither Orya nor Choral appeared to be shaken at his sudden appearance. In fact, the king stood to greet him. "Good morning, Brogan! My sister and I were just bringing our concerns before the Eternal One. I hope you don't mind that we didn't wait for you."

Brogan sat at the table. "I don't quite know what you mean. Who's the Eternal One?"

Choral raised a smug eyebrow at Orya. "I believe you call him God."

Brogan shrugged and dismissed her self-righteousness. "I don't really believe that stuff."

She gestured to their surroundings. "Perhaps your experience here is easier to believe?"

He didn't reply. She didn't need fuel for her assumptions.

"Good enough for now. Let's eat, then get to work," said the king. "Today we are going to spar. I think it would be wise to prepare for battle as we await word on Daisy's location."

Brogan nodded, and the trio ate in silence. As he placed the last bite of a pastry into his mouth, Orya motioned for him to follow outside.

Couldn't this guy just wait until he choked it down? Brogan stood and followed the king.

They meandered through the garden and entered a courtyard where other men were training with practice swords and staffs. Orya tossed a long staff to Brogan and gestured toward a training ring.

Everywhere Brogan went lately, he was being told what to do —and now with sticks.

"Brogan, you will feel sluggish today, but as you are nourished by our elements, your movements and reflexes should grow faster and easier."

He could not have prepared for what came next. Although he had grown up learning several types of martial arts, he couldn't counter any movement made by the king. He tried to swing a kick from his hip, but his body moved too slowly, like when you dream and can only run a fraction of your normal speed.

The king blocked and countered with a hard, painful strike on Brogan's thigh with his staff. "You will have to acclimate, Brogan. Not only does this extreme altitude lack oxygen, but we gain much of our strength from an electrical charge in the air. Your body doesn't know yet what to do with it." The king eased off, which Brogan hated even more than being beaten around. No one ever treated him with kid gloves, but as his muscles shook, he couldn't argue that he needed help.

Orya relaxed from his fighting stance and motioned to one of the warriors watching from the side, who came forward carrying a chalice of water.

"Drink this," Orya commanded.

Brogan grasped the chalice and drank the sweet liquid inside. It saturated his senses and cleared his mind. His tired muscles stopped shaking. Soon he was standing again with his full breath.

149

"Your skill is competent," Orya said. "I will pair you with Lord Lightfleet. He is your age, and I think you will learn well from each other."

Something about the way he said *competent* made Brogan indignant. It didn't help that a smiley, blond teenager with radiant, white teeth bopped in front of him. This Lord Lightfleet also had brilliant caramel eyes that sparkled with dewy joy.

Brogan didn't wait for the signal to begin but quickly swung his practice rod at Lightfleet's side. He struck him hard, and the kid doubled over in pain.

It brought him satisfaction to see that the happy, smiling eyes weren't happy anymore.

A quick motion came from Lord Lightfleet's weak side. Brogan felt a pain in his head and a pressure in his nose. He fell over in a stupor, recognizing the taste of blood in his mouth.

He couldn't remember what happened after that. He awoke in a warm room with lights dancing around him. Yes, dancing. They undulated and transformed their contours while rotating through the air. The light radiating from them comforted Brogan's aching head. Once his eyes focused again, he recognized the same kid from the practice field, watching him with an air of annoyance and boredom. No one else was in the room.

"I'm glad to see you're finally awake, Brogan," said Lord Lightfleet. The inflection of his voice sounded anything but *glad*.

Brogan sat up, his head aching. "Where am I?"

"The infirmary. My punishment is sitting here making sure you're not permanently damaged. Fortunately for you, our best healers were in the castle today."

Blood-saturated bandages overflowed a nearby bin. "Those are mine?"

"They're not mine," Lightfleet said, his light brown eyes staring into space.

Another man entered the room and hustled to Brogan. He touched the side of his head and whispered something Brogan didn't understand. It sounded like Ellesse, but the words had power, like fingers that dug into his head and felt around inside of it. Memories and movements were being triggered. His left foot involuntarily pointed and flexed like a ballet dancer. His left hand opened and closed. His right hand counted from one to five and back down to one before the brain fingers released him.

"You appear to be functioning normally. That was a close call. We caught the breakage to your arteries in time. I'm afraid we couldn't replace your blood. It isn't like ours, so you will need to rest until your body replaces it for you. Really, Lord Lightfleet, you almost killed him."

The blond kid shrugged just before the room spun. Brogan lay back down.

"The king instructed you to stay here with him until he's able to walk. You must also stay at his villa for now and make amends."

The kid didn't reply before the healer left the room.

Lord Lightfleet grabbed a cup of water and helped Brogan drink. It had a tangy flavor to it. "It's an herb that fights inflammation," he explained. "Once you finish it, you will need to keep drinking water."

Brogan didn't say anything in response. He simply drank. A few hours went by where neither of them said a word. Bored, Brogan began counting to himself in various languages. When he ran out of languages he knew from Earth, he counted in Ellesse. "What's after ninety-nine?" he asked.

Lightfleet shuffled. "*Grael.*"

"It doesn't sound like the other numbers."

"There is a more uniform word for one hundred, but everyone speaking high Ellesse uses grael because of its significance."

"Significance?"

"It has magical properties. When you have *grael* of something, the collection sometimes bonds and functions singularly with surprising effects." He delivered the intricate response in a rote and very bored tone.

"Sounds exciting."

"Yeah, maybe if I hit you grael times, something interesting will happen. Should we try it tomorrow?"

Brogan sighed. "Stand down already. I shouldn't have come at you. I was angry and you were all smiling and happy."

Lord Lightfleet didn't answer right away. "Fine."

"Fine?"

"It wasn't exactly an apology. I accept that you are spineless and spoiled—*fine*."

Heat rushed to Brogan's face, but he held back. "I'm sorry. I shouldn't have hit you. I was being a jerk."

There was a long pause before Lord Lightfleet answered. "If you are sincere, then I will accept your apology."

Brogan was keen to change the subject. "Lord Lightfleet, what does it mean to be a lord here?"

Another pause. "I'm from the king's lineage. I own a good measure of land along the coast, but I'm young and it hasn't been tamed yet. I have the privilege of making whatever I want out of it."

"Are there a lot of lords?"

"Right now? Me and three others. Lordship skips many generations and even siblings. I still don't know why it landed on me."

"How did you know it landed on you?" Brogan was sincerely interested now.

"A small, wild light rested on my mother's abdomen while she carried me. No one could shepherd it away. I guess that's the sign." A groan of boredom escaped Lord Lightfleet. "Are you ready to go to the villa yet?"

"I probably need help. I feel strong but still dizzy."

Lord Lightfleet moved over and hoisted Brogan up by his armpits. His sturdy frame had no problem lifting him, and now that Brogan could see him more clearly, he was not at all goofy in the way he had imagined him upon their first meeting. Lord Lightfleet held him steady as they walked back to the villa and didn't release him until he lay on the bed.

"I must have really lost my mind," said Brogan aloud.

"What now?"

"You're different than how I remember meeting you this morning."

"Less congenial?" suggested Lord Lightfleet.

"I was just . . . so angry, and you piqued my anger."

After a thoughtful pause, Lord Lightfleet said, "Maybe there was misfortune tied to our meeting. Tomorrow I will try not to be happy at you."

A flicker of a sarcastic grin crossed Lightfleet's face.

Brogan nodded, feeling like a jerk.

Lord Lightfleet nodded back and walked out toward the other bedroom.

BROGAN SLEPT until the smell of breakfast lured him to stand on his own. His head still felt heavy and unbalanced. He used various items of furniture to steady himself as he wandered into the kitchen. Instead of a servant, Lord Lightfleet stood at the stove, cooking. He had set the table for the two of them.

"There's hot tea waiting for you. The healer suggested you drink it. It should help you restore your hemoglobin count. He thinks that's why you are still dizzy."

Brogan sat. "Thanks."

Lord Lightfleet nodded and continued cooking in silence. A few minutes later he served Brogan a plate full of strangely colored foods. Pink eggs, blue bacon, glowing fruit. Everything on Lord Lightfleet's plate looked normal enough. When Brogan glared at him, Lord Lightfleet laughed and started eating. "It won't hurt you."

"Really? Because it's glowing."

Lord Lightfleet pointed at the fruit and the glowing stopped. "It's harmless."

Brogan ate what tasted a lot like humble pie. "Are we sparring again today?"

"Nope. You have to heal, and I have to *befriend* you while you do."

"What?"

"It's my assigned duty. The king wants me to make amends. Since we don't have a choice, I'm going to try to find good things I can like about you. Anything like that in there?" Lord Lightfleet pointed toward Brogan's heart.

Brogan scoffed slightly. "Good luck. You might have to dig deep."

"What are you so angry about anyway? We've determined that friendly people irk you. Did friendly people try to shank you back home?"

Brogan laughed in spite of himself. "I get a lot of admiration back home. Most people are friendly, but I don't like aggressive friendliness. It feels like manipulation to me. And then the king was sort of friendly in a weird, assuming way just before he started ordering me around. But then he beat me with various objects on the practice field."

"I see my mistake. Obviously, Brogan, I don't know you, but you are the first traveler that I've met. My position in the royal family has afforded me that unique opportunity. I didn't stop to consider that you might not be in a befriending mood."

Brogan's chest loosened with relief. "I will overlook your mistakes if you overlook mine."

As the day progressed, Lord Lightfleet helped Brogan sort through his limited clothing options, even adding to it from his own wardrobe. They laughed about the insecure feelings they both sometimes got when they know they are dressed well, but the public staring inevitably made them second-guess their choice of clothing.

"It happens to you too? Are you royalty?" Lightfleet's eyes became pools of warmth.

The expression took Brogan aback. It was the same look that he'd reacted to earlier when he'd hit Lightfleet. Blind admiration had always put him off people. Only . . . he'd misinterpreted it here. Lightfleet was not adoring him. Rather, he emanated an innocent curiosity.

"We don't have royalty. My father is famous. It might be a close equivalent. Speaking of . . . do I have to address you as Lord Lightfleet all the time? Is that protocol?"

"You *must*." Lord Lightfleet frowned. "I prefer Your Grace Most Honorable Lord Lightfleet, to be exact."

Brogan scoffed. "Lightfleet it is."

"Just don't call me Greg. My mother named me after one of the travelers. It's so weird."

"Is it short for Gregory?"

"No. Are you saying it should have been something more regal sounding like Gregory, but my mother only knew the casual, truncated version?"

"It's possible." Brogan laughed. "But Greg has become common."

"Common. Maybe I require a common name so I won't become arrogant, being this handsome and intelligent." Lightfleet motioned to his face and body.

"And you hit hard," added Brogan.

"And I hit hard!" The words resonated in the small dome under which they were sitting.

Brogan held up a pointed finger. "Greg! The hard hitter!"

"Greg, the defeater of Earth men!"

"Greg, the superior cheap-shot taker!"

CHAPTER SIXTEEN

A FEW DAYS after the healers had rescued him from head trauma, Brogan stood without the room spinning around him. This was the all the sign he needed. He could start over and prove he wasn't a waste of magical space.

Lightfleet whooped at the sight of him in the practice court-yard. "Right on time! Dewberry just beat me without mercy, and I need to redeem myself." He gestured toward a tall man with thick, bolder-like calves. Everything about him bespoke terrifying masculinity, except for his dark pink hair and the name Dewberry.

Brogan picked up one of the practice swords and weighed it in his hand.

"They're all the same, Princess; just hop to it."

Brogan felt heat rush to his face, but Lightfleet's enormous smile infected him and he chuckled. "You just called me Princess."

"And I'm not sorry. Are you going to use that sword or preen with it?" At this, he threw one of his boots at Brogan.

Dewberry whistled. "He never gets enough good beatings, that one."

"I can believe it," Brogan grinned.

As they sparred, the movements perplexed Brogan. As badly as

Brogan wanted to oblige him with a good beating, Lightfleet outmaneuvered him in every skill. Brogan knew how to fight. He just *couldn't*. He couldn't get enough air, he couldn't think clearly, and he couldn't move fast enough. He often had to stop and drink the strange water that steadied him.

The day stretched on in a brutal pattern of Brogan getting beaten by Lightfleet until he succumbed to a lack of oxygen. He got a few good shots in but not often enough. Each set ended as he fell to his knees to catch his breath. He was sure his diaphragm was going to be as sore as any of his other muscles simply from struggling to breath.

At different intervals throughout the day, colors flashed through the sky. At green they took their lunch. At red Orya finally gave the order to stop, adding, "Brogan, an herbal bath waits at your villa. It will help the welts. When you feel whole, meet us at the dining room for dinner."

Brogan eyed Lightfleet.

"Greg, you are welcome to join us," Orya said.

Lightfleet nodded, then pouted at Brogan for commiseration at the use of his name. Brogan shrugged and put on his best pity face.

The next day was the same, and the day after, and the next. Throughout the week Brogan was beat up, mended, beat up, mended. Eventually, his love of martial arts lulled him into a contented pattern of daily, intensive practice.

On the sixth day Orya broke the pattern at noon, when the green light flashed. "Let's call it a day," he said. "Brogan, I'd like to take you on a tour through the city."

"Sure." Brogan heaved as he pulled off one of his socks. "What city?"

Lightfleet pointed at the high gray wall. "The one behind that."

It took Brogan a minute to comprehend. "We've been so busy training, I didn't consider what's on the other side of the wall."

Lightfleet chuckled at him. "The castle grounds are extensive, but they're not our whole world."

Brogan threw his sock at Lightfleet, who grimaced and flung it back with two tentative fingers. "Stinky human. Go shower and meet us at the gate."

"Sounds good." He stood and dragged his sore body to the bath.

WHEN BROGAN CAME to meet them later that afternoon, the gate courtyard was a flurry of people and horses. A hand fell heavy on his shoulder and he turned to see Lightfleet's serious face.

"Forget the city. There's been a change of plans. Orya finally got the news he's been waiting for." He handed Brogan the reins of a chestnut mare. "I saddled her for you. She's fast and spirited. We weren't sure of your riding abilities, but you need to keep up."

"Wait! Where are we going? Have they found Daisy?"

"Yes, though the king hasn't shared many details. Just that we're on our way to the swamps."

Brogan's adrenaline kicked up, and he mounted the beautiful chestnut. He shifted in the saddle and felt the twitchy movements of the mare testing his abilities. He reined her in and gave her no opportunity to toss him.

The king mounted his horse and called for all warriors to follow him. He led them to a steep roadway that led down to the base of the mountain peak.

The initial decent took several hours, but at the bottom the road widened and mellowed. A small brigade waited to join them.

Orya turned to his men and said, "We're expecting a fight once we get to the swamps."

He pressed forward and kept a steady pace the whole day, even while planning strategies and working through different possible scenarios with his generals. Apparently Orya respected Lightfleet's advice because he hardly stopped conferring with him. As a result, Brogan didn't have his familiar friend to talk with.

"You ride well, young one," said a regal man with black hair and dark gray eyes. His low, deep voice made his singsong speech sound something of a baritone.

Brogan nodded. "Thank you. It's not my first time."

"I should say not. That's my wife's mare, and she's spoiled her. Don't think my wife wanted anyone else to ride her."

The man sat tall with a broad chest, and he had an intelligent look about him. Brogan wanted the conversation to continue because talking eased his fear for Daisy. "If I'm not mistaken, this horse is quite an athlete."

"Her name is Splatter because she passes all others in a frenzy of mud and dirt. She absolutely hates to lose."

Brogan snorted. "How was I so lucky to ride her today?"

"When the king says, 'Bring a fast horse,' you bring a fast horse." The man actually did a spot-on impression of King Orya by raising his tone of his voice and slurring his enunciation.

Brogan chuckled. He liked this guy. He looked into the clever gray eyes and said, "I'm Brogan."

"My name is Storm. I have three sons about your age. They were not called to come along, which rankled them a bit."

"Storm," Brogan repeated the name, liking the way it suited this man, "what do young lightmen do with their time anyway?"

"I keep them busy so they don't get into trouble. It takes a few decades to teach contemplation and patience. I'd say the next years are the most dangerous of their lives. A man thrives on danger and adventure but needs to learn how to respect limitations first."

"Here's a man who gets it." Brogan said, gesturing toward himself. "I couldn't agree more. Men need danger."

Storm guffawed. "You've already forgotten the contemplation and patience part, my young friend!"

"I didn't forget. I disregarded."

"Aye. I know, son. I know."

They continued talking until they came up to the edge of the dense forest that Brogan had noticed from the villa terrace. The foliage wasn't as charming now that its canopy choked out light and cast dark shadows. Fortunately, the roads were well kept, and as they traveled fields of fruit and grain situated themselves stubbornly against the wild green. Large, richly adorned manor houses peaked through the trees. Farmers stopped their happy work to check out the movement of the king's men. They all waved. A few approached with concern on their faces. Orya would wave back or ask one of his men to speak with them while the soldiers continued on.

They camped that night in a clearing. A man with long, light brown hair introduced himself as Lord Phoss and invited Brogan to join a few of the men at the campfire. Brogan sat himself next to Phoss, as Storm had duties elsewhere.

Despite the sense of tension and urgency, Dewberry strummed a strange stringed instrument, high pitched like a ukulele. It was tiny in his massive, veiny hands. The rest of the warriors jumped in, singing about epic battles with twists in the story. Brogan would have been lost if Lord Phoss didn't explain some of the hidden meanings, and he found himself awed by the stories of valor. "Thank you for helping me understand."

Lord Phoss exclaimed, "Oh, but how could we not be a friend to Leo's son? We only wish he were here with us as well!" A chorus of agreement went up from the other men.

Brogan's heart turned cold. His father had been here?

A dense pressure built in Brogan's nose. "Excuse me." He stood and exited the circle to pace outside of the campfire's light. His dad had never said anything about Elleson. Of course, what *could* he say without sounding crazy? He could only paint and brood over memories.

"Brogan?"

Brogan jumped at the sudden intrusion.

Yellow light from a nearby campfire rimmed Orya's face. "I can see that this isn't pleasant for you, learning about Leo."

"Why didn't you say something sooner?"

Orya put a hand on Brogan's shoulder. "To be forthright, his leaving here and what transpired after . . . they were sorrowful events to us and to all involved. It is Leo's secret to tell or not tell."

Brogan groaned and brushed off Orya's hand. "Is this why he shipped me to outskirts of civilization? Did he know I was coming here?"

"No one really knew. There were signs, and he probably

wanted you to have the opportunity to experience the adventures he had. His time here left us all with a great love for him. It just didn't end well."

Brogan searched what he could see of the king's sincere expression. "What happened?"

The king sighed. "I guess he didn't tell you anything. At this point, your need may supersede his wish to keep it to himself."

"Look! He's not the only one in the equation. Don't I deserve to have some idea of who I am and where I came from? I'm sick of subterfuge!"

"Calm down, Brogan." Orya placed his hands on his shoulders and pressed down.

"Help me. Help me calm down."

"Your father was only allowed to come here because he was with Ophelia at the time of her summoning. It's her family line that is connected with us. But as he came, we treated him like a royal guest." Orya pulled his hands off Brogan's shoulders.

Brogan attempted to pull all of the erratic thoughts back into some kind of order. "He came here with Ophelia. And then what?"

"They were already in love, and while here . . . they conceived a child."

"A child?"

"Daisy."

Brogan's jaw dropped. "Daisy is my"—he almost couldn't say it—"half sister?" The heat and pressure in his nose returned. "A sister I didn't know my whole life?"

"As you can imagine, when we learned that Ophelia was pregnant, we had to send her and your father back immediately. Our wild magic is violent against children conceived outside of covenant. It would have killed both Ophelia and Daisy. We had no choice. The next news I received, Ophelia had married another man. Leo had a second child in the womb of another woman. That second child was you. And that, Brogan, is how you are connected to us."

Rage pressed against Brogan's temples. He knew it wasn't

logical to take it out on Orya, but the king represented the entire cluster of events creating the lie that was his life. He shoved Orya aside and strode toward his tent.

Upon entering, he sat alone to deal with the spiral of agitation. There was no Emmy here to draw him from his darkness. Only a single candle flickered on a stand.

He had to get Daisy out of the swamp. Away from the Ahlforr. If he had known about this sooner, he wouldn't have stayed at the castle training for a whole week. He'd have gone into the swamp alone, if needed.

"Brogan?" A familiar voice rang into his tent, and one that didn't spur him to anger.

"Lightfleet?"

His friend ducked as he stepped through the tent entrance. "Orya told me to check in on you. What is this about?"

"Daisy, the girl in the swamps. I guess—" Brogan couldn't keep himself from choking his words. "She's my half-sister. No one told me."

Lightfleet sat on the ground next to him. "She is still alive. We're putting everything into getting her back. The Ellesian army is suitable to the task."

Brogan nodded in appreciation, but it wasn't enough to reassure him.

It took two more days to clear out of the forest. Early afternoon on the second day, they assembled on horseback on an open plain. Orya drew his horse up to Brogan's and said, "We will increase our speed now. Your mare will set the pace for a small team. She is feisty and fast. The rest will follow us as they can."

The most elite men kept up with them, Lightfleet one of them. The horses worked like marathoners, stronger than any Brogan had known on earth.

Soon, blue trees with yellow leaves met them like a wall. As soon as he could distinguish individual leaves, a heavy, wet stench hit him, and he reined Splatter back. The king spurred his horse past Brogan, slid to the ground, and fell on his knees before an object that was impaled on a signpost in the ground.

Horror struck Brogan as soon as he could make out what was on the post.

Lightfleet leaned over and said, "Now *that* is the work of Demonclaw."

CHAPTER SEVENTEEN

As soon as Zerek had gone, the lights circled furiously around Daisy's feet. Her heart thumped.

"Okay, I'm coming."

At her words, they shot ahead on the path. She darted after them.

She ran as hard as she could, suddenly realizing that she was running. She hadn't run in years. She might have taken to leaping had her lungs not already burned with the effort.

She bent over and rested her hands on her knees as she caught her breath. "I'm so out of shape, aren't I?" Her tiny calf muscles might as well have nodded their heads in tiny spasms.

The little lights ahead of her on the path escalated into frantic spins like a dust storm.

"I'm sorry!" Deep breath. She would try to keep jogging.

As she raced ahead, the lights grew brighter and brighter. Then other things around Daisy started to glow. Trees radiated, first with only a soft illumination. Then rays of light burst from their knobs. A yellow, glowing bubble formed around her. Her face grew hot, and when she looked down, the rest of her skin gave off a warm, yellow light.

"How do I make this stop?" She halted and took long, even breaths until the colors and lights calmed down around her. As soon as she stopped glowing, she marched forward for what seemed like hours, sometimes glowing, sometimes not. When she glowed, silence permeated her surroundings. When the glow faded, she heard the buzzing of wings.

A tall figure fell onto the path in front of her and stood up again. His height towered over her. "Are you Daisy?"

She must have jumped a mile into the air. "H-how did you know? Who are you?"

The man was lean and wiry with a very light complexion. She wondered if he was albino, except that his brown eyes shifted about the swamp. She remembered albino people had little pigmentation in their eyes. "The king's scouts have been looking for you for days." He scanned the canopy of the trees. "I followed the glow you projected earlier. My name is Feather." A glopping noise from the bog triggered a twitch in his shoulders.

"Which king?"

He stopped looking about, turned to her, and squinted his eyes as if confused. "The Light King—Orya of Ells."

"Then are you a friend? Am I in Elleson?"

"I am a friend, here to help you to Elleson. I'm afraid we aren't there yet." He let out a low, long whistle. "Danger lurks every which way in this swamp. I am surprised to find you whole."

He didn't give off the I-wanna-kill-you vibe the way Zerek did, but that remark creeped her out.

He motioned for her to keep walking. "By all means, think yourself in circles. Just do it *as* we walk. I will keep step behind you. Alert me immediately if you see anything. And forgive me if I ask you to walk silently, my lady. I need my ears to be alert."

"Okay," she said, but she was disappointed not to be able to ask questions when a great source of information trudged only a few paces behind her.

Walking in silence, she had all day to process her experience with Zerek. Her thoughts, however, were troubling. Zerek was not good. He was actually bad. He was enslaved to a dark king. He might not be human. It was fortunate to be away from the young general. Away from his dark destiny. But something about that didn't sit well with her.

"Here, my lady," Feather said, pointing up to a tree shelter like the one she had just stayed on with Zerek. "We can rest here until morning."

Daisy climbed the ladder to the platform and Feather followed.

"Is it okay to talk now?" she asked, desperate for information.

"Yes, but keep your voice low. Demonclaw isn't the only monster out here."

Daisy didn't know who this Demonclaw was, but the mere sound of his name made her skin crawl. "I just want to know about King Orya. What do you know about him?"

"My lady has not met him?" Feather sounded surprised.

"This may sound strange, but I'm not sure."

"Of course. Magic is as unpredictable as realm jumping." He knitted his brows and explained. "He is our beloved ruler in Elleson, and though his youth has been known to make him rash, I find him engaging and warm. I met him last year at the Sapphire Solstice. He took a whole moment of his time to compliment my attire."

"Magic? Realm jumping? Sapphire Solstice?" Daisy's heart beat faster as she sifted through these words.

"I feel, my lady, as if I have spoken out of turn. Perhaps I am not the one meant to explain mysteries to you." He shook his head with a goofy smile. "As if I *could* explain them."

"No, really, I like trying, at least—"

"Nonsense. You don't need to hear this stuff from me."

Couldn't this man see she needed information? That she was from a different freaking world? She decided to drop her questions about magic—for now. She asked with forced calm, "Can you at least tell me about the king?"

"Of course." This made him smile. "The women say he is handsome, though he is not overly tall. Maybe only a hand shorter than me. He is strong and athletic. Before he was king, he would fight in tournaments. Often won. He is also witty. Stories circulate, you see. His lines are repeated around the kingdom."

Just as the details interested Daisy, the sky turned purple.

Feather released a great yawn and said, "That's our mark for bedtime. It will be dark in exactly one hour, and we need all the sleep we can get." He plopped to his side and said, "Goodnight."

THE NEXT DAY, Daisy continued her silent trek on the path, this time behind Feather. His back annoyed her, and it irritated her further that she had to keep up with his super-long strides. Why couldn't she travel with someone who had a personality?

A few hours into the day, however, her opinion changed.

The same kind of reptilian monster that had attacked Zerek now sat on the trail in front of them. Feather materialized a near-blinding ball of light between his hands, then flung it at the creature's eyes. The beast hissed and rolled into the swamp.

"My lady, keep your wits about you. You've just seen a swamp lizard. They are tenacious and never stop hunting once they have targeted their prey."

Daisy recalled how the one she hit with the branch recoiled into the swamp never to bother her again. Was that not normal?

Feather created another bright orb and pushed it between the lizard and the trail. It kept the beast off the trail, but the light attracted more creatures and the splashing increased. Throughout that day, Daisy tried not to imagine how many hungry animals worked through the sludge, hoping for an easy meal.

They camped again on a platform high in the trees. Daisy fell easily into an exhausted sleep. When she awoke, the last thing she wanted to do was to climb back down and continue walking.

"We don't have time to waste," Feather urged her as he hopped back onto the trail.

Daisy forced her body to follow.

The tails started swishing again down in the gloop. "How many things in that swarm could eat us?"

"It's best not to think about them all. I'm afraid the light attracted more, but they cannot pass through it."

She forced them out of her mind despite their tenacious flopping. "This swamp must be massive," she said aloud.

"It is indeed. Finding you here was not an advantage to Demonclaw either. He must not have had a choice and likely lost a few men on the way in. Not to frighten you, but I worry that he was able to pull his troops out faster on the other side."

"So, when you say Demonclaw, you mean—"

"The young general who captured you. We should be out of the swamps by this evening. If all goes according to plan, we will meet the king at the exit."

Daisy's burden lightened a bit. Leaving the swamps for tamer landscape gave her something to hope for.

But as they rounded the next corner, they stopped at the sight of Zerek. Ten fierce warriors blocked the path behind him. His hard eyes had a glassy quality about them, and the alabaster seal again encircled his neck.

Feather stepped between him and Daisy and unsheathed his sword. A bright orb formed in front of Feather, blowing massive heat forward. Part of the trail caught fire, and all of the men drew back, except Zerek.

Zerek chanted something and passed through the orb unscathed. He took two curved swords and charged at Feather, who blocked the parry.

Daisy backed away from the scuffle, and one of the beasts nipped at her heel. There was no longer an orb of light between her and the dragon, and she screamed.

Feather turned and shot an orb at the beast, while Zerek slashed completely through his neck in one swift motion. Feather's body crumbled to the ground while his head rolled a few feet away.

Zerek tossed the head to his captain. "Post this as a greeting to our friends in Elleson."

Daisy watched in horror. Her scream lodged itself deep in her throat and only tears spilled out.

Zerek grabbed Daisy by the hair and pulled her to his horse. Daisy couldn't believe this was the same man who had stayed with her in the swamp.

He mounted the shadowbeast, and one of the men handed Daisy up to him. He hoisted her astride his unicorn just in front of himself and barked the forward charge.

At that moment, several of the monsters pulled out of the swamp and took down three men and two horses, then dragged them, as well as Feather's body, into a feeding frenzy.

Zerek and his remaining guards ran their horses at unmerciful speeds. They left the swamp sometime in the late morning.

The other warriors unmounted to let the steeds rest in a pleasant meadow. One of them mounted Feather's head on a post in the ground. Zerek nodded to his captain, then charged the shadowbeast forward, leaving the rest behind. Apparently the creature had supernatural stamina because it ran for hours. The road they followed ran alongside the swamp. Eventually the large trees were replaced by a stretch of barren land on the left side. On the right side of the road, a rich forest stood alight, occasionally wafting fruity and flowery scents toward them. Daisy wanted nothing but to dive into it and shake off the death she had just been through.

She never had the chance.

Zerek took a sharp left turn onto a road that barreled straight into the barren landscape. The unicorn did not stop running until they reached an outpost that was definitely not in the blessed land of Elleson.

ZEREK PUSHED DAISY INTO A ROOM. She fell onto a cold, ceramic floor covered with coarse dust. Pebbles of dirt lodged into her palms.

"Get some sleep," he said in a low voice. The door lock clicked behind him and his footsteps faded down the hall.

She stood and rubbed the pebbles out of her palms before walking over to sit on a straw bed. She couldn't keep the tears from falling. She cried until she shook, shocked by multiple griefs at once. Her imagination kept replaying the scene of Feather's head falling to the ground and Zerek's emotionless face splattered by blood. She finally crashed into a deep sleep, medicated only by sheer exhaustion.

She had a dream where doctors lined up through a great room to take care of healthy, happy people. On the other side of the same room, sick and dying patients were ignored and neglected. Her heart went out to them, until she recognized Zerek among them. A tall man surrounded by light approached her and handed her a stethoscope. "Light does not go into darkness without being seen," he said. He pointed to Zerek. "Carry my mercy."

But she objected. "That man is a murderer."

"Many of my friends were murderers once. Remember?"

A gentle knock at the door awakened her.

Daisy sat up and studied the room for the first time. Stucco walls surrounded a tiled floor. The few items of furniture included a table with three chairs and her straw bed. It didn't appear to be a prison cell, but the door unlocked from outside.

A small face peeked in. "Hello, miss. I'm to dress you and take you down to breakfast."

The words *carry my mercy* resounded through Daisy's conscience. She rubbed at her temples before looking again at the small girl, who wore a threadbare brown dress, no shoes, and looked to be around nine years old.

"Come in," Daisy said.

The girl shifted her eyes to the ground as she walked in with a stack of clothes. She placed them on the bed, then turned back to pull a heavy washbasin from the hallway.

She seemed strong for her age, able to drag a washbasin full of water to the table without trouble. She prepared some lotions and turned to Daisy. "I'm to wash your hair."

Daisy then noticed that the folded clothes were her dragon skins, and they had all been laundered during the night. A fresh shirt sat next to them. "Did you do this?"

The girl nodded. "General said they needed a wash, so I came and got them from your room."

Daisy's chest constricted. She couldn't think about him now. "Thank you. My clothes smelled bad."

The girl bowed. "You were in the swamp for many days. Sit here and lean your head over the water."

Daisy sighed and obeyed. The girl jumped into the work and massaged soaps and lotions through her hair, scrubbing her scalp. It felt glorious for her head to be clean again.

The girl sat Daisy upright and towel-dried her wet strands before pulling them into a French braid. As the child finished the last touches, she said, "You may finish bathing with the soaps. Breakfast is ready downstairs."

"Would you like to eat with me?" Daisy asked.

The girl blushed. "I'm not allowed. I would be punished."

Daisy tried to make eye contact, but the girl's gaze penetrated the floor.

The child curtsied and ran out the door.

Once Daisy buttoned her jacket, she left her room and flitted down to the dining hall. Stairs used to be cumbersome, but she moved now with effortless mobility. A rush of gratitude flooded her heart before she stopped herself. "Stockholm syndrome much, Daisy?"

She pressed forward into the dining hall where a breeze swept through from several open doors. She looked over unknown faces until she saw Zerek at a table with two bar maids. One of them massaged his shoulders, the other sat next to him, leaning against him. They might as well be groping a chair for all the response he gave them. He held a bottle and his eyes were only half open.

When he saw Daisy, his slackened facial features tensed, and he stood to his feet. The maid next to him tried to pull him back, but he pushed her away by the neck. Still clutching his bottle, he exited through the outer door.

Everyone in the room continued whatever they were doing as if this were normal.

A maid plunked soup and bread in front of Daisy without a

word. She was hungry enough that she didn't need pleasantries. She tore into the bread, inhaled the soup, and allowed the sustenance to calm her tense body.

The men at Zerek's table continued their conversation without him.

"The master says we won't leave until tomorrow. It don't make no sense why we would wait here another day. It's just inviting Ellish forces."

"Somethin' ain't right when he takes to drink anyhow."

"Ain't the king eager for the girl to be in Ahl?"

Daisy couldn't think about the king. She grabbed half a loaf of bread and headed toward one of the open doorways. No one moved to stop her, so there must be little prospect for escape outside.

Still, she scanned the barren outpost. No fences. A few practical, military buildings stood without flourish. Stables, bunkhouses, and a warehouse of some sort. Outside the camp there were no trees or foliage as far as she could see. She wouldn't get anywhere if she tried to run away.

She looked around for horses that might be left alone. As she approached the stables, a soldier stepped between her and the entrance. "You should stay out of trouble. I'm sure we can find plenty of soldiers to keep you company, if that's what it takes." He leered down at her with a yellow-toothed smile.

"I'm fine." She raised her hand and backed away. She turned and meandered back through the various buildings—a few paltry stone cottages along the main road, followed by a secluded garden. It might be more accurate to call the garden four ruined walls within which vegetation had found some desperate will to live.

She wandered in and cozied into a rock pile that mostly hid her from view. She found herself praying again, inviting a holy God into an unholy place. It struck her as a familiar metaphor. This same act of praying invited him into her wasteland of a heart.

She stayed there a while until her fought-for serenity was shaken. Zerek tore into the enclosure. Daisy squeezed more tightly behind a few fallen stones to keep her presence from his view.

Meanwhile, he sat on the ground, put his head in his hands, and wept.

She had to fight to keep back her own tears. *Is his heart this tender?*

After several minutes the warrior's heaving sobs abated. He stood and lifted his chin, all traces of vulnerability disappeared from his face.

Daisy barely breathed until he had left. The lights were fading, but she didn't want him to have the slightest inkling she'd been spying on him.

She slipped out of the enclosure unseen and tiptoed back to the inn.

CHAPTER EIGHTEEN

THE NEXT MORNING Daisy wandered out to the street. Brown dust hung in the dry, cool air. It reminded her of Eastern Colorado after a windstorm. It would probably be hot later in the day.

Soldiers prepared their horses on the street with ample space between themselves and the shadowbeast. The black monster twitched for action and dug its claws in and out of the dry earth.

Out of nowhere, Zerek grabbed her arm and pulled her toward the beast. Perhaps it was an improvement over the hair-grabbing, but she still didn't love it.

One of Zerek's captains approached him. "We found an extra horse, master. It would keep you from having to carry the girl."

"I will not risk it," replied the general in his low, toneless voice. He lifted her onto the beast's saddle and then hoisted himself up behind her. "Let's move."

The pack of horses left the outpost, and Zerek let them move ahead multiple paces. Now that she had rested, she became aware of his breath, his warmth, his physical presence directly against her back. She could not shudder with disgust because at some point her disgust had been replaced with confusion. Zerek was a person, a person with uncontrollable circumstances who wept. A person who had played with her and had been like a friend for a brief interlude.

They rode deeper into the land of Ahl. Vegetation and houses appeared on the landscape. People tended crops. Thatched roofs dotted the countryside.

"This is Lord Goring's land," Zerek said, breaking a long silence.

His voice startled her, but she listened.

"Those are his serfs. He is said to be fairly lenient toward them, though his reputation makes you wonder if many of them are his bastard children. If it is true, the crime is all the worse because he is descended from the light nobility. They will have to live centuries in servitude and probably take their own lives out of desperation."

Daisy shuttered.

Zerek put one arm around her waist and drew her tight, which didn't calm her either.

Later in the day they approached another outpost where foot soldiers had gathered along the road. Their faces were mangled in the same manner as the faces of Zerek's own men.

"Why all the scars?" Daisy asked, unsure if he would answer.

"It is a sign of my king. He wanted a way to distinguish his most trusted soldiers. The scars are both their initiation into the special guard and their reward. Everywhere they go, people give them deference and preferential treatment."

"But you don't have scars."

"You will also notice my king's hypocrisy. He is particularly drawn to beauty and does not allow anything less in his court."

Daisy didn't like the assumption that she would witness this herself. The more she saw of this king's land, the more she wished to avoid him.

"I'm scarred, so he shouldn't like me so much."

"He is fascinated by you already, but he will be disappointed."

He had no time to expound.

A dozen or so riders were upon them, halting Zerek and his men in a half circle. Daisy saw that their commander was an attractive, unmutilated man with an arrogant air. He half smiled at Zerek and said, "Hello, my prince." But there was a mocking tone in the title.

Zerek unmounted, fell to a knee, and crossed his chest with his right fist. "My Lord Taph."

"I'm here to relieve you of your baggage. I will deliver the girl to Ahl."

Zerek switched to his calm, deadly way of speaking—the one Daisy found more terrifying than agitation. "The task was given to me."

"Yes, and you botched it. Our king sent me to guarantee the delivery." Lord Taph grimaced as his eyes scanned Daisy's face. "But I will allow you to put her away for the night."

Zerek stood and bowed his head. The rest of his frame held rigid until he hopped back onto the unicorn. His arms shook as he reached around her for the reigns.

Taph and his men maneuvered their horses to the side of the road, allowing Zerek and his men passage on toward the next outpost.

APPARENTLY, the accommodations became nicer as they neared the castle. More people populated this outpost than the first. Its cleanliness also evidenced more care and commerce. People milled about, and chatter filled the street where pockets of merchants or soldiers gathered.

Zerek pulled Daisy inside and sat her at a long wooden table in the dining hall. At least twenty soldiers ate dinner. Five sat at the other end of her table, staring at her.

"You don't have to sit so far away, dove," said a large man with sweaty brown hair and a red face.

Zerek stepped between her and the man and said, loud enough for all to hear, "If anyone talks to or approaches this girl, they will have my knife at their throat."

The man's red face turned ashen, and he refocused all of his attention to his soup. The threat left Daisy pretty much to herself.

The smell of soup wafted from the kitchen. Her stomach growled, but the barmaids didn't glance her way. They flitted about, chatting with one another. One woman exclaimed, "The general has arrived, ladies! Pity the girls who aren't here tonight!" They all swooned.

A woman blew through the doors at the news. She had dark hair and large brown eyes framed by perfect eyebrows. Her deep red lips pouted, while the top of her dress dangled seductively off her shoulders. She glided to Zerek and sat on his lap. "Hello, sweetie." The soldiers laughed their approval. Zerek looked at Daisy with a strange expression, and Daisy averted her eyes in discomfort.

"Dahlia. You are looking lovely as ever."

"I heard you were nearby, so I did what I could." Her voice sounded growly, like an angry French kitten.

"I'm afraid I will have to disappoint you. My baggage is slippery. I've already lost her once."

Dahlia stuck out her lower lip. "Can't we lock her in a closet?" She drew her forefinger along the bridge of his nose.

"I'm sorry, dear." Zerek pecked Dahlia's forehead with a kiss, then firmly pushed her from his lap. He brushed past her and grabbed Daisy by the collar of her dragon skins. "Bring the weed's dinner to her room!"

Daisy pulled against her collar the whole walk down the corridor, but he didn't lose an inch of control. He maybe didn't even notice she had resisted. Blast her weak body. He closed the door behind them, placed her in a chair at a small round table, sat next to her, then exhaled. He ran his hands through his long hair as if shaking off what had just happened.

Daisy crossed her arms. "You don't have to stay with me. Where would I go?"

"Maybe I'm more concerned about you than your escape. You looked scandalized." He chuckled.

Of course she was scandalized—not that she was happy he could tell. "Why should you care? A lady is begging for your attention."

Zerek watched her with a deepening smile. "Dalia is merely one of my distractions."

"Why do I need to know about your *distractions*?"

He jumped and covered her mouth with a strong hand. "Shh! If Taph doubts my control, he will take over from here."

Daisy began to shake as her reserves finally snapped. Tears gushed from her eyes. Zerek let her go and stepped back.

She grabbed a napkin and covered her face as she sobbed.

He cleared his throat, stood, and paced. "I'm not saying this to be mean, but if you insist on crying, it's going to be a problem for you."

She ignored him. She needed to cry. He paced while she worked some of her tears out.

A knock came at the door.

"Come in," Zerek ordered.

"I'm here with the girl's food," said a maid.

"Bring mine as well."

The maid set a tray on the table, curtsied, and left.

Zerek paced through the room. "Tomorrow you will arrive at the castle around green. I should prepare you for what you encounter there."

She dabbed her eyes with the cloth. "You are helping me?"

Zerek shrugged. "Fortunately, you aren't pretty."

"Seriously? What does that have to do with anything?"

He settled again on the chair opposite hers. "My king likes pretty women the same way a cat likes mice. He likes to collect them and keep them. Until he decides he is finished, they get to wear lovely things and be his intimate companions. He charms them. They don't even realize they are going to be trophies. He does not want them to get old, so most are made *still* while they are quite young." He leaned forward. "I think he may have planned this for you, but your looks will not suit him. I don't know what he will do."

"He *stills* them?"

"They no longer move. They stand or sit in his favorite chamber where he can admire their beauty. They do not age, but they are no longer alive. Their skin feels real and warm. He does it from his magic."

"I might throw up."

"Try to control that impulse."

"Are you scaring me on purpose?"

"Yes, but not because I enjoy it. I do not like my king or his hobbies, and it is better that you are shocked here with me than in front of him. For him, weaknesses are exploitable. He would love to see your horrified expression as often as possible. So calm your fears. No matter how he tries to shock you, look disinterested. Don't play his game. The safest place for you is in the dungeon, which is where he will send you once he is bored."

"And then what?"

"I don't know." He studied her. "But you will be alive, and then I can think of something."

"So you *are* helping me."

"I think so." He didn't shift his gaze.

Daisy looked away to diffuse his stare. "Lord Taph called you prince. What did he mean?"

"I am a prince."

"So, your king is—" She couldn't help turning back to him to see his expression.

Zerek held up a hand to stop her. "Enough. He brought me into the world. I am not his only progeny. Taph, my older brother, is by far his favorite. But I am his only child born from marriage."

"You are the only prince?"

"Sure. I'm *the* prince."

"That's kind of a big deal, isn't it?"

"If it were, Taph would have killed me already. I am honored as an extension of the king, which gives me some privilege. I don't know if privilege is worth much in this place, beyond keeping me alive. In a good kingdom even peasants are happy. In Ahl, the king can kill his best friend without warning."

"Will I have to talk to the king?"

"Of course."

Daisy shivered. How could she play a game and keep her wits

about her with all of these things to consider? She thought back to some of the stories she'd read about ancient Chinese dynasties and all of their power plays. She'd been grateful that her daily choices couldn't be misconstrued as treason. Yet, was this the life Zerek lived?

Warmth rushed around her and the room brightened. *Light does not go into darkness without being seen.* That's what the man in her dream had said.

Zerek's expression changed from unreadable to noticeably surprised.

"What?" she asked. "Do you feel a change too?"

He pointed at her. "You are glowing."

She looked down at her hands and arms. Sure enough, light radiated around her. "But this has happened before, in the swamps. What causes it?"

Zerek scowled. "You don't know?"

"It never happened before you brought me here. Does everyone here glow?"

"Only the light people and those descended from them." His glare did not relent.

"Why are you giving me that look? I'm not a 'light person.' I am a girl who doesn't glow in my own world."

"Mortals from your world are still mortal here. It seems that your mother and her family's journeys have given you an unusual gift."

Daisy poked him. "Do *you* glow?"

Zerek brushed her hand away. "I have no control over it."

"So that's a yes?"

"I can't wield my light or even *glow*. It comes out with force. I *explode*." He was full-on pouting.

Daisy held back a giggle. "Exploding isn't desirable?"

Again, the scowl. He could be so childish.

"How should I know? I thought exploding might be something you would like."

"What good is being out of control?" he asked. "I used to blow things up when I was a child. I caused no end of damage to a fountain in Ells—some national treasure or something. The light-people could only teach me how to control my adrenaline and keep the light dormant."

"You were in Ells? Are you descended from the light people?"

"Only by my mother."

"How are you here? Do you move between the two kingdoms?"

"No one moves between enemies. You are with one or the other, and maybe you will have the opportunity to switch once."

"Then why did you leave Elleson?"

"Many decisions we make, even in our youth, are lasting ones. I grew to hate Orya, who hated me first. Now we enjoy a mutual hatred. It's less confusing than trying to figure out what I did to piss him off all the time."

"But this place is a nightmare. Why would you want to be here?"

Zerek's eyes flashed for a brief second.

Feeling the urge to comfort him, Daisy reached across the table and placed her hand on his.

He snatched her hand between his palms. She tried to pull it back, but he held it tighter. "In *Jane Eyre*, Mr. Rochester says, 'And this is what I wished to have. This young girl who stands so grave and quiet at the mouth of hell.' " His voice grew so quiet that Daisy could barely hear what came next. "When I first read it, I committed treason. I prayed to the Eternal One. I told him that if he brought me such a woman, I would give him my allegiance." Zerek forced his gaze up at her. "Imagine my surprise when I met you, who is thoughtful and brave in the face of all kinds of horrors."

A glassy sheen overtook his eyes, and she knew what it was like. Pretending to be fine every day while going through tasks and living, not daring to want anything.

And now she saw . . . longing. But for what? For *her*? Her breath caught. That was just unthinkable.

Zerek bent toward her and kissed her cheek. "Tomorrow

morning will be chaotic. I can't refuse Taph, but don't be afraid. This exchange will work in your favor."

He stood and cleared his throat. "It is time for me to see to preparations." Then he left the room.

DESPITE HER EXHAUSTION, Daisy couldn't sleep after Zerek left. Her thoughts ran circles through her brain until a dull light eased into the sky.

Her door flung wide, hitting the wall with a bang. Lord Taph filled the doorway.

"We're leaving now," he ordered. "You have two minutes to dress."

The door slammed shut again. Daisy had barely pulled on her coat when a soldier walked in and grabbed her by the wrist. He dragged her toward the stairs, then through the tavern and into the street.

Outside, she scanned the chaos in search of Zerek, but he wasn't there. Fear eclipsed whatever small faith she had mustered. For all of his collar-grabbing, Zerek had guarded her safety, but Taph's men shoved her around. Someone pushed her forward and smacked the back of her head. "Get on the horse, you twit."

She climbed up onto the saddle of a gray horse. Before she could settle herself securely, a soldier whipped the animal toward Ahl.

CHAPTER NINETEEN

BROGAN LISTENED in horror as the light men identified the head on the spike. It was the guide who had found Daisy and beaconed the news back to Ells. Brogan barely heard Orya making arrangements for the proper treatment of the man's remains.

"Brogan."

He snapped his head up to see Orya pointing eastward.

"We must catch up with them before they reach the road to Ahl. Keep Splatter near the front. She urges the rest to run harder."

Brogan wasted no time in charging down the road that ran along the edge of the swamp. Soon, the swamp and its stench were behind them, and the landscape opened up into a strange contrast. On the north side of the road, thick clouds hung in a heavy sky, and barren, exposed ground stretched as far as the horizon—if the dusty air allowed one to see that far. On the south side, dense woods crawled to the edge of the road. He could smell sweet flowers and fruits; colors speckled the terrain under a happy light.

Orya passed him, stopped at a crossroad, and turned back to the few men whose horses had kept pace with them. His face betrayed frustration.

Lightfleet leaned over to Brogan. "They've outrun us. Our horses can't keep going, and besides that, the dark lands are poison to us. Even if we *could* take the path to Ahl without being poisoned, we would meet small armies at each outpost. And even if we made it to the castle gates alive, there are fates worse than death inside."

Lightfleet perked up and addressed the other men. "Brogan wouldn't be affected by the poisoned air. If he had help, he could avoid the outposts. He might be able to intercept them."

Orya glared at Lightfleet. "Send my young guest alone into the lands of the dark king? And what would he do if he reached them?"

Brogan wondered the same thing.

"There is help to be had," Lightfleet insisted.

"Greg, we're talking about Demonclaw. I simply cannot allow one so new to our world to—"

Brogan pushed aside all thoughts of *fates worse than death*. "I'm willing to go if it means keeping Daisy from that castle." Turning toward Lightfleet he asked, "Who would be my help?"

Lightfleet cocked an eyebrow at Orya. "We have *other* friends."

The men shifted on their mounts and peered around them.

As if on cue, a sleek, elegant panther strode up to their small group. Horses stomped their hooves and backed away, allowing the enormous animal room to sit in front of a newly formed half circle.

Brogan stared at the svelte creature. It moved like water flowing over a rock, but rather than water, short yellow tabby fur glistened over a lioness frame. Its heart-shaped head angled toward Brogan, and its large, green, intelligent eyes drew him in.

The cat winked at him and shifted its gaze back to the Light King. It meowed and growled repeatedly before Brogan realized it was speaking.

Brogan nudged Lightfleet. "What is it saying?"

The cat turned to Brogan and locked eyes again. A deep, feminine voice rang out in Ellesse. "I asked if the king called me."

Orya huffed. "No, Maomao. I did not call you."

The cat blinked. "Yet, you are here, where I was waiting, and my curiosity compels me. It will be the death of me one day."

Brogan smiled at her wit. This drew the cat's attention to him again. "You are not one of Orya's subjects." She drew closer.

"He is a guest of my kingdom, and thereby under my protection and rule," Orya interjected dryly. "The Grar are narcissists, Brogan. If you even acknowledge their existence, they will become insufferable."

The grar? he mouthed to Lightfleet.

"Yes, Brogan." Maomao drew a paw up to her face and inspected a claw. "We cannot help it. We are quite fascinating, if we say so ourselves. But Orya, you are not in a position to play cold. I saw Demonclaw dragging your lady toward Ahl three hours ago. Is this not more important than putting me in my place?"

She tilted her head and continued. "I considered stopping him myself, but the warrior is too much for me alone. The shadowbeast too. I would need tricks. Had you given me warning, I could have prepared something. You knew I was guarding this border."

Orya narrowed his eyes. "What do you propose, cat?"

Maomao stood and stretched. "I will take the boy. He will be safe off the roads. He looks to be sturdy and ready for adventure. The enemy doesn't know he is here, so no one will know there is a human at your bidding. If we manage to free the lady, however, there will be fury. Our escape will require at least one strong child. If she is hurt, I need the boy to help carry her."

"Could that work?" asked Brogan. "My horse can't run through unknown fields with that kind of speed."

"You are right Brogan. You will not bring the dumb creature. You will run. With me." Maomao smiled.

"Do cats smile?" Brogan whispered to Lightfleet.

"Grar do," Lightfleet responded, his eyes big and dewy. "I can't tell you how much I envy you right now."

"Why? I don't know how am I supposed to run fast enough to catch up to horses."

Orya's shoulders must have been tense, because they fell hard and he sighed. "The cat can share her stamina and speed with you. It requires that your body have more than your natural nutrients. Burning that many calories is dangerous, even for a young, strong man."

Excitement welled up within him. Supernatural endurance? "How do I get more nutrients?"

Maomao purred so loud that Brogan could feel the vibrations. "Almost anything is possible with the right magic," she said.

"We don't use that kind of magic," Orya insisted.

She rolled her eyes. "I'm not subjecting him to dark magic. I smell a gonji tree even now. Remember the fate of the girl. Your time is short."

Orya's face contorted in frustration. He spied out something almost immediately, jumped off his horse, walked up to the forest edge, and shook a smallish tree with wild, twisted branches. Yellow berries rained down around him. A few of his comrades in arms dismounted their horses to pick the berries off the ground, including Brogan. Before long, they collected enough to fill a satchel.

Orya handed this to Brogan and spoke in a much different tone than he had been using with the cat. "I don't want to do this, but I have been backed into a corner. I think if Daisy were to see you, she would muster the strength to return with you. It might give her the courage she needs to escape. My friend, this is a dangerous task, and these little fruits should not be eaten unless you are about to run with the cat. They will destroy your body if you are not using the energy contained in them. Do not be afraid. The cat will not betray you, though I dare say you will find her company abhorrent. Be patient and do not fight her. Her race is powerful and cunning, and she is personally renowned for being ever more so. Even if you were to win, you will walk away with considerable scars and fewer limbs."

"Sir, I don't know what the plan is . . . for when we find Daisy."

The cat laughed. "There is no planning in chaos, dear. We will keep moving until we find her. We can weigh our options on the journey. We might have two days. If we get within sight of the castle, it is too late."

Maomao padded to the side of the road and turned her great head to face the barren lands.

Brogan handed Splatter's reins to Storm.

Orya put a hand on his shoulder. "I will ask the Eternal One to guard you, friend."

"Yeah. Whatever you think will help."

The rest of the men also bid Brogan goodbye, saying they would pray for him. Brogan wasn't sure if prayer was their typical adieu or if they really were afraid for his life.

"Eat three berries now, Earthling," said Maomao.

He popped the berries into his mouth. "How do you know to call me Earthling?" asked Brogan, curious about the alien reference.

"I heard your mind saying it, and I find that familiar things put people at ease."

"You read minds?"

"Not always. I love fun, so the Eternal One lets me hear fun things. Once in a while, though, he means business, and I hear serious things."

"But you heard my thoughts?"

Before she could answer, Brogan started to get light-headed.

"Touch my shoulder, Brogan," said Maomao.

As he did, his chest was lifted upward and his mind cleared. He could see, in detail, the landscape as it stretched into the distance. He understood how they must proceed to move quickly over it, and he realized the plans were coming from Maomao's mind. Following her directions, he jogged forward. The cat laughed and pranced alongside of him. The two laughed together as they ran faster and faster. Brogan leaped over rocks, shrubs, and dried streambeds. He leapt like a stag and ran like a cheetah. His muscles had never moved so quickly nor with such power.

Nothing could slow him! If anything, this experience might make the whole trip to crazyland worth it.

Barren horizons stretched around them. Occasional mud houses and herds of livestock dared to take on the sorrowful, forsaken landscape, but no real agriculture thrived.

They kept the pace for hours, sprinting until Brogan's chest tightened and his breath suddenly escaped him.

Maomao slowed. "Eat three more berries, Brogan." The gentleness in her voice eased his panic.

Her tenderness surprised him, and he wondered about Orya's stern caution toward the cat as he ate three berries.

"We will run until you feel like this again. Then you must only eat one berry, because we will rest."

Again they ran, and great reservoirs of the cat's joy moved through him. Her magic kept him alive and impervious to the sickened land around him. Laughter rang out from his mouth, not so much from his own heart but from hers.

An hour later, when Brogan's body could not continue, he ate one berry as instructed. The sustenance of the fruit moved like warm syrup from his stomach through his limbs, providing immediate recovery and relief.

The cat panted, though her head remained upright and alert. Brogan stared at her in wonder.

He had never shared in someone's heart so intimately. He had been given insight to this creature's soul. And Maomao was so . . . happy and at peace in spite of many weighty things pressing in on her. This levity was something Brogan had never experienced before. It wasn't flippancy, but the weight of the circumstances was missing. And there was something else—it felt like *love,* but Brogan didn't understand it.

"I haven't run with a companion in years. I forget what fun it is."

Brogan wanted to know more about her.

"You have questions." She purred as she flopped down on a patch of grass.

He laughed. "I have many."

"You may ask them."

"Where are you from? What kind of animal are you?"

Maomao flipped upright and held her head high. "I am Maomao of the Grar. We are the rulers of the Peralinal." She relaxed and peered into Brogan's eyes. "I have been told that in your world it would be like the Savannah. We are a cat-people —*not* animals. Fierce hunters, fierce warriors, fierce lovers." She smiled. "Mostly, we are just fierce."

"But you seemed so gentle before."

"Ah, well, I stumbled into something strange and it has changed me. Those few of us Grar who have come to follow the Eternal One no longer fit easily into the hierarchy of Peralinal. I was held in high regard before, for my skills in fighting, for my beauty, and for my eloquence. I was a poetess and a comedian. I still am, of course, but my style has changed. It upset my king, who fancied himself my mate for a time. His wrath at my conversion was deadly, and so those of us who follow the Eternal One fled. I hope to return and continue my work one day."

"Your king? Did you love him?"

"It is a good question." She stared up into the sky for a while, then started licking her paws.

Brogan leaned back. *I guess she refuses to answer that question.*

"You are mistaken," Maomao purred. "I *cannot* answer the question. Feelings of love are merely a hint—a pointer to love itself. When we meet love for real, we understand that we only knew a shadow of it."

"I've never been in love."

She smiled. "You are a young soul. You will see: Love is a powerful thing. It can be life-giving. But nothing can hurt you like your own selfish appetite seeking what can never feed it."

"What do you mean?"

"Like another soul. Another soul's body. Another soul's possessions. If you seek something, seek what is greatest, then allow love to grow out from that."

Brogan didn't want to talk about the Eternal One, so he ventured toward another topic. "How do you know Orya?"

"I don't know Orya." She looked at him and blinked her eyes slowly. "He is right not to trust the Grar. They have been too long on the wrong side. But he is wrong to mistrust his God."

"I'm not certain that God is even real, so I can't blame someone else for doubting."

"I did not come to my beliefs in a day either. Wait and stay alert. If the Eternal One has spoken to me, he has also spoken to Orya. Plus, the king was not surprised to see me."

Brogan thought back to the interactions on the road. "I think you are right. But did Lightfleet also know you were waiting there?"

"He is a sensitive child. Very astute."

Brogan narrowed his eyes. "Do you know him?"

She only closed her eyes and smiled.

"Okay. Fine. How about the Demonclaw?"

Maomao stopped smiling. She looked sad and bowed her face downward. "He was not brought into this world in peace but as an act of aggression. Yet his life has been granted, so whether as an object of wrath or salvation, we have yet to understand his purpose."

"Is he evil?"

"He has been given the power of death, so the Dark King uses him for such purposes. He is not a simple man, however, and I would not categorize him."

Brogan leaned back against a rock. "You sound like you admire him."

"Brogan, it is important to distinguish subtleties. I admire the works of the Eternal One. This man is one of his most unique, innately interesting creatures. I wonder why the Eternal One even let life come into being there, in that darkness. I wonder over his destiny, but I pray for his soul."

"Everyone here prays a lot."

Maomao only blinked her eyes.

. . .

THE DAY ENDED and light faded into darkness. When the night was very black, Maomao stood. "Follow me."

Brogan pushed himself off the ground and followed after her, trying to keep his feet as quiet as her paws. Not that stealth was necessary when he couldn't see his hands in front of him. They walked for what seemed like an hour through black darkness. Cold gusts of wind tore through his dragon skins.

"We will sleep here. Lean against me to stay warm, Brogan."

Brogan drew close to her warm, soft fur and fell into a deep sleep, his body spent. A few hours later the light flashed yellow. He sat up and discovered they had rested atop a high hill. Beneath their perch stood a small settlement with tents and some crude buildings.

"Eat a berry now. You need my sight."

As Brogan ate the berry, his view of the activity below magnified. He could see the outpost as if it were across the street.

Servants stirred, preparing horses. Brogan's fascination fell on one particular, massive black horse. A blade-like horn extended from its head. Its muscles twitched like an athlete ready to race—a beautiful and frightening creature.

"That's Demonclaw's unicorn. The beast is a warrior as much as any man."

Brogan drew another breath. "I believe you."

"We will not attack. When the path provides surprise, I will lure the girl's horse away. You pull her down and I will catch her. Most importantly, avoid the shadowbeast. We can outrun him, but we cannot fight him."

They kept watch as the light grew. Then, Brogan saw a man walking Daisy out of the building. He was not overly big, maybe six feet tall, but he was strong and trim and his movements looked effortless. His hands tied and shifted saddle paraphernalia in quick, specific movements. The unicorn nuzzled up to the man's auburn hair. He caressed its jaw and whispered to it before vaulting on with one graceful move. Could humans even move like that? He was a ballet dancer, a gymnast, and a ninja combined.

"Yes, I think so too," said Maomao.

"I didn't say anything."

Maomao smiled at him. Her smile disappeared, however, when Demonclaw pulled Daisy onto the shadowbeast with him.

"You said we can't fight the shadowbeast, so if that's what she's riding, what do we do?"

Maomao agreed, "This compromises our plan. Quick, eat two more berries."

As Brogan ate, the warrior looked directly up at them.

Brogan fell low to the ground. "Did he see us?"

"I don't think so. He would not leave us alone if he had. We will meet them at the next outpost. We must take her from her quarters in the night. We cannot fail again or we will lose her."

Brogan's chest tightened, taking in the new situation. There was too little room for error. In his distress, he didn't even want to stand up.

Maomao approached him, purring. She nuzzled his cheek for a minute before softly growling. Her growl sounded like a song that vibrated into Brogan's chest and relaxed the clutch of worry from his physical body. He stood and knew that he could run again today.

So they ran. This time Maomao lent more determination than joy. They arrived at the next outpost just as the last light faded from the sky.

They waited behind brush and rock for several hours until the sounds of people talking and moving settled in the outpost and the camp around it. Something about the stillness in the air felt eerie to Brogan. No wind blew, no bugs chirped, no lights shone in the sky. The only light in the great sphere of darkness came from the settlement. Brogan could barely make out Maomao's silhouette. It challenged their ability to communicate, and he was determined to remain silent.

Maomao pricked her ears upward when a figure appeared a few feet in front of them, sword in hand. He said something to Maomao in a growling, cat-like language. Brogan never understood how someone could just appear like that, when he was certain he would have seen or heard a pebble drop within a fifty-foot radius.

Brogan drew his knife, but Maomao pushed him aside and stepped between him and the warrior. "Put your knife away, Brogan."

Hearing her command, the figure switched languages. He spoke in lilted Ellesse, accented exactly like Orya's. "Hail, mighty grar." There was amusement in his voice. "To what do I owe the honor of your presence?"

Maomao bared her fangs and lowered her shoulders. When the figure made no move to fight, her body relaxed. "We are here for the girl, Prince."

The man sheathed his sword. "How convenient. I was just wishing someone would take her."

Brogan stared in astonishment.

"But you cannot have her on my watch, since I am bound to obedience. Taph is planning to take her in the morning. He will not have my shadowbeast, and you can steal her from him." He laughed softly. "He is no match for you, cat. Who is the boy?" He stepped toward Brogan.

Again, Maomao moved between them.

"I see. He is human?" The figure gripped his sword again. "Was he sent here to rescue the girl?"

Maomao answered, "He is the girl's brother."

Her answer annoyed Brogan. Why would Maomoa disclose such sensitive information?

Demonclaw relaxed his stance, however, and bowed courteously. "In that case, may your journey be easy." He turned and walked away.

Maomao whispered, "But is it really to be *that* easy?"

"Why did you tell him I am Daisy's brother?"

"I told you. I sometimes hear thoughts, and I have never known the Prince to be vulnerable before."

"So we can trust him?"

Maomao narrowed her eyes. "All I know is that Demonclaw does not play when he kills."

THE NEXT MORNING, Brogan followed Maomao's lead in hiding behind rock formations. A mile from the outpost, an opening in the rock formation revealed the road. And on that road Brogan could see Taph's band of warriors approaching.

In a single leap, Maomao had cleared the rocks. She landed in the road, obstructing the way with teeth bared.

The horses reared. Warriors yelled in surprised.

Maomao was, indeed, terrifying. She seemed even larger than ever. She cocked her head and let out a chilling roar.

The soldiers turned their mounts to flee. Taph's men weren't stupid enough to grapple with a grar.

Brogan felt some relief at their retreat because most of the men were twice his size. As they left, a horse and rider bolted toward him, clearing the rocks. The man hit Brogan with his scabbard and swiped the satchel of berries Brogan carried.

Still empowered by gonji berries and by Maomao, Brogan turned to chase the horse when something caught his eye.

On the road Taph snatched the reins of Daisy's horse and turned his mount toward Ahl.

He had to choose between the berries or Daisy. He used Maomao's speed to run after Daisy, then leaped up behind her and onto the horse, pulled out his knife, and cut the ropes binding Daisy's hands. As he did, Taph lunged at them with his sword.

Brogan grabbed Daisy and pulled her backward from the saddle. The move was a desperate one, and he heard his collarbone snap as he hit the ground, Daisy on top of him. Taph whirled his horse back to reclaim his captive, but Maomao jumped between them. With the agility of a tiger, she jumped onto the back of the horse, sending the creature racing for its life.

Taph cursed at her, but she calmly leaped from the horse and made her way back to where Brogan lay on the road.

Pain radiated from his shoulder to his neck. He saw Maomao

through wincing eyes and gasped, "One of the soldiers took the gonji berries."

Maomao bowed her head in understanding. "We need to get away from the road before they regroup. Can you walk?"

Brogan didn't answer and struggled to sit up.

Daisy reached an arm around him to help him stand, sending bolts of pain through his shoulder.

Brogan ranted through his pain. "The berries were our fuel, Daisy. They allow us to run with Maomao. Now, we have none, and I don't know how long it's going to take to get back to Elleson."

Maomao broke in. "Speed is our only advantage. We must have it to leave this place. Brogan, remember what Orya said about the other magic?"

"The magic he said I should never use?"

"Yes. The magic that can help your body the way the berries did. It's dangerous but less dangerous than the alternative. The two of you can both use it. It will allow you to run in your condition and even temporarily ease your pain."

"Maomao," Daisy said, "it's important that Brogan does not fall into the hands of these soldiers."

Maomao gawked at Daisy. "You forget about yourself, young one?"

"No, but I'm okay wherever I go," came her strange, soft reply.

Maomao studied her before she released her peculiar growling laughter. "Well, there is no need to be reckless about it, my lady."

Brogan didn't understand the exchange. It seemed to him that this was the point at which Maomao began to speak to Daisy deferentially, even calling her 'my lady' where he was 'child.' In fact, to Brogan she spoke as a mother. The difference bothered him a little. It bothered him a lot that the two were talking about getting *him* out of the dark kingdom and protecting *him* from danger. *You're welcome for the rescue*, he thought, wincing at the sharp stab of pain.

Maomao pulled him back to the present with a startling assertion. "Brogan, this kind of magic asks for a price. Your body must pay for the exchange. The simplest one is to offer up your future facial hair. That means you will never grow a beard as a man."

Brogan covered the lower half of his face with his hands. "Wuh-what? That's not something I want to exchange."

"Would you rather exchange a hand?"

He swallowed, sighed, then let his hands drop.

"It's more costly for women," said Maomao. "The price is your hair."

"Oh." Daisy looked sad for a moment but wiped the despondency from her face and asked, "How do I give it?"

Brogan cringed at the thought that his mistake would cost Daisy her hair.

"The magic will take it."

Daisy nodded her head in approval.

"Well then, shall we begin?" Maomao growled an incantation. She looked comfortable doing so, and as she finished, an energy pulled on him and filled his body. It was different than the gonji berries' magic. It was more constricting and commanding and did not lend any companionship with Maomao.

Maomao began to run, prompting him to run after her. Daisy followed. The three ran without stopping, even through the night. A day and a half later they crossed a road into a dense forest.

Maomao halted and turned to Daisy. "There is a house over that hill. They will welcome you and send word to the king."

Brogan stared at Daisy's now completely smooth head. He could never complain about his beard. Daisy needed all the help she could get when it came to her looks, and now she was so pitiable.

Maomao turned to Brogan, "It was a pleasure, my young friend."

As the magic released them, Brogan fell to the ground in terrible pain. He had forgotten about his broken collarbone.

"I am sorry I cannot make the magic hold until you get to the door of the house."

Brogan looked up at her through wincing eyes. "You are leaving?"

"I am not yet a welcome sight to those who dwell in Elleson, especially after what I just did to return the two of you."

Daisy stood silent, a dazed look in her eyes.

Brogan asked, "Will we see you again?"

The cat smiled and said, "I hope so, Earthling." At that, she turned and prowled away.

CHAPTER TWENTY

DAISY BUCKLED under Brogan's weight as he leaned on her, but she managed to heave him toward the manor house. As they approached the large, stone structure, three men ran out to them.

"The king informed us that you might come to a home somewhere along the border," one of them said in Ahlfang. They relieved Daisy of her burden and carried Brogan through massive double doors.

Daisy followed them inside where she was greeted by a dozen men and women, all of them with concerned looks on their faces.

A woman spoke with commanding gestures in a language Daisy didn't understand, sending a few running into various parts of the manor house.

Though exhausted, she couldn't help notice how beautiful all of these people were. Their faces were shining with health and vigor. They looked young, strong, energetic, and happy.

Daisy followed the men who carried Brogan into a peculiar room where they set him on a bed. Other beautiful people buzzed about, giving Brogan this and that, while Daisy stared around her. Soft, white light flooded the room from several directions at once. It was a stark contrast to the darkness she had just been through.

A different woman touched her elbow and guided her from the clamor. "We have a room for you, too, my lady," she said in Ahlfang.

Daisy let herself drift in the path of the woman's guidance to another room also filled with light; once inside, it immediately altered her mood. Daisy's chest decompressed, her shoulders fell, and her eyelids pulled themselves downward.

The woman handed her a soft sleeping gown and gestured at a doorway. "You can bathe in there. I'll bring your meal around quickly."

Daisy took the gown and trudged into the bathroom. By instinct, she reached up to unfasten her braid but found only smooth skin on her head. At least there were no mirrors to see what her hands now felt. She climbed into a bath full of hot water and let it pull the tension from her exhausted limbs. It took everything she had to crawl back out, put on the bedclothes, and wiggle under the covers. Eating would have to wait.

When she awoke, the light in her room barely glowed. Within minutes it grew brighter, mimicking a sunrise. Warm and soothing peace fell around her.

A knock sounded at the door.

Daisy sat up, unsure if she should open the door herself. "Come in?"

A woman entered, the same one who had led her to the room earlier. Now that Daisy could keep her eyes open, she noticed a glimmer reflecting around the woman's golden hair.

The woman smiled brightly. "You fell asleep without eating. I would assume you are hungry now." Even her voice was alight.

"Are you Ellesian?" Daisy wanted to touch her billowing tresses.

"Yes, my lady. You are now in Elleson. The king is delighted that you are safe."

Daisy's thoughts drifted at mention of the king. The king. Elleson. Brogan. "Brogan!" She blurted his name and the woman jumped. "I'm sorry to startle you. Is he okay?"

The woman laughed. "Brogan is fine. He is still with the healers."

A cold current of air blew across the back of her head, reminding Daisy of her baldness. She touched her head and recoiled. It was somehow even more humiliating in the presence of this beautiful creature.

The woman set a small table next to the bed. "If you are still hungry after eating, we have more. In fact, if you need anything, pull that cord." She pointed to a cord hanging next to the door. "My name is Aurora, and I'll be right up."

Aurora left, and Daisy ate the most delicious bread she'd ever tasted. It was even better dipped in the stew. The food warmed her insides and relaxed her achy muscles. Again her eyelids struggled to remain open. She would find Brogan and ask him questions.

Later.

The lights dimmed as if in response to her closing eyelids.

Daisy drifted in and out of sleep. Each time she awoke, her eyes sprang open, but she didn't see the dingy outposts or swamp tents she'd been expecting.

Instead, singing spontaneously erupted outside her room at various distances and people laughed. Laughing was the most indisputable sign that she couldn't be in Ahl. Even in their sarcasm and coarse joking, she never heard laughter among Zerek's men.

Her heart panged at the thought of Zerek. *God, is he going to rise above all of that? Could you at least give him a choice to not murder?*

A knock at her door interrupted her thoughts. This time Brogan stood in the doorway, strong as if he had never been injured.

Daisy surveyed his collarbone. "You're okay?"

"My bones have been mended. The bruises are still here, but that's nothing. They really have some incredible healing arts. And you have guests." His attention drifted to her head, and she wished he wouldn't look at it.

"Guests?"

He moved his gaze back to her eyes. "Yes, King Orya."

"I keep hearing about that guy," Daisy said, flopping back onto the bed.

"Are you well enough to go downstairs? I think he wants to escort you to the castle."

Daisy nodded and waved an arm, motioning him out of the room so she could change. When she stood, her body felt better than it had in days. Not only did her knee feel fantastic, everything else was whole and easily mobile. She put on her unchafable leather ensemble, like a cartoon character who never changed clothes. She kept feeling air moving over her scalp, but she willed away the tears pressing against her eyes. Instead, she jumped and squatted. A brand new knee was something to celebrate. And though meeting strangers did not appeal to her, her curiosity gave her the strength to walk out toward the living area of the house.

Five beautiful men stood at the bottom of the stairs dressed in leather with swords sheathed at their sides. *Don't worry, Daisy*, she thought to herself. *Your facial scars are much more arresting than your head.*

She scanned the scene for Brogan—her one, bizarre familiarity.

The men all smiled up at her, then stared at her mercilessly as she made her way down to them. Her face grew warm as none of them had the decency to direct their gaze elsewhere.

Brogan flew to her side. "Daisy, let me introduce you to my new friends. This is Lord Lightfleet, Lord Phoss, Dewberry, Storm, and Orya King of Elleson." Each of them bowed. A palpable energy radiated from them, shimmering especially from their hair.

"Daisy, I am relieved that you are safe." King Orya addressed her in lilted English. He tilted his head and angled his eyebrows in a compassionate expression.

She was beginning to understand what it meant to be descended from the lightpeople. Zerek had a similar unearthly beauty. And now she stumbled into a country full of them.

Daisy managed a smile. "Thank you."

When she said nothing else, Brogan broke in. "They have a

carriage waiting for us. The king thought you should ride that way rather than on horseback."

He assumed correctly.

"Let's get to the carriage then." King Orya offered his arm to Daisy, which she took. He led her outside, touched her hand, and said, "Brogan will ride with you."

His warm hand almost tingled with kindness. Birds sang and aromatic smells wafted around them. It was like a fairy tale. She half expected one of the birds to open the carriage door.

Instead, the younger one, Lord Lightfleet, ran to open the door for her. She nodded her thanks and climbed up. Brogan followed her.

Inside the carriage, Brogan sat opposite her. He handed her a pillow. She took it and leaned against the carriage wall, remembering their first bus ride to Denver where he fell asleep against her. She would ask him how he found himself in Elleson, but not yet. She closed her eyes and waited for the hot tears to stop pressing against her lids.

The ride back to the castle took several days. They stopped and slept in various houses, each one magnificent in completely different ways. One was earthy, with plants growing from the roof. Another was cut from polished stone. Each manor bore an expression of the family that lived in them—refined, artistic, fun, relaxed.

The landscape also changed. It continued to become more and more lush; the flowers grew more profuse, their perfumes mixing with deeper scents—coffee, moss, and cedar. They mingled with her already confused emotions. What must her parents be going through? What was she going into now, and what did she need to know?

And then there was Brogan, who sat across the carriage trying to make pleasant conversation. He had, at some point, shared how he got to Elleson, his training in the castle, and how the king wished for them to stay. "Daisy, there are things we need to discuss. Are you ready for a shock?"

Daisy snorted a laugh. "More shocking than what exactly?"

Brogan smiled, but the expression didn't reach his eyes. "There's not an easy way to say this, so I hope you forgive the delivery. It's just that I wish I had known sooner, so I imagine you would want to know. My father, Leo Lukes, used to date your mother. It turns out he's your father too."

Daisy's face heated. The fact that Dave Bloom was not her biological father was not news to her. She had never questioned his devotion to her; therefore she accepted her mother's promise to tell her about her biological father when she turned eighteen.

But Brogan? Her brother? Now *that* was shocking. She gave her head a shake, trying to process the information. "Wait, what?"

"I know, right?" Brogan agreed. "I saw my dad's painting in your house, so I knew there was some connection to your family. And then there are the photos of your mom with my dad. It kind of makes sense the weird ways we relate."

Daisy searched his face. Something about his eyes had always been familiar, but how could she have thought to connect them to her own?

* * *

On the long carriage ride, Brogan finally had the time he needed to piece together the puzzle that had been his life. He didn't want to wait any longer to ask questions.

"Your birthday is in November, right?"

Daisy nodded. "November fourteenth."

"Mine is September twenty-third, so I'm two months older than you. My parents met at a basketball camp and dated on and off at various international tournaments. They broke up some time in March, I think, but she didn't tell him about the pregnancy until she was eight months along. That means my dad had been with my mom before he came to Elleson. Probably before the relationship with your mom. That means several months of your gestation happened here in this world."

Daisy's eyes widened at the term *gestation*.

Brogan rolled his eyes at her innocence. "They were here

together, Daisy. Your mom and my . . . *our* dad. That thing in the dark said you were conceived with magic, and King Orya said it happened here. In Elleson. Where Leo and Ophelia traveled together. But the time shift may mean you were en utero here, so the length of time between my birth and yours isn't an accurate representation of when our parents were together. I can't imagine Dad dating them both at the same time. Despite how it appears, he's not exactly a player."

Her mouth fell open. When she recovered, she said, "It makes sense, doesn't it? My mom won't talk about my biological father or the pregnancy. She didn't even want me to know my dad isn't my biological dad. I overheard them telling the nurse when I was in the hospital why Dad couldn't give blood."

"And my dad won't talk about anything pre-college," Brogan said.

"Do you think they were both pretty wounded by it all? By each other? I can't imagine my mother reacting well to hearing he had gotten another girl pregnant."

Brogan sighed. "I don't think my parents were happily married either." He wasn't prepared to tell her *how* unhappy. From what he remembered, his mother was never the docile, forgiving type, so Brogan had blamed her for being crazy. The tragedy of his parents became clearer.

"What is your dad like, Brogan? Even though he's a town hero of sorts, I've never bothered to google him."

"You can say *our*, if you want. You're my sister."

Daisy gazed at him with moistened eyes and nodded. "I want to know if he had a choice to meet me."

"I can't imagine him not wanting to know you. To be honest, he's really cool, just oddly sensitive over certain things."

The carriage took a steep upturn, forcing Daisy off her seat.

Brogan snickered. "It's a steep road up to Ells. Might as well get comfy on this side."

Daisy climbed to the bench on the side of the carriage where gravity held them both to the wall. She opened the window and sighed. "It's beautiful."

"Unearthly?"

"I wouldn't go that far."

They turned a corner to the massive castle gates. The enormous blocks were polished quartz-like stone of various colors.

Daisy's breath caught. "Okay. *That's* unearthly."

"Really? Just that? Not this entire wacky planet? We just took a four-day carriage ride through a thick, cultivated rainforest. You stayed in houses like nothing I've seen on earth."

Daisy continued oohing as the carriage drove through the grounds.

AN HOUR LATER, Brogan watched as men removed Lightfleet's things from the second bedroom of the villa. Orya had made an executive decision to move Daisy into the room, which meant his friend had to move out.

And Lightfleet bent over backward to accommodate Daisy. He trudged stacks of feminine clothes and fabrics into the villa before his things were even removed.

Brogan stopped him. "Where are you going to stay?"

"I've always had a room in the castle. This was only temporary so that we wouldn't kill each other, remember? Does she like dresses?" Lightfleet dropped a pile of flowery, shimmery robes onto the sofa.

Brogan stared in disgust at the shimmers. "Why do you care?"

His friend lowered his brows at him. "Seriously, Brogan? After what Daisy has been through? Not to mention"—he lowered his voice—"she might be our queen one day."

Brogan's stomach lurched at the words. "Has Orya told you this? Why would the king start those kinds of rumors?"

"I'm more like a little brother than a cousin, so I get the family version of news. He hasn't announced anything."

"I seriously doubt Daisy will marry Orya."

"How do you know?"

Brogan sat on the coach next to the pile of silks and picked one up. "Because he's one hundred fifty years old and more like a demigod, while poor Daisy's a normal little human. I don't think she'll be comfortable with the idea."

Lightfleet sat on the other side of the robes. "I don't think Daisy is entirely normal, Brogan. Did you *really* watch her when she walked down the stairs of that borderland manor?"

Nope. "I was watching Orya's eyes pop out as she came down. Thought I was going to have to pick them off the floor. It's like he doesn't even see how bald she is."

"Right. Because she was *glowing*."

"Pfft. We call that blushing, and from what I've witnessed, she's always embarrassed in front of guys." He recalled the countless times he had to help her speak in front of Dean.

"No, Brogan. She was glowing *light*, and her light was beautiful. There were aspects about its purity that you wouldn't see and certainly couldn't understand, not being a light person yourself. But trust me, Orya didn't miss it."

"Light?" Brogan harrumphed.

Lightfleet shrugged. "You said you weren't looking at her."

Brogan sat up straighter, piecing the ideas together. "Are you serious? Like a light person? How is that possible?"

"Orya said she was conceived here in our world."

Brogan threw the fabric back on the heap. "I know, Fleet, but that's too weird."

Just then, the villa door opened and they heard Daisy calling, "Hello?"

"We're in here!" Brogan barked without moving.

Lightfleet ran to open the door from the foyer to the small atrium like an eager beaver. Queen Daisy was already getting the royal treatment.

"A few of the houses look the same. I wasn't sure I'd returned to the right one." Her musical laughter reminded him of glass breaking. It shattered the stillness as she entered into the domed atrium. She stood, unglowing, in all of her ordinariness. All of her baldness.

"Your room will be ready soon." Lightfleet gestured toward the bedroom directly across from the entrance. "Is there anything you need us to bring in?"

"Just my collection of hairbrushes."

Brogan raised an eyebrow. "You brought hairbrushes?"

She scowled. "Where would I get hairbrushes? I thought a little joke might lighten the mood."

"By 'the mood,' do you mean *Brogan*?" Lightfleet asked.

The traitor.

She released another musical chuckle. "Is that my room?"

"Yes. The last of my things were just removed. I also brought these." Lightfleet grabbed the pile of clothes off the sofa and ran into her room. Daisy followed.

Brogan could hear them discuss each outfit as Lightfleet hung them in the wardrobe. "These are for working out. They are in the fashion of the light women who spar and train acrobatics. This one is like a day dress, and the king himself picked out the fabric for this robe."

Without waiting for Lightfleet's return from girl-world, Brogan went out to the garden.

CHAPTER TWENTY-ONE

THE NEXT MORNING, Daisy laid light silks out onto the bed. *These are for working out?* she thought, amused.

She pulled on the dark blue pants and tied a light blue tunic around her waste. The fabric and shape of the clothes flowed well. And now that she had perfect range of motion in her knee, she had no reason to avoid exercise. Donning a pair of sport moccasins, she rambled out to the gardens in search of a gym or something.

She asked first lightman she encountered if she could find a place like that. But he didn't understand English. She tried again in Ahlfang, but he winced and shook his head. So she mimed exercises.

He flashed a bright smile before pointing his finger down a path, giving directions or something in the beautiful, lilting language she now understood to be Ellesse.

She nodded her thanks, followed his pointing finger, and found a double door at the bottom of the path. She pulled one of the doors open, then caught her breath. This was the gym where she had trained in her dreams.

Large skylights filtered daylight into the space, while the

equipment smelled clean and fresh. Several large square mats were laid out in the center of the room. They weren't like the ones she used to train on in gymnastics, but she knew them from the hours she'd spent working out on them.

She had the place to herself, so she kicked off the moccasins and stepped onto the soft surface. With a familiar joy, she moved through a warm-up she knew by heart. Side-squat, side-squat, standing straddle. Jumping-jack, squat, jumping-jack, squat. Adrenaline kicked in like a drug to her bloodstream. Sweet release. She jogged around the room, skipped, lunged. Her hamstrings protested when she reached for the floor in her standing pike.

"Oof!" she muttered. "I'm not as limber as I used to be!"

"It will come back. Right now your skill level is higher in knowledge than in physique." The clear voice rang like a bell, and Daisy shot up from her stretching position. Before her stood a woman with silver, curly hair and deep gray eyes.

"Parshant!" Daisy cried out before standing to bow with joy.

The woman bowed back. "Now that you are here, I will share my real name with you. It is Choral. *Parshant* simply means instructor. I was wondering if you were going to train with us."

Daisy frowned down at her untoned legs and her skinny arms. "I am not exactly in shape. I haven't practiced with *this* body since I was twelve." She flexed her nonexistent bicep to prove the point.

"I know. It limits me, too, not having access to your dream translation." Choral smiled as she said it, but the smile felt cold. Her lips tightened as her eyes moved over Daisy's form. Her evaluating gaze reminded Daisy of her mother.

Daisy shrugged. She had shed some of her naiveté in the past weeks. She had always felt such respect towards her teacher, but today Choral's demeanor cautioned her. "It's different being here in body," Daisy admitted. "I feel heavy and stiff right now, and I'm not even trying to do tricks."

"Start slow. We have healing arts here, but you still need to strengthen your tendons and ligaments before we get into anything exciting. It'll take longer than you think."

"So . . . no special assignments." Daisy meant for her statement to be a joke. Of course she couldn't parkour through villages.

Coral snorted. "Now that you're really here, you'll never be allowed to do anything dangerous again. My brother, the king, is a force of will like you've never met before."

"The king is your brother? Why would he—"

"Treat you like a doll? Because your importance no longer has anything to do with your talent or what you contribute. Welcome to royalty."

"What do you mean by that?"

Coral didn't answer the question. Instead, she joined Daisy on the mat and started one of her typical gut-wrenching workouts, which Daisy followed. By the time they were finished, she was too exhausted to remember that she had asked the question.

DAISY LABORED across the castle grounds to the threshold of her villa. Her quads and calves shook with fatigue, while simple movements taxed her fine motor skills. She heaved her bathroom door closed, wiggled out of her sweaty gym clothes, and nudged the faucet handle to start a bath.

Good thing she didn't eat breakfast, or she'd be tossing chunks right now.

Little electric jolts ran through her tired muscles as she slipped into the steaming tub. "What's in this water?" She pulled her hands above the surface and marveled. Each of her ten digits twitched as if playing an air piano. Within minutes, everything steadied. Relaxation sank deep into her muscles. She'd better get out of the water before she fell asleep in it.

She dried herself and dressed in one of the loungewear ensembles Lightfleet had explained to her. Tie this, loop this. She held five different straps out from the tunic, lost as to what each tied on to. When she finished, fabric bubbled on her right side.

"This will work for exploring the house," she said with a laugh.

She wandered through the circular main room, past Brogan's closed door. A clanking noise emanated from another doorway.

She peaked her head around it. A small breakfast room sat against an open kitchen where a man stood flipping pancakes. When he saw her he said, "The princess thought you would be hungry. We didn't know what kind of food you like, but this is a protein-rich snack Brogan requests daily." The man spoke to her in Ahlfang. It sounded rustic and harsh compared to the elegant surroundings.

"Thank you, I'm sure it's tasty. It's strange to hear the Ahlfang spoken here."

"Only the royal family and a few scholars have learned English, and I was told you weren't given Ellesse upon coming to our world." He shook his head and tsked. "Any ogre can speak Ahlfang."

She rubbed her bald head, wondering if she could avoid looking like an ogre to the Ellesian people. The man poured a fruit compote over the pancake creation and took it to the table. It smelled delicious, and she sat with eagerness.

"Thank you . . . ah—"

"My name is Kehal." His named rolled out like a melodic Ellesian song.

"Ellesse sounds quite musical, doesn't it? My name is Daisy."

"Yes, I know. In our language, that flower is called Boshem. I like it better than Daisy, so I'll use our word if that's okay."

She stopped her fork midway to her face. "Kehal, I prefer Daisy, please." She could handle Zerek making fun of her name, but in this instance, Kehal seemed to believe her name was vulgar. If she didn't draw a line somewhere, she wouldn't have the confidence to talk to anyone.

Kehal raised his eyebrows, but before he could respond, the creek of the front door echoed through the house. Brogan and Lightfleet's voices chattered.

Brogan said something about showering before his bedroom door opened and closed. Then Lightfleet rounded the corner, his skin near-glowing from exercise. "Greetings, Kehal. The king must have been trying to impress Daisy to send his best chef."

"He doesn't speak English." Daisy motioned over to Kehal, who shook his head and shrugged.

Lightfleet said something in Ellesse, then grabbed a full plate from Kehal and sat at the table next to Daisy. "What are you waiting for? I'm sure it's tasty." As if to demonstrate his assurance, he shoveled a mouthful and smiled in delight.

Daisy put the bite in her mouth. It was delicious—much better than her pancake creations. The fruit compote, especially, presented her taste buds with spicy, sweet, and savory all at the same time.

"I'm glad to see you are enjoying the pancake, *Daisy*," Kehal emphasized her name.

Lightfleet chuckled. "It's been so long since I've used Ahlfang. How unfortunate that you weren't given Ellesse."

"Yeah, yeah. I hear any ogre can speak Ahlfang."

Lightfleet side smiled, though his eyes were wide with kindness. He switched to English. "I simply meant Ellesian is a more difficult language to learn. I still resent my Ellesian teachers. They spent centuries developing their linguistic snobbery, and then they cast equal expectations on every courtier in the capital."

Daisy let her shoulders relax a little. "You're a kind soul, Lord Lightfleet."

He brightened. "I'm like my mother."

They exchanged a few stories from the morning until Brogan strutted in, his hair wet. He sat down as Kehal served him. "Can you explain, Fleet, why I can't seem to keep my balance in that last maneuver. I don't think it's a lack of strength."

Lightfleet answered, and Daisy was left out of the conversation. She walked to the sink where Kehal took her plate just as she attempted to wash it. He didn't say anything, just raised his eyebrows again.

She grunted an ogre-like thank you in Ahlfang and escaped the villa.

The meal had given her new energy. As the sweet air tingled her senses, the castle grounds begged to be explored. She followed an outer castle wall until she came to a narrow gate big enough for only one person to squeeze through.

A single guard stood at the gate. His face bore a serious expression as his gaze traveled over her lumpy, misshaped tunic.

She had forgotten all about her half-witted struggle with the clothes earlier. Now she had given yet another lightperson reason to judge her. The guard's eyes softened, however, and a slight smile broke over his face. "Lahorateteh grah zhoulas farroah fraisonme."

The language barrier was going to follow her everywhere. She asked in Ahlfang, "Can I go through this gate."

The guard's eyes grew wide, but he answered. "I never believed I would need to know Ahlfang to guard this castle. It's a good thing I learned it anyway." For a moment he lost his smile, but it came back twice as big. "My lady, you may indeed use this gate when it's open. Let me instruct you, because it's not easy to find from the outside."

He disappeared through the doorway. Daisy followed him to the other side of the wall where a vibrant meadow opened before her. From the clearing, several paths led into a dense, aromatic forest.

"The paths are safe," the guard broke into her thoughts, "but take care to learn your way before exploring too aggressively." He walked several strides into the clearing and turned back to her. "Stand here and look."

She followed him and turned back toward the wall.

"Do you see the gate?"

She saw only a large, smooth castle wall.

"It's magic. There's no way to see it unless the guard on duty— that's me—gives you his name. When you come back, stand in this clearing and say, 'Grovian.' No need to yell. I don't need to hear you." He turned toward her, his face eager. "Try it!"

She couldn't help smiling back at him and whispering as small as she could, "Grovian."

He belted out a guffaw, distracting enough that she almost didn't notice the small gate materializing.

"I think it passed your whisper test, my lady." Grovian pointed up to a quaint iron door adorned with an elaborate design of flowers twisted from different colored metals. "The flowers represent the gardens inside. The late queen herself made the door and set its magic. Once you can see the gate, your touch will open it."

"Thank you."

"Enjoy your walk, my lady. If, for whatever reason, you cannot find this gate, follow the wall westward. In half a mile you will meet the main gate to the city. Although not many guards speak Ahlfang."

She cringed. There had to be a way to study Ellesse. Weird languages were her thing, after all.

She bid Grovian goodbye and let herself be carried away into the glorious woods outside of the castle walls.

* * *

BROGAN DRAGGED himself out of bed, rubbing sleep from his eyes. If it was his day off from training, why was someone knocking at his bedroom door so early in the morning? "Lightfleet, if you think I'm going swimming at this hour—"

But it wasn't Lightfleet. Daisy stood at his door, a sheepish, annoying look on her face. "Did I wake you? I'm sorry, I didn't think anyone could sleep through the raising of the light."

He pointed to himself. "Somebody can, but I'm awake now. What do you want?"

"I've been studying Ellesse, and I was hoping you would let me practice with you."

"We can practice at any time. Doesn't have to be at the butt crack of dawn."

She slumped away from him. "It's just that . . . you're always gone. So I wanted to catch you before you leave for the day."

It was true. He crossed his arms and died a little inside looking at her bald head—her price for his mistake. "I can help. In exchange, teach me Ahlfang."

Her eyebrow shot up, even the one mangled by scars. "Why would you—"

"I don't know. It's something to do, I guess."

"It's a deal." As he closed the door, she blocked it with her palm. "Wait. When?"

"After I shower, eat, and am awake enough not to hate people."

She grinned. "Fair enough."

And the door shut, maybe a little louder than he meant it to.

BROGAN CRINGED as Daisy stumbled over beautiful Ellesian expressions. "Like a German speaking French," he told her. Sure, he could have told her she learned the mechanics freakishly fast, but he didn't feel at all generous with complements that day.

Daisy scowled back at him.

"Try it again, kind of like you're singing."

"I hear it, Brogan, but it's like there's a melody in there that keeps changing. That's the part I don't get."

She was right. It did keep changing, but it made perfect sense to him. "I think the change comes with the atmosphere somehow. Or the feelings the person has toward the one they are addressing. Like . . . it's under the mechanics and communicates its own nuance of meaning."

She sighed, tapped her forehead on the table, and cursed in Ahlfang. He had no idea what she was saying, but it sounded like it came straight out of a gutter. It was hilarious, made even more so by her cackle. "I've never been able to curse so well in my life."

A begrudging grin spread across his face. "Say it again."

She repeated herself, smirking as she said it.

Laughter forced itself from his chest, and tension escaped from his neck and shoulders. "It so visceral."

"Everything in Ahlfang is debased. I could ask for soup, and somehow I'm insulting you at the same time. The upside is no one gets bent out of shape over a gruff word. These two languages are opposites, not only in sound but in spirit."

"Ask me for soup."

Daisy poured out a horrific string of syllables.

"Wow."

Why had he been so annoyed with her?

BROGAN FOUND himself talking to Daisy more often and on purpose. One day she ran inside from the terrace, screaming, as an eagle screeched behind her.

He couldn't contain uproarious laughter at the expression on her face. "Was it holding a bloody carcass this time?"

"You've seen it? I just hope that the mangled animal in its claws wasn't somebody's sweet puppy."

"Your imagination is a little dark, Daisy."

She shrugged. "It's gotten darker since being here."

Of course. She'd been through hell. He sometimes blocked that out of his own memory.

Brogan grabbed a long loaf of bread and thwacked her with it. "Just fight it off with a sword. Like this." He hit her several times as the roll broke and flew into tiny pieces. She ran into the kitchen, grabbed a roll, and hit him back. He proceeded to give her mock lessons in swordplay, using the longest rolls of bread stored in the kitchen. By the time they finished, bread crumbs lay all over the atrium.

Daisy fell onto the couch laughing. She picked up a chunk of bread from the seat and ate it. "If the lightpeople saw us just now, do you think they would think we were lunatics?"

"Do you think they would think that we think we are lunatics?" Brogan countered, sending Daisy off the edge of her seat in peals of fresh laughter. "I would be disappointed at their powers of observation if they missed it."

CHAPTER TWENTY-TWO

Daisy stood in the doorway of the library, wondering if she should strike up a conversation with the light woman inside. The lady wasn't reading, so it probably wouldn't disturb her. *Just act like Brogan. Act like you belong everywhere. People are waiting to talk with you.*

She drew a breath and strode forward. "Hello." Her voice shook, but she pressed herself to continue. "I was told this is the library?" The word for *library* twisted in her mouth, and she couldn't quite hold its tune. The lightpeople probably wanted to envelop a sense of sacred learning in the single word, but she wished they hadn't been so lofty about it.

The woman lifted her chin up from her work. Her soft lips flattened into a serene smile, and her skin released a soft, warm light. "What an honor to speak with you, Daisy. Yes, this is the library. Would you floyant sul vollarez?"

She hadn't learned those last words, and now she couldn't remember what she had practiced.

"It's organized by tone, if that helps." The lady pointed up and down through the melody and said some more stuff Daisy couldn't translate quickly enough. Something about *sadness* and something else about *botany* perhaps?

A shorter woman rounded the corner and stepped straight up to Daisy. She looked normal. Like *Earth*-normal. While the other lightpeople looked young, this lady had streaks of gray running through what probably had once been black hair. Her small, thin frame also contrasted against the tall, strong women around the castle.

In English, with a soft Ellesian accent, she said, "I suspect you were looking for language help."

Daisy blinked in shock. "Y-yes."

The smaller woman turned to the tall one and said in Ellesse, "Thank you, Ahalinan. I will take it from here." She walked away.

Daisy looked at Ahalinan. "Am I supposed to follow her?"

The woman nodded, her eyes big with surprise. "Her name is Mabel. You should listen to her."

Daisy ran after Mabel, but the library was a maze of nooks and shelves. She had to stop in the center of a convergence of aisles, totally lost. She turned in a circle, peering down each row.

After she rotated a second time, she spotted Mabel at the end of one row. "This way, child."

Daisy ran after her. After each turn she would barely catch a glimpse of Mabel's white skirt around the next corner. She finally caught up to where Mabel stood before a section of books and scrolls.

Her chubby finger pointed along the edges of scrolls. Ellesian runes on each scroll lit faintly as her finger touched them. "Here." Mabel pulled a scroll from its perch and handed it to Daisy. "One of your people wrote this one in English. It's a parsing guide."

This was fantastic news. Daisy hadn't been able to make enough sense of the language to create a parsing guide on her own. The linguistic features were too squirrelly, but if someone else had managed to nail them down, it would be a great help to her.

"This is so helpful. I—"

"You may take the scroll with you. Good day."

Mabel didn't wait for thanks. She turned on a heel and

marched away, leaving Daisy alone to figure out how to get out of the library.

Now that she had met Mabel, Daisy kept seeing her around the castle and made it her mission to engage Mabel in conversation. Each attempt brought a strange kind of look to Mabel's face, which Daisy couldn't decipher.

One morning Daisy left her villa only to find Mabel waiting for her by the path. She stood and handed Daisy a pretty hat woven with blue and silver thread.

"I can't look at your head anymore. It's too pathetic. This will help."

Daisy didn't think Mabel had meant to insult her, so she took the hat and placed it on her head.

Mabel lifted a small mirror and pointed it at her. Daisy had formed a habit of avoiding any and all mirrors, but she didn't want to show signs of displeasure after receiving a gift, so she peered at her reflection.

It was a nice surprise. The hat suited her and matched her eyes perfectly. She even looked kind of pretty. "Thank you, Mabel."

"It's lovely, young one. It will do well until your hair is given back to you."

"What do you mean, given back?"

Mabel remained expressionless. "The Eternal One cursed certain magic so that it would not be abused. You, however, used it for someone else's benefit. The curse will not keep its hold."

"But how could you know my motivation?"

Mabel shrugged. "I have already looked into the matter, as the Light King requested. I see many things."

"Like, with magic? Can you tell me about it?"

Mabel winced at the word *magic*. She picked up a broken pot from the ground and inspected its pieces. A long pause ensued, where it seemed like she wasn't going to answer. "My aged body is residue from having delved into the forbidden. There is no end to magic." Mabel raised the broken shards up to Daisy's face. "Do not seek it on your own if you don't want to give up more of yourself."

This information was more exciting than scary. "Is there a book or something, just to know a little more?"

Mabel dropped the pottery pieces and walked away, flicking her hands in the air. "There are many, many books. They fill up caverns, there are so many."

Daisy followed at her heels. "Caverns?"

"In the desert. Where else can millions of books be left without rotting?"

"Millions? Left? There is no one to care for them?"

"There is no one to read them. We almost destroyed them altogether, as we found them either useless or dangerous. Many are in a language too old even for Gleyo, our eldest elder."

"Who is how old?"

"Only the Eternal One could say. Gleyo doesn't have any idea. There was a time when our people didn't count years. It was the increasing evil that brought about the numbering."

The numbering? "How long ago was the numbering?"

"Fourteen hundred years ago. It was near the end of Orya's grandfather's reign."

And so the conversations with Mabel went, often lasting for hours at a time — so many answers bringing even more questions.

* * *

A FLOWERY-SWEET AROMA washed over Brogan as he and Daisy crossed the threshold into the palace corridor. Warm light embraced them and flooded along both sides of the hallway where softly hued mosaics formed patterns of flowers and plant life intertwined.

Brogan recalled visiting palaces in Europe, wondering if the throne room in Ells would be anything like those stone halls covered in elaborate paintings, sculptures, and tapestries. They always struck him as cold and overly decorated. So far, everything was perfectly tasteful, if not understated. The beauty of its decor couldn't be denied, but it wasn't screaming to get your attention, like Versailles or Peterhof.

This would be their first time walking into the king's official court. Daisy twitched each time one of the lightpeople bowed to them, but he had experienced this kind of treatment with his father, so he didn't have a problem with it. "It's just protocol. Calm down, country girl."

Daisy scowled at him. "Don't judge me."

What a funny command. "But I'm always judging you." He couldn't keep the chuckle from his voice.

She seemed about to retaliate as they passed through the doorway into Orya's throne room, but both were stunned into silence. The large, domed room overtook them. Dancing lights circled beneath a ceiling that mimicked the night sky of Elleson. Rather than stars, swirls of subtle colors undulated through a textured blackness. The walls bore no paintings or draped fabrics. Only a subtle pattern repeated over the light stone. Semiprecious stones tiled the floor, and though vivid, they remained subdued by their placement. Overall, the effect demonstrated wealth and taste without losing the charm of a warm and happy atmosphere.

Lightmen and women stood to their feet as Brogan and Daisy entered the great room. An excitement buzzed as the crowd rushed around them, leaving the delicate benches that lined the sides of the room.

Then the crowd parted like a curtain, and King Orya stepped through it. He offered his arm to Daisy. Brogan sensed her rigidity as she placed her hand on the king's arm to be escorted to the front of the room up to the throne platform. Brogan followed them up. From there, they could see over the sea of eager faces, many smiling but all bright and alert.

"My dear friends, it is my pleasure to introduce our guests." He gestured to them. "Daisy and Brogan." No applause or cheering broke out, but an increased glow radiated from the crowd.

"How does my Lady Daisy like Ells?" a woman with black hair asked.

Orya leaned close to translate into Daisy's ear. A deep blush crawled across Daisy's cheeks. Brogan couldn't tell if the attention or the king's whisper caused it. "It's beautiful, of course," came Daisy's light, Ellesian reply. The musical quality sounded forced to Brogan's fluent ear, but the entire audience murmured their approval.

A lightman spoke up as Orya leaned close again to translate. "We heard you kept your heart steady through your ordeal in Ahl, Lady Daisy." The court murmured in agreement. "You must be very brave."

Her blush was in full fury, and suddenly Brogan could see the glow. He wouldn't have called it beautiful, but the light emanating from her face certainly wasn't a human phenomenon. It increased as she struggled through her answer. "Is it brave if I didn't choose to be there?" The audience smiled and glowed their approval.

The questions kept coming at Daisy, and Brogan realized that no one asked him anything. He might as well have been a potted plant. He, who had grown up trained for such occasions, was forgotten in the presence of his glowing half-sister.

After the questions, the king introduced Daisy to individuals and small groups, his chest puffed up the entire time. If he remembered Brogan at all, it was an afterthought. Whenever Brogan tried to speak up and contribute, all eyes were polite, but they quickly shifted back to Daisy.

Brogan peered around and locked eyes with Lightfleet, whose shaking chest betrayed his mischievous laugh. He motioned for Brogan to join him.

"You aren't used to being unimportant, are you?"

"No one listened to me at all, and I speak fluently."

Lightfleet put his arm on Brogan's shoulder. "No one's talking to me either, even though I'm second only to Orya in the kingdom. But they see me as a child."

"So they see me as a child too? And what about Daisy? She's our age."

"Doesn't matter. She has already proven herself in their eyes. It's no longer a secret that Orya wants to make her his queen."

"He announced it?" A protective surge ran through Brogan, conflicting with his indignation.

"Didn't need to. Look at him."

He watched as the king clung to Daisy through each introduction.

"Every word she speaks. Every action. It's drenched in charity, kindness, and wisdom. At least that's what I heard one of the elders say."

Brogan huffed. "They don't see her insecurity and fear?"

Lightfleet chuckled again. "I'm sorry it has to pain you, but you should not get roiled up in that mess. Orya himself is seeing only what he wants to see."

Brogan stopped and studied Lightfleet. Maomao called him an astute child. "What else do you notice when everyone is ignoring you?"

Lightfleet's lip curled into a half smile. "You should sit on the sidelines with me and be educated."

Brogan's mind flew through the corridors of his memory. He had always been in the game, not on the sidelines. So what had he missed all these years? He nodded his head, followed Lightfleet's tutelage, and sat along the wall. To watch.

* * *

ONE FACE DRIFTED into the next for Daisy, each resplendent in its beauty. And each a reminder that her averageness did not belong there. She might have run out of the great room had she not come face-to-face with someone she recognized.

"Hello, my friend," said the woman with silver, curly hair.

"Choral?"

"You've forgotten protocol already?" She smiled a bright smile.

"No, my *parshant*!" Daisy bowed in the manner she had hundreds of times. She had exercised on her own for several days now, Choral nowhere to be seen. "I haven't seen you in the gymnasium lately."

The princess nodded. Her luscious curls swayed and her shoulders remained ramrod straight throughout the motion. She would make an incredible ballerina. "Don't work yourself too hard, Daisy. It will take a long time to reach any kind of level worth mentioning."

Daisy's heart took the shot with a thud. She curtsied as Choral moved on to chat with someone else, leaving her mood so low that the king must have caught on. He paid a great deal of attention to her that evening, introducing her to his friends and engaging her in conversation. She appreciated his attempts to cheer her, but for heaven's sake, he could stop touching her at every turn. Personal space was a thing.

When the event finally slowed, Daisy eyed Brogan sitting with Lightfleet. How did he get so lucky? She caught his eye and he nodded his head toward the door with eyebrows raised. Yes, she nodded back, God bless him.

He approached the king and said, "I think Daisy and I are ready to head to the villa."

Orya's smile faded and he searched Daisy's face. "I can escort you."

"N-no." She pulled her arm away from his hold and latched onto Brogan. "Stay with your guests. I'm tired, and I'm happy to turn in as fast as I can."

"If you insist." His eyes stayed on her.

She curtsied and silently thanked all that was holy as she and Brogan made a beeline for the door.

All the way back to the villa she repeated, "God bless you. God bless you a thousand times."

"God?" He sighed. "Well, I hope you sleep well."

THE NEXT DAY there was a knock on the door of Daisy's villa. Lightfleet never knocked and no one else visited them. She and Brogan rushed together to the door to see who it was. Daisy wrenched the door open while Brogan shoved her from standing center. King Orya presented himself on their doorstep, looking impressive in white dragon skins, his face glowing in angelic unnaturalness.

"Hello, your highness," she said, pushing Brogan aside.

The king smiled. "I'm here to see if the lady would like to go to town with me."

The lady? Daisy resisted the urge to look to Brogan for help. Instead, she motioned to herself. "Me? I'm wearing my workout clothes."

"I commissioned a robe for you. I hope you don't mind wearing it." A servant appeared behind him, carrying a rich, silk dress—knee length with a floral print.

Daisy's guts twisted. What exactly was going on here? Why would he bring a dress for her to accompany him to town? After an awkward pause, she reached out for the dress and matching slippers.

Orya stepped forward, pressing past them, and waved a hand inside their foyer. "I can wait in your common room." He entered the atrium and seated himself on a comfortable chaise, admiring the dome.

Brogan raised his eyebrows at Daisy and followed after him.

She stared for a second in disbelief, then scurried past them into her room. She pressed her door closed and took deep breaths.

Great. She could smell herself. How did the lightpeople always smell good when she still smelled like a gym sock?

She threw her sweaty tunic on the floor, pirate-bathed her pits, and pulled the dress over her head. It fit perfectly, and the stunning pattern of subtle whites and yellows displayed an artistry she'd never seen on fabrics back home. It charmed her until her eyes followed the reflection up to her misshapen nose, scarred face, and very bald head. With a groan, she threw Mabel's blue hat over her shame. The hat almost made her look like a girl.

Daisy forced herself to open her bedroom door and step into the common room. Orya stood and said some nonsense about how nice she looked. She focused her eyes downward and pressed straight to the door.

. . .

WHEN DAISY SAW that King Orya had planned an elaborate lunch on one of the canal boats, her face grew warm. *This was definitely a date.* Orya helped her into the long, stylized vessel for two —three if you count the gondolier.

As they drifted along, Daisy found herself surrounded by beauty she never imagined possible from architecture. It reminded her of Venice, only the entire city was made from carved white stone. Bright accents of colored stone were inset in designs and murals. The canal passed open squares filled with people eating outside and milling about. They all looked serene and beautiful.

People swam in the canal, many chatting from the water to others sitting on the bank or from window ledges. Children played games as if the canal was a swimming pool, throwing balls and jumping from the second-floor ledges.

A floral scent wafted over Daisy, followed by the smell of freshly baked bread. She tried to take in as many details as she could as she scanned the scene until her focus landed hard against the man lounging next to her. It was like hearing the screech of a turntable on vinyl in the middle of a beautiful song.

The king's smile radiated beauty, but his grandeur didn't incite attraction for Daisy so much as discomfort. When had he made himself so comfortable? She wished for another portal to suck her away

"Your highness. I think we have something to discuss."

"I would agree." His confident gaze locked onto hers. "Do you want to go first, or shall I?"

The staring threw her off, and after a pause Orya began. "I don't know if you remember the letters I sent you."

Daisy must have squinched her face.

"I see. You do, but maybe they confused you."

Ugh. Should she swim for it?

He leaned toward her. "Daisy, I have been watching you for years. I have watched you grow up. I have always felt that you are an extraordinary young woman, and I was hoping I could persuade you to consider me. Our families have long been connected, and it was my father's wish that I marry from your mother's line. You can't imagine my delight when I found you so remarkable. I am not asking out of duty but because I hope to share my life with you."

"But your life will go on after mine ends. I'm going to grow old. How can that even be appealing?" Someone had to say it.

Orya's face actually glowed. "There are ways around your mortality. Our marriage would involve magic, as has long been known and expected, and so you would share the lifespan of the lightpeople."

Our marriage. Daisy looked down at her clenched hands. If she cringed any further, she might become a black hole.

The king continued, "It was my intention to bring you here on your seventeenth birthday. I want you to take all the time you need. Years. Decades. I will wait for you. But I wanted you to learn our court and our language while your mind is still young. The dark king must have guessed my plan, because he sent for you himself. I don't know how to make that up to you. I can't imagine what you have been through. If you knew how much I desired that I had been there first—"

Daisy shook her head. "This is really weird."

King Orya flinched but paused and regained his serenity. "Fair observation, Daisy. You do not know me the way I know you. Perhaps you can give us a chance to become acquainted?"

Daisy had never dated. Her crush on Dean had been one-sided. What was she supposed to do with Orya? Could she simply get to know the king without thinking about all of his plans to marry her and make her immortal? And what about her life back home? She let herself drift into a bubble of her own thoughts without inviting King Orya in with her.

After she deflected all of his efforts to keep talking, he turned the boat around. Daisy hopped out of the boat as they arrived back on the castle grounds and escaped to her villa as quickly as she could.

She threw the dress into the wardrobe, pulled on her dragon skins, and left to find solace somewhere. She avoided her usual walks and took a detour into the library. She would nestle into one of the nooks or little rooms hidden throughout the stacks. The thoughtfulness put into each reading space might lull her mind to peace.

She wandered for a while until she came across Mabel sitting in one of the rooms, the door open and inviting. Daisy approached in a way to make intentional noise so she wouldn't startle her. Mabel's face, however, remained in a scroll. Two steaming cups of tea sat on the table, one with a small cake next to it.

"It's for you, dear. Please sit down." Mabel clasped the scroll and set it next to Daisy's tea. "This will be interesting for you."

Daisy tried not to overreact to Mabel's foresight. "What is it?"

"It's a story about a young woman who questioned the elders. Youth interests us because it rare and fleeting. It is also accompanied by iconoclastic ways." Mabel brought a finger up and tapped her temple. "New eyes see things anew." She snorted. "How boring would life be if nothing were questioned! But elders can sometimes be caught in fear when they don't understand the young people. They spent so much time getting everything to work for them in the ways they understand, and now you want to change the paradigm? I wonder if it's harder for the young ones to raise the elders than the other way around."

"Is that a problem here?"

"It wouldn't be if the elders weren't selfish. For example, they are terrified that Lord Lightfleet has been granted half of the kingdom to develop however he sees fit. But they cannot contest it, for it was from the Eternal One himself. That's not to say they didn't try! Fortunately, his father utilized a great deal of his own power to protect his son—even from his other sons."

Daisy nodded. She found the lecture and information interesting but not relevant. Maybe Mabel was just trying to get her mind off her date with the king.

"The king also has his assumptions," Mabel continued.

Ok, here it is.

"He has inherited a crown and he wants to protect that crown. He also wants a wife. He is not wrong in wanting these things. I think he sincerely admires you, but I think he is a little pig-headed at the moment. He is only seeing things the way he has always seen them. You may need to teach him and coax him out of ideas that have never met opposition."

Daisy stared at her tea. "I don't understand what you mean. How am I supposed to teach the king?"

"I don't know, exactly. You were given your adoptive father for a reason. Your mind is more important than you or your father guessed. His obedience in raising you to think well is integral to your calling here. Don't dismiss your own understanding or ideas just because someone else is so certain of theirs. Their experience should not minimize what you can contribute, for you are bringing completely unique things."

Daisy nodded. "But how did you know I needed this?" She held up the scroll.

"I am observant, dear. It's sometimes hard to say if any of it is magic or not."

Ellesian script danced across the velum. She had no idea how to read it. She didn't want to disappoint Mabel, so she took it back to the villa where it taunted her with all of its possibilities.

CHAPTER TWENTY-THREE

BROGAN LAY UPSIDE DOWN on the couch one morning, his feet in the air. As Daisy wandered into the main room, he took the opportunity to whine. "Daisy, I need to do something. Anything. As long as it's new."

Daisy sat opposite him and deadpanned. "We could stare at the other wall."

Brogan glared up at her. "People here can't always be bored."

"Maybe you can ask Lightfleet to introduce you to a new sport or something."

He flipped his body right side up. "Of course. He's always getting into trouble. Let's go."

"Me?"

"You're bored too. Or boring."

She huffed at the remark but ran behind him into the gardens. They found Lord Lightfleet in the gym, trying some acrobatic moves.

"Lightfleet!"

At his summons, Lightfleet fell out of a handstand. He groaned and frowned up at them.

Brogan ran to him and held out a hand. "Sorry, man. We were

hoping you could help us find something fun to do. Anything that isn't staring at the inside of our villa." He nudged Daisy in the side, who shoved him back.

Lightfleet's face flashed from annoyance to delight. "I have been thinking about riding the eastern waterfall off the edge into the pools below. That would require a long hike back up, which takes more than one day. We would need to prepare, and there's no time. So as an alternative, we have hatchlings."

"Hatchlings?"

"This year's babies."

Brogan and Daisy shook their heads.

"Dragons?"

"Ohhhh," they responded together.

Daisy's face turned ashen.

Brogan, on the other hand, couldn't wait to start. "What do we wear? Do we have to fight off the adult dragons?"

"Ha! You don't fight adult dragons. You don't fight babies either. But we do mess with them while their mommy dragon is out hunting." His grin was evil.

"Messing?" Brogan asked.

"Yeah, they can't talk very well, so they mimic whatever they hear. My favorite is to make other animal sounds or twang an instrument. They're incredible at matching the noises perfectly. And I get a kick out of a dragon doing a gong."

"What happens if you idiots are caught?" Daisy asked in a typical girl-afraid attitude.

"By the big dragon? Nothing. She squirts a little fire and gets irritated."

"How do we get there?" Brogan brushed off Daisy's concern, eager to be going already.

Lightfleet motioned them toward the small castle gate that led eastward into the forest. Daisy ran to keep up with them.

The journey to the hatchlings began by riding horses about four miles, until they came to a steep foot trail. They tied their horses at the trail and followed the steep path up to a mountain ledge where the path narrowed and continued on along a cliff face.

Lightfleet pointed up the crags. "We can follow that trail and then hide behind those rocks until we know the big girl is off."

Daisy heaved great breaths, but she stayed with them all the way up to the rocks. The nest sat unguarded, and Lightfleet strolled over to it.

"Hi! Hi! Lightfweet! Hi!" Cute little creatures jumped up and down, greeting their familiar friend. Brogan had expected gruesome lizards. They *were* reptilian, but multicolored, shiny, and even kind of cuddly.

Brogan laughed. "I take it you've been here before?"

"Of course. It's like a cat. If they know you as a kitten, they are less likely to tear your face off when they're grown. These little guys have already let me teach them a few things." He projected his voice. "You all ready to review what we did last time?" The little voices responded with noises Daisy and Brogan had heard around the castle. Trumpets, bells, and a loud siren-like sound that would go off from time to time for some reason.

Per Daisy's idea, they taught the hatchlings the "Hallelujah Chorus" in harmony. They were laughing so hard that they didn't notice the mother hovering over them until a shadow made her presence unmistakable.

Lightfleet threw himself against the cliff edge.

Lady dragon hovered down until she was eye level with them. Her pink face glistened in the light. Though her purple eyes had narrowed, she did not give off the vibe of animalistic rage. She huffed warm air from her nostrils, which blew the hair away from Lightfleet's face. With a commanding voice she said, "Lord Lightfleet, did your older brother not warn you what happened to him when he visited my children?"

"He did, but his eyebrows grew back," Lightfleet squeaked.

"Your *inspiring* noises gave me a terrible headache last week. Stop teaching my hatchlings, or your eyebrows will the least of your worries. And greet your king for me. Do not give me offense by forgetting." She growled and maneuvered up to sit with her children.

Brogan and Daisy let out huge sighs of relief as they scrambled back down the trail. When they arrived at the horses, Lightfleet wore a sullen expression.

"What's wrong, Fleet?"

He huffed. "I'm not supposed to be near them. Orya will be so angry."

Brogan shrugged. "So don't tell him. What trouble would that cause?"

"Offense! Did you not hear her? I have no choice. She will know and come hunting for us."

"Will we be in trouble?" Daisy asked. Lightfleet didn't reply, though an answer came later that evening by another knock at their villa door.

King Orya stood in the doorway with Lightfleet, his jaw set tight. "I am here to speak with you both on the matter of Quillo the dragon. Under the circumstances," he glared at Daisy, "it would be embarrassing to do this in my court, as I would typically proceed."

Brogan looked over at Daisy, whose face betrayed a remorse that made *him* feel guilty. She probably didn't get into trouble very often. Brogan's father chastised him often enough that getting scolded here didn't bother him. And Lightfleet—it was just another day for Lightfleet.

They invited the king to sit and talk in the atrium.

"You two are new here." Orya locked eyes with Daisy and then Brogan. "I am expecting the culture to be something to which you must acclimate. But *dragons?* Surely you have a concept of danger? Daisy, you know I moved a small army for your safe rescue, and then you do this? Do you have any respect for me or my kingdom?"

Brogan cringed. This man, who was trying to woo Daisy, now had to lecture her about proper behavior as if he were a father or a teacher.

The king's face also reddened. "Dragons are our allies— formidable allies. They are not tame and they are not predictable. We do not need a reason for them to grow weary of us." He stood and walked through the room with his hands on his head. "In the future, if you have questions about what is appropriate, please ask me." He glared at Lightfleet, "I have no choice but to make amends with Quillo, which I don't have time for. Tomorrow you three are coming with me. Be ready by yellow."

He stood. "Greg, I'm going to walk back by myself. Goodnight."

It would have been a great downer of a night had they not heard the king laughing as he walked away from the villa.

* * *

DAISY HAD PLANNED to help prepare the horses for the ride, but the next morning the king knocked on their door earlier than expected. Four horses stood saddled behind him, Lightfleet astride one. Brogan brushed past her, leaving her surprised in the face of the king.

It's a good thing she woke up *early.*

The king smiled and gestured her toward the horses.

Orya may have been busy, as he had claimed the night before, but his eyes shone when he asked, "How many hatchlings are there, Greg?"

"Seven. Four female, three male."

"Seven?" Orya's voice inflected with great surprise, and he let out a long whistle. "It isn't going to be easy when they dispute territory. You'll want to keep them out of your lands, for sure. That last quiver nearly burnt the lower eastern woods."

"What's a quiver?" Brogan interjected.

Orya explained, "It's the name for a dragon herd or pack."

"I guess it's good they know me already." Lightfleet peered sideways at the king, who shook his head with a grin.

"Brogan, Daisy, I refuse to let Greg think this was a good idea, but he may have a point. Dragons are certainly the least dangerous as hatchlings than any other time of their lives."

"Where will they go to live when they leave the nest?" Daisy knew so little about the land of Elleson or its magical creatures.

"They are territorial," Orya answered. "Most will leave our

lands and fly beyond the desert, searching for a home and a mate. We have made it clear that our lands are spoken for, but Greg hasn't tamed his territory yet. That will be the work of centuries, and he doesn't want dragons to take root there in the meantime."

Brogan screwed up his face. "The idea of a dragon infestation makes cockroaches seem less horrific."

"I'd still take them over cockroaches." Daisy didn't think twice before she let her declaration slip, and her face grew warm when Orya smiled at her.

Lightfleet asked, "What important business did we pull you away from today, my Lord King?"

"A critical meeting was scheduled with the song elders. And I must thank you for freeing me."

"I'm at your service." Lightfleet made a circular gesture with his hand.

"Give your services sparingly, dear cousin. They are like salt—too much is too much."

"Song elders?" asked Brogan. "That sounds intriguing."

Orya let out a great exhale. "They are mired in tradition. One said the morning song should never lose its simple four-part harmony, but we need the extra treble. The daylight has had a red hue for several weeks now, and there's only one way to correct it. I may or may not have suggested she looked sallow in the reddish light."

Daisy remembered the Dixons at her church, who constantly made a fuss over the music being too trendy. "Can you fix the hue with an additional song? After the traditional one? That might appease your elder friends while giving some of the younger musicians an opportunity to utilize their talents. It might shame the elders a little, which is the only downside."

Her companions all nodded. Orya cocked an eyebrow. "I'll suggest that at our next governing assembly. Do you mind if I credit you for the idea?"

"It's not a new idea. Just something my father did with our church. You'll leave out the part about shaming, right?"

The king smirked. "But that's where your argument is the most compelling."

Brogan shared how he experienced Daisy's piano version of a pop ballad before the morning service. "Afterward, my grandparents asked me what that lovely hymn was called." He and Daisy snickered, though their two friends missed the joke.

They came to the point where the path continued upward, craggy and narrow, only safe for walking. They tied the horses to a low tree branch and continued.

Orya often stopped to point out specific foliage and their uses. "Now this plant here," he used his sword to lift a droopy red flower, "is one of the deadliest poisons in our world. It's called a *saraph*. In very small, diluted doses, it cures fungal infections and fevers. The trick is in harvesting it without getting hurt."

Lightfleet looked as if he were filing the information away for another day.

"Greg. Perhaps it would be best to learn more from the apothecary before you come back to play with this one."

Lightfleet narrowed his eyes and tilted his head, still staring at the plant. "What if I use gloves?"

"I'm going to have to take you there myself, aren't I?"

Daisy and Brogan burst out laughing, knowing that there was no other way to save Lightfleet from death by curiosity.

Orya shook his head and continued walking. Rather than climb the cliff path as they had before, he stopped at a clearing, pulled out a horn, and blew. Soon, a great windfall of dragon wings changed the air pressure in measured beats as the beast landed before them. She had lost none of her terrifying stature.

"I expected to see you today, my king."

"Yes. I was displeased to hear our children had bothered you. As an apology, may I offer one of the sheep from my northern flock? I have already alerted the shepherds, and they will be expecting you."

"This is an acceptable gift. Might I also add that my father's skin looks fine on you?"

"Thank you. It is one of my favorites. He was a splendid creature. One of the most attractive dragons I have ever laid eyes on."

Quillo bowed her great head. Then she used her talons to dig up a stone.

Daisy watched with curiosity as the beast suddenly released a great burst of fire over it. The intense heat forced her to step back and turn away. After the heat dissipated, she turned back to see the dragon chipping away the edges of the stone before handing Orya one walnut-sized, circular blue diamond clenched in her massive talons. The stone had transformed into a gemstone.

"I foresee your need for this."

The king held out a trembling hand to receive it.

Quillo continued, "It's been imbued with softhue. In blackness, it will shine still. It shines even when your heart fails."

"This is an honor," he spoke softly.

"An honor, perhaps, but one that comes with a dark task."

Orya turned to his companions and said, "If you three don't mind, Quillo and I have something to discuss."

They nodded and returned down the path to wait, much to Daisy's annoyance. They had just witnessed something significant, but what, exactly?

Lightfleet buzzed. "The diamond has softhue! No one else in the kingdom has one! Its power is legendary."

"How did the dragon know he needs it?" she asked.

Lightfleet threw his hands in the air and gestured in his excitement. "Dragons have magic that is unpredictable, even to themselves. Prophecy is one of them, but many of their powers depend on other elements of existence. The softhue diamond was not her magic alone."

"But aren't you worried about the darkness that would cause a lightperson's heart to fail?"

The young lightman shrugged while Daisy marveled over his flippancy.

After half an hour, Orya caught up with them. He did not reveal anything further about his encounter with Quillo. His light and happy demeanor pried Daisy out of her morose dread.

With a glint in his eye, Lightfleet suggested the Sugar Falls as a faster route back to the horses.

Orya chuckled, "Yes, but it is a waterfall. Brogan, Daisy, are you up for swimming?"

"Is it safe?" Daisy didn't trust Lightfleet's judgment after the dragons.

The king put a hand to his chin. "Yes and no. I mean, yes. It is safe." He nudged her arm. "But only because our healers can put most injuries to right."

"How about I carry your things down and meet you at the bottom?" Daisy suggested. Her companions laughed and handed her their jackets, shirts, and one sword. Orya tore off his shirt, and Daisy had to work desperately not to stare at his chest. What was this witchery? Not only did every one of his muscles gleam in perfection, his long silver hair accentuated the unearthly vision. She stared into the sky, away from the falls, then headed down the trail.

She focused her thoughts on kittens. Cute, fluffy, unmanly kittens.

What was that?

Strange music hummed from Orya's jacket. She opened his pocket to find the blue dragon stone. It sang a song Daisy found familiar, though she couldn't detect actual words. Daisy stared at its crystalline shape. Streaks and clouds of light moved inside of the stone. "Weird," she murmured.

The stone responded with a wispy giggle. Could she call that a giggle? It reminded her of a young child being tickled.

Spooked, she put the thing back in the jacket. It kept humming a happy song while she walked. Despite her misgivings, Daisy absorbed its joy. Mirth and elation filled her with each step. By the time she arrived at the bottom of the trail, she had never felt so amazing in her life!

Brogan, Lightfleet, and Orya were playing in a pool of water, dunking one another and yelping. Brogan and Lightfleet had ganged up on Orya until he shouted, "Mercy! Mercy!" She grew warm at the sight of them. An overwhelming sense of love and acceptance opened her heart. As the day went on, she zeroed in on Orya's gentle kindness and the happy expression in his beautiful gray eyes.

This, the king of all the light realms, deserved every accolade she could ever find words for!

THE NEXT MORNING Daisy woke with thoughts of Orya, but perhaps a sobered version of his greatness. Her thoughtful frame of mind led her to the library. She couldn't focus on reading the fancy Ellesian script, so she rolled up the scroll—the one Mabel had given her. As she made her way back to the villa, she spied the King sitting on a carved stone bench, his head bowed.

He glanced up and saw her.

Daisy lips twitched as she forced them into a smile-like shape —the rest of her face cemented in embarrassment. Orya's warm gaze followed her approach.

Don't blush now. Curse the blush! If she walked faster, maybe she could just brush by him and continue toward the villa—

"I heard you were studying Ellesian poetry. Do you recognize this garden?"

Daisy forced herself to face him. She couldn't even read normal stuff in Ellesse; how could she grasp poetry?

A lemon tree grew in the center of the garden, surrounded by rosemary and geraniums. The three worked together to create a zesty, deep, romantic bouquet. But she had no idea which poem he was talking about, so she shook her head.

The king sang in a perfect, heart-twisting tenor:
"The rosemary and lemon tree shall rise and remember thee;
The deeper the decay, the greater the scent of victory."

It hadn't occurred to her before, but now that he mentioned it, there was a sad song that used a garden as a metaphor, but she'd only understood a handful of the words.

"It's called "The Song of the Queen," written by my grand-mother. This garden inspired her."

"It's about loss, isn't it?"

He nodded. "My grandmother watched her beloved garden wilt in a drought. Like many others at that time, she wrestled with the Eternal One. Why would he withhold life? Why would he allow something precious to die? Of course, she was referring more broadly to her kingdom."

"The drought was pretty bad?" What a dumb thing to say. Of course it was *bad*. Someone had written a dirge all about it. Was the stupid hammer going to strike her brain every time she saw Orya, now that . . . that what? She gasped in the realization that she saw him as a man she could be interested in.

The king's dewy-skinned face drew into a thoughtful frown.

Does he even have pores?

"Food was scarce. Every Ellesian man and woman older than eighteen fasted three days each week. Even the queen. But the Eternal One had his reasons. While fasting, they all prayed earnestly." Orya's deep gray eyes became the backdrop to his story. "Fasting prepared their hearts for the war that came a few years after the drought ended. The most righteous army ever to march from Elleson took their enemies within weeks, and many individuals even helped our enemies rebuild afterward. They taught them the ways of the Eternal One for many generations. Trade with distant lands thrived like never before."

He picked up a leaf and twirled it between his thumb and forefinger. "So you see, the song was about poverty but also about how the Eternal One is wise in knowing when to bestow life and when to relinquish his protection over it."

He closed his eyes, releasing her from his trance.

She should say something. "That makes sense. Like how David was anointed king but had to live as a fugitive in a desert for decades."

Orya stood and stepped toward her. "I don't know this story." The tone of his voice invited her to open up and share more.

"My storytelling isn't as beautiful as Ellesian poetry."

He laughed like wind chimes. "There is a slight difference, but I cannot believe you lack skills of captivation. Let's meet here again, and you can tell me next time."

His beautiful eyes flashed — like the dragon stone. Like a bear trap. Daisy had been caught in them. Mercifully, he bowed and turned toward the castle.

DAISY LEARNED that Mabel had a cottage just outside the castle grounds. There was one particularly daring question she felt she needed to ask someone, and Mabel might just be the loose canon of truth she needed. Daisy stood outside her cottage the next morning, working up her courage.

Without warning, the door swung open and Daisy felt her chest lurch in fright.

Mabel's eyebrows arched high over tired eyes—her gray, streaked hair wild and long. A teapot steamed in one of her hands. "Are you going to knock?"

Daisy took in Mabel's pink robes. "I wasn't sure if I should."

"Well, since you're here." She held the door wide. "Your tea will be cold if you wait."

Daisy bowed her head and entered. She should have known Mabel would be waiting for her.

The cottage reminded her of Merlin's from the cartoon she had seen so long ago. There were hundreds, if not thousands, of cupboards, baskets, boxes, and pots all full of spices and herbs. Sweet smells stewed over an open fire. Lights bent and twisted, ministering to sick plants. Daisy felt good about the room, like it was a place of healing. An idea occurred to her. "Mabel, are you the apothecary?"

"I am *an* apothecary. One of a few in Ells."

"Are you making medicines?"

"Some are medicines. Others are simply experiments. I like to know about the world."

Daisy studied the room.

"Are you going to sit down, dear, or do I need to serve your tea in a sippy cup?"

"Oh, I'm sorry. Yes, I am sitting . . . now."

"Indeed." Mabel raised her eyebrows again.

The tea warmed Daisy from fingers to toes. The room exuded a joy that overtook her. She released soft giggles, almost forgetting her purpose in coming.

"It used to have this effect on me too." Mabel's eyes lingered from place to place. "Now it is just my home where I find comfort. I also find the Eternal One in my own way here."

"Yeah, I feel like he's here. Like a menagerie of him."

Mabel smiled. "I knew you would understand."

"Mabel, how do you know about sippy cups?"

She went to a cupboard. Upon opening it, a cup fell out, which she caught. "I know a few things about your world," she said as she placed a small ceramic cup with a spouted lid on the table. "I thought it was ingenious. Every time a friend has a child, I make a few."

The conversation continued into Ellesian pottery and the famous glowing goblets of the dragon era. They talked some more about art, government, and various plants. The sky flashed red.

"Have I been here so long?"

Mabel chuckled. "Since this morning. Have you remembered your quest?"

Daisy had to think back about why she had come. "I have a question."

"And do you *remember* your question?"

"Yes, but it seems unimportant now."

"It will be important again when you leave. Perhaps you should ask it."

Coming and asking had seemed difficult. Now it wasn't a big deal at all. "I had questions about Prince Zerek of Ahl."

"Oh?" Mabel leaned forward, her eyes wide. "What could you need to know about him? And dear, please do not refer to him as Prince Zerek of Ahl. We shall not assist in that destiny. Instead, we —*you and I*—will refer to him as a prince of Ells, for that is surely what he is."

"Prince of *Ells*? What do you mean?"

"He is not only the son of the cursed king; he is the son of our late queen, whom the cursed king wed after he killed her husband,

247

our late king. As their son, Zerek bears all the curses of one lineage while receiving all the promises of another."

Daisy's heart thumped hard in her chest. "Why would the queen marry him after he killed her husband?"

"She was forced to vow so that her child would not suffer as much."

Daisy's eyes opened wide. *She was raped?*

Mabel sighed and grabbed a flask from which she took a large swallow. "You must excuse me. We do not speak often of these matters."

"Do you know Zerek?"

"We all know him . . . that is, everyone in the castle. He was a kind child"—she released another heavy sigh—"but wounded and lonely. I watched, but what could I do? The royal family was in deep mourning through his formative years. The late queen died while smuggling him to Elleson. The borders are poison to light-people, but no one knew at the time. And Zerek looked so much like his father, whom we all remembered with disdain." She took another drink. "The crown prince, broken inside, could hardly put himself aside for the boy. No, I suppose he was the king already."

By that point in the conversation, the sky was dark and Daisy had more information than she thought to ask for. But she had to know. "Is he lost? Or can he return?"

Mabel put her hand on her chest and shook her head. "Return? Oh no, dear, not if he wishes to live. But perhaps, by returning and dying, he will be unlost."

Unlost? Or would it be better to say undamned and spared of that dark, sulfurous chasm? It was like all of her breath fell out of her chest at once. Was there no hope for this young man, who, for whatever purpose, would not leave her thoughts?

CHAPTER TWENTY-FOUR

ONE MORNING as Brogan made his way to exercise with Light-fleet, Orya stopped him in the castle courtyards.

"Did you know that our science of light taught your father what he needed to influence LCD technology? I understand he did very well in business on account of it."

Brogan's jaw dropped. Of course he didn't know, but it made sense. Dad had revolutionized the industry and taken many people by surprise while he was still young.

"I'm bringing it up because you may want to study while you're here. Our understanding of science is advanced. Much of it translates to your world, but it wasn't easy for Leo. We will have to get you his old notes as he struggled to keep up with what we already know by nature."

As if there was anything to consider. Brogan was ready to read every book they had. He'd always been an eager student—to please himself rather than his father or some ideal. The countries he'd lived in put a high regard on academics, and while that rigor shocked him at first, it developed his mind into a place where he could delight himself in science, history, mathematics, and art.

What could he learn in this magic-infused world?

"The library is through the arched blue doors, on the same path to the practice pitch."

"How did I not know about the library?"

"Daisy's been going there for weeks."

Brogan shucked off his annoyance. He'd been busy enough with the books Lightfeet had brought him.

Still, he didn't waste time finding the arched blue doors. He showed himself in, smiled at the woman at the desk, and made his way through a maze of stacks. Many volumes were bound like books, but he noticed several shelves of scrolls interspersed throughout. Some scrolls were plain, with ordinary wooden disks at the edges of the rolls. Others displayed gemstones and ornate carvings with gold, silver, and other colorful metals trailing through the reliefs.

He reached out and trailed his finger along *Medicinal Horticulture, Volume 11*. He pulled the scroll from its shelf and unrolled it. Rich illustrations displayed sprouts, trees, vines, fruits, and seeds. They demonstrated where to find the plants, how to care for them, and how to harvest and produce medicines. It was so detailed they nearly rendered the elaborate script unnecessary.

He grabbed a second volume and wandered to a nearby nook. He spread the ornate scrolls across the table. The beauty of the pen work arrested him, not to mention the illustrations of various plants and flowers. He recognized one of the plants. *Seraph: A deadly toxin, essential for the treatment of Prolkol fungus.* It was the same plant Orya had touched with the tip of his sword in the forest. The image showed dragon-skin gloved hands cutting the stalk and placing it in an oil press. *It is essential to sterilize press and gloves with grovin fire after use. Dilute oil 30 to 1 with neutral carrier oil. Store anywhere, potency does not decrease. Such poisons, though deadly, free patients from pestilence when handled properly.*

Another entry followed *Seraph* and described a plant that created depression and pain with no physical side effects. *This has been known to cast out the unwanted.* Brogan studied the vine that grew symbiotically with a narrow tree. The two twirled around each other and, like a double helix, together at points.

A bound leather codex kerplunked on the table next to the scroll he'd been using to take notes.

"The king says you need this. It's in the memoir section of the library since we don't really need it for research ourselves."

A short woman with wild black hair stood over him. Her face had absolutely zero wrinkles, but something else about her bespoke a lack of youth that other lightpeople manifested, and it wasn't just the gray streak in her hair. She didn't emanate warmth like all of the others. She reminded him of someone in mourning.

"I've seen you with Daisy, haven't I?"

"Yes, young warrior. Fight with your wits first." She padded away in the ninja style they all possessed, only it had the effect of floating because of her long skirt.

Brogan shook his head. The most preposterously weird things happened in Ells.

He picked up the codex and opened it. He recognized his dad's handwriting immediately and lost himself in countless pages of his old notes. He also recognized the runes now clearly legible to him.

Apparently Dad loved studying something called *Illuminated Organics*.

Brogan rubbed his eyes and leaned back into his chair, fighting off the emotion of having been left out of his father's confidence.

He read until after the lights faded and realized he was the only one left in the library. No one shooed him out, but the lights had gradually faded until reading was impossible. He stretched and grabbed his father's notes and a few volumes of *Luminated Organics* on his way out. It would be enough to keep him busy for several days.

"GAH!" shouted Lightfleet one afternoon when Brogan again declined going into the forest for a ride. "You can't only want to read!" He grabbed a scroll from Brogan's hand and dropped in on the floor.

Brogan watched it roll across his bedroom, then looked up

into his friend's narrowed eyes. "Have I really disappeared into my studies?"

"When was the last time we went riding? Or swimming? Or anything?"

Brogan leaned back in his chair and smirked. "It's kind of endearing how much you miss me."

One side of Lightfleet's mouth lifted in a snarl.

Brogan couldn't contain his chuckle. "I could pick this up again later."

His friend let out a great sigh, grabbed Brogan's arm, and pulled him from the desk. "I've already saddled two horses so you wouldn't have time to change your mind." He pushed Brogan toward the gray gelding standing just outside his front door. Brogan almost protested, but Lightfleet's smile grew too bright for him to be upset.

Brogan wanted to ask Lightfleet a ton of questions anyway. The more he learned about light, the more it fascinated him. And his friend was another source of information. "What part of shepherding light is science and what part is magic?"

"Magic is the part that transcends the science." Lightfleet blew out a rough breath.

"Like breaking the rules?" asked Brogan.

"More like knowing other rules."

"But which is which?"

"I don't know, Brogan. What part of *walking* is science for you and what part is instinct? You just know how to do it, and your muscles obey you. I've never stopped to think *how* I shepherd light. It's my birthright, but it's more like a monotonous duty. I have to wake up and help the lights awaken each day. *You* get to sleep."

"*You* get to live forever."

"So do you. You just have to die first."

"What do you mean by that?"

Lightfleet mumbled something about ignorance, his tone rough. Brogan didn't want to needle him for clarification if he was already bent out of shape. He was lost in these thoughts when he spotted a shadowy form under a tree maybe twenty feet away.

"Who is that?" As Brogan pointed at the form, his arm hair stood on end.

Lightfleet checked in the direction Brogan pointed. "I don't see anyone."

A face peaked from under a hood that was just visible enough to stare at him before it turned and ran into the trees. "He's running away now."

"I don't see anyone."

"How can you not see him?"

Lightfleet narrowed his eyes. "How can you not be more pleasant?"

"What's your deal? That guy doesn't look pleasant."

Brogan watched the figure disappear into the forest. Lightfleet stared as well, annoyance thick on his face.

THE NEXT MORNING, Brogan awoke to a different tune in the dawn—a sad one. And though the light did arise, it seemed to arise out of obligation rather than joy.

"What does it mean?" Daisy asked as he trudged into the common room.

He yawned and shrugged as a hard knock boomed from the front door. An out-of-breath Lightfleet stumbled in. "The dark king has sent his forces into Elleson. The northern borderlands have been burned. The manor house you stayed in has been leveled. The people are all dead."

Daisy's eyes widened as she thought of Aurora. "D-dead?"

"They suspect only Demonclaw would have that kind of audacity. The warrior counsel gathered late last night. The king and his forces are moving out now."

Brogan's heart jolted. He needed to pack. "How long do I have to gather my stuff?"

Lightfleet shook his head. "They asked us to stay behind as part of the castle guard. There's always a possibility the enemy could attack here. He's used such strategies to steal magical items from other kingdoms, and there's much to guard in Ells."

A light knock came from the door; this time Orya stepped in. He nodded to Brogan, then locked eyes with Daisy. "I'm saying my adieus. Please don't wander from the castle while I'm away. For my sanity, keep yourself safe, Daisy."

She nodded without a word.

"And you, Brogan, guard her well." Orya bowed his head and left without giving him an opportunity to respond.

* * *

THE FOLLOWING days were long and tense. Daisy tried not to be annoyed by all of Brogan's frenetic energy. Because he had long shifts with Lightfleet guarding the castle, he didn't work out as often. He probably needed running and sparring in the same way she needed alone time, and he kept knocking things over when he wasn't on a guard shift. He even broke a vase while practicing flips.

She should take him for a walk or something.

All she could think to say was, "I'll race you around the castle walls." She couldn't really compete against him, but he would agree as long as Lightfleet joined.

Lightfleet wasn't hard to convince either. He had been reclining on a bench near the castle's main entrance as if waiting for them.

"Lightfleet, will you race us around the outside of the castle walls?" She hoped her lack of enthusiasm wasn't too pronounced.

"Sure, I'll beat Brogan for you." He winked at Daisy.

Brogan guffawed. "Save your bragging for after the race."

Lightfleet's lip quirked. Brogan had just increased the intensity of the competition.

"Okay, okay. Line up." She hated racing against boys, and Brogan wouldn't even be grateful. "On your mark. Get set. Go!"

The two testosterone-laden young men took off in a dead sprint, leaving Daisy to her not-sprinting-but-kind-of-trying trot. The air was warm; sweat poured down her face and back. When she finally met them back at the main gate, they had already recovered their breath.

"Lightfleet for the win," said Brogan, still sweaty. He motioned for Daisy to join them.

As she approached, her headscarf fell off, leaving her bald head to gleam in the sun.

Brogan picked up the scarf and helped her tie it back on. "It's strange, Daisy. I expected you to look different by now. Not that it's important."

"Why would I look different?"

"Didn't Orya tell you about the spell? You are supposed to stand on the altar stone, or something like that, and the spell will break."

"What spell? What altar stone?"

Brogan eyes widened and he glanced around. "I don't really know anything about it. Just a passing conversation."

"The altar stone in the cathedral?" Lightfleet asked. "People don't normally stand on it. Maybe on their wedding day or coronation or special event."

"What do you mean by *spell*?"

"I don't know anything about it. Like I said, just something Orya mentioned." He shrugged and urged Lightfleet toward the villa as if the conversation were already in the past.

Daisy growled and trekked over to the cathedral.

She was a sweaty mess when she knocked on the heavy wooden door. It opened to a serene monk, who'd probably never sweated despite his agile, trim physique. The lightpeople were always perfectly composed.

"You need access to the house of prayer?" His smile appeared genuine even as he took in Daisy's unkemptness.

"I want to explore inside, if that's okay?" She widened her eyes and forced a small smile. She didn't need him to question her intentions.

He stood to the side and motioned toward the sanctuary. "You are welcome to wander freely. Only be careful with the altar."

Daisy brushed passed him and shivered as the cool air hit her moist skin. A light, floral aroma danced around her, hopefully overpowering her body odor. She drifted farther into the main atrium, awed by the way individual lights floated around the sanctuary. The architecture was so grand and warm that she almost couldn't ignore the sense of peace and joy inside.

Almost.

She looked up toward the apse and eyed a large, deep-red crystalline rock—the altar stone. She didn't know the ways in which it was sacred, but something instinctively told her not to treat it lightly. Begrudging reverence eased her pace as she approached.

She came to a full stop at the stairs leading up to its surface. She took a breath, stepped to the top of the stairs, and looked over into the stone's depths.

It was alive, like the blue gem from the dragon. She could see movement, but instead of hearing laughter she heard prayers. They were protective, as if they represented the prayers of all the light people to have ever passed through the cathedral. As if by instinct, Daisy knew these prayers guarded Elleson.

She remembered Brogan's words. *You are supposed to stand on the altar stone . . . or something.* But now that she was here, she couldn't walk onto something so sacred.

As she stared down in to the rich, scarlet depths of the stone, an active force, like invisible hands, pushed her forward. She caught herself from falling by taking two steps.

She regained her balance, only now she stood directly on the stone. Her fear evaporated as a single tenor voice rose up from its depths, singing a sweet tune. After one chorus it was joined by a baritone, then an alto, then a soprano. Another and then another voice arose in ranges she couldn't describe, until the songs stored in the stone enveloped her.

Then the visions started. Like the single voice that had been joined by so many, multiple visions gathered toward a crescendo. The images flashed by so quickly, she couldn't keep track of them. Kings and queens were born, crowned, wed, and died through ages and ages. Elleson was much older than she had guessed. And she saw the wars, the pleas of the people in times of imminent doom.

Scenes kept coming and coming until the folds of elation, sorrow, and grief nauseated her. Their weight pressed against her chest. She labored for each breath until the pressure was held back by the man made out of light—an ancient man.

His hands touched her face and held it gently. Other hands peeled off what felt like garments from her head, her hands, her entire body. She felt sorrow at losing the garments. She had no choice. They were not true, and they were already discarded forever.

Her uncovered body burned from head to toe. The pain of exposure overtook her and she screamed. The man's fingers lifted her chin up toward his face. Daisy swallowed her scream when two dark purple eyes arrested her. They became a crimson pool, and she swam. The pool had no bottom. It reached down into eternity. As it washed over her, the burning subsided and she was aware again of the person in whose eyes she had been swimming. His unending glory focused itself on her little problem, and she didn't even question that it was worth it to him. He was pure love; it was all that she wanted forever.

He used his thumbs to pull her eyelids down. She woke up alone and cold on the floor in front of the altar stone. As the room drew into focus, Daisy checked to feel that her clothes were still on. Her smooth silk tunic remained stuck against her skin, drenched in sweat. What was it, then, that he peeled from her body? She moved her feet to stand. The world tilted and spun, so she lay back down on her side. Vomit pressed up into her esophagus, but she pushed it back. A monk ran toward her. His form blurred as the world again became black.

CHAPTER TWENTY-FIVE

THE NEXT TIME DAISY AWOKE, she was in a comfortable bed. Sunlight warmed the room.

Sunlight? There was no sun in Elleson. So, was she . . . home?

Hope surged from her heart to all of her extremities. She bolted up and immediately regretted it. The room wouldn't still. Smears of color traced across her vision and pulled into solid forms. A few beds came into focus. Chairs were placed opposite each bed, and windows lined the wall high above them.

The lights hovering near the ceiling wouldn't stop spinning. That must be what a concussion does to your senses. Did she fall out of her bedroom window last night?

She refused to let them be magic lamps spinning just under the ceiling. She lay back and stared at the undulating forms. As she watched, they grew sharper on the edges and emanated the same color of light the sun releases.

She blinked back disappointment.

A man opened the door and stepped into the room. "Hello. My name is Raphi. I am a healer." He spoke in Ellesse.

Daisy blinked back her tears and asked, "A healer? Like, a doctor?"

"Much like a doctor, yes." The man glanced at Daisy and then shifted to a scroll on which he scratched something.

What had happened? She fell on the altar stone, and the rest wasn't clear. "Raphi, I may have done something wrong."

He turned his face to her but shifted his line of vision above her head. "We know. You went to the altar stone. That is indeed dangerous. It is a deep magic, as old as this world. While it is usually just decorative, no one knows what will happen on the stone. Also, magic in this world is bound to react differently to you."

She sighed.

The man smiled as he turned away from her. "I'm afraid your problems are just beginning."

The healer pointed Daisy to a mirror across the room.

Curious, she rose from the bed and toddled over to it, using various chairs to hold her balance until she gained her equilibrium. Her heart grew cold at the sight. She looked at a girl who looked like herself, yet very different. Her skin was more than blemish-free; it was radiant. Zero scars twisted her now perfectly shaped eyebrows. Her eyelashes were heavy and full, causing her light blue eyes to pierce through them. She had hair! And what hair she had! Her old hair had always limped in straw-like clumps, but these tresses gathered in large waves and curls. Its color was no longer dirty-blond but rich with reds and coppers—more akin to her mother's, only lighter.

She raised strong and perfect fingers in front of her face. Each perfectly manicured nail glistened. Her forearms exhibited shaped muscles, still feminine but strong. Her shoulders, her neck, her feet—her entire exterior frightened her with its beauty.

She poked at her abdomen to make sure she wasn't simply looking through a window at someone else, but she felt the jab of each finger on her muscled abs.

She faced the healer. "Why did this happen?"

Raphi continued focusing his eyes on his instruments. "I think you need to speak to the king. He may know something about it.

The bishop as well might be able to answer some of your questions."

Was he kidding? The king was fighting on the northern front, and she couldn't wait months for an explanation. "I want to go to my villa." She tried to keep her tone from being icy and clipped, but she preferred that to panicked and terrified.

Raphi handed her a simple frock to wear over the infirmary nightgown. "Your clothes were wet. They are being laundered and will be returned to your villa."

She threw on the frock and left, *not* ready for what happened next. Every courtier and servant she passed stared her down. One dropped a tray full of goblets. Glass shattered on the walkway.

Lightpeople simply didn't drop things. Control and grace accentuated even their micro-movements. The young man's eyes manifested some kind of whimsical pool of adoration in their hazel depths; the mess of glass and wine lay forgotten.

Daisy bolted. As she ran from the scene, she picked up unbelievable speed. The wind around her grew strong, and when she stopped at the villa, her hair bounced heavy and lively on her shoulders.

At the door her hands shook, but she couldn't avoid the inevitable, so she opened it. Brogan's and Lightfleet's voices filled the main room. She breathed deep and marched in.

Brogan glanced at her, then stood with his mouth agape. Lightfleet turned around to see what the commotion was about, and he, too. stood, eyes wide.

Tears burned her eyes and poured onto her cheeks. "You have to tell me what you know about this, Brogan."

"What . . . ? I—"

"Brogan. You know something. You knew about the altar stone." As her voice steadied, it came out clear and strong in a way she'd never experienced before. Before, she was unheard, quiet, but now she could likely command an army with this voice.

"Daisy. I'm sorry. I was careless about the information." But he didn't continue.

"It's not about you being careless. Look at me! Please, anything you can tell me."

Brogan's eyebrows knit together. "I don't know much. Orya mention, offhanded, a long time ago that he put you under a spell. He said he regretted it because it wasn't his idea; he had been sad and intoxicated at the time. But Daisy, I know he didn't mean to—"

"A spell?"

"Yeah." Brogan sighed, eyes wide with compassion. "To keep you from being beautiful, like your mom. So he would have the chance to know you before you fell in love with someone else."

Hot anger engulfed her. She turned from Brogan and Light-fleet and flew into her bedroom. There, trembling, she confronted the stranger in the mirror. A stranger that glowed with burning, beautiful skin.

The bishop. I should go see the bishop. Daisy wrapped her head and face in a scarf and walked through the main room toward the entrance of the house.

"Are you okay, Daisy?" Brogan tried to move in front of her, but she threw him aside in a quick judo-like move. She was fast *and* strong. Really strong. And her body obeyed everything her mind remembered from training in her dreams.

She almost stopped to help Brogan back up, but she needed to go to the cathedral. "Sorry," she whispered and darted outside. She ran through obscure garden paths until she stopped at the grand door—not as eager to enter the house of worship as she had been the last time. She pressed herself forward.

Inside, the altar stone stood at the end of the great room, pretending to be dull and innocuous. She would not approach that thing so casually again. Instead, she edged alongside the atrium wall toward the door where the first monk had disappeared yesterday. Several doorways presented themselves, so she chose one, which led to another, until she met another monk in the traditional bright blue tunic. He looked surprised to see her, but not alarmed. "The bishop went to the battlefront with the king," he informed her, "but one of his students might be able to help."

He ushered her into an office, which reminded her of her father's study with its absentminded hodgepodge of study materials and books. A man glanced up from a parchment. his warm eyes sober and steady. "You are the lady who fell from the alter stone yesterday."

Yesterday? Was she asleep an entire day? Her new body countered the shock with easy breaths. "Yes. Can you help me understand what happened?"

Again, her voice carried power by the clarity of its tone.

Despite her vocal authority, the monk responded with ease. He gestured toward a deep, comfortable chair. "I am at your service to try. I need to know the what before I can help with the why."

She sat. "I'm not sure what happened."

The monk nodded. "I am in no rush. Tell me what you remember."

This assured Daisy, and without removing her veil, she spoke. The man listened so intently that she found herself spilling everything from her deformities after the accident, to overcoming her insecurities by the help of her father, to finding joy just in being herself only to discover that it was not enough for other people.

Then to discover the thoughtless command of a drunken king caused all of her torment, months in the hospital, scars, and humiliation. Then to change physically again, which is probably what he had hoped for. Is being beautiful the only thing she was worth? Was her soul disregarded until her body could please a man's appetite? Or did the king see her as a possession who wasn't allowed to be beautiful to others? And what could she do with this new, terrifying face? She was both sobbing and raging by the time she finished.

The man listened to it all while maintaining his peaceful sincerity. Neither her despair nor her anger shook his kind eyes. "May I call you Daisy?"

"Yes," she whispered between sniffs.

"Good. My name is Montanit, but you can call me Monty. First, give yourself permission to feel grief and anger. If you push it aside, it will turn into hatred, fear, or worse. So I am glad you are expressing it now. You can address your anger once you've dealt with the underlying vulnerability that has been transgressed."

This man was good.

"Next, I believe you are looking for explanations before sympathy. So while we could address your pain when you are ready, perhaps we should do our detective work first?"

He spoke so clearly. How did she follow all of this when she didn't know the language?

"Are we speaking in Ellesse?"

He nodded with a smile barely creasing his eyes. "We are, and your accent is perfect."

Yesterday that would have pleased her, but she didn't care at the moment. "Let's deal with the incident first, if that's okay? I want to know what happened . . . what is happening."

Monty took a deep breath. "Yes, well, I can tell you what I suspect more than what I know. The altar stone, as you have discovered, is a deeply magical thing. That our king used it in a curse could only have been the product of drunken stupidity. It is likely that he has born a weight of guilt ever since. You see, the stone belongs to the Eternal One, and the Eternal One is not bullied into cursing people. The satrap who cast the spell could only curse you and use the stone as the means to set the curse right again. But he was playing above his knowledge—with a future queen no less."

Daisy winced. Even Monty accepted Orya's plans to marry her. She would set that right later. Time to focus.

He drew his thick eyebrows into a thoughtful pose. "Whenever the Eternal One touches us, it is to his discretion how extensively he works. What you are right now is not an accident, but it might reveal more than just how you *would have* looked without the curse. It reveals the extent to which the Eternal One trusts you. You could have been regenerated to an image of your future glory. In which case, you would be conspicuous, to say the least. In my own belief, this is only a fraction of your future glory, or all eyes would be strained toward you—face covered or not." He sighed and sank back in his chair. "The Eternal One must have wanted you, and others, to see yourself like this and to feel the power and resilience of a more perfected body. It is possible you will fade back to normal once his purposes have been carried through."

"What do you mean by 'future glory'?"

"Surely you already understand, Daisy. This is not our final home. Even the lightpeople, though we do not age, we are not perfect. What we once were has been touched by evil, so it is less than what the Eternal One has intended for us. And what we will be is all a mystery still uncovered. If I am to encourage you, it is only to remind you of the love you have encountered."

"But what do I do now?" She searched Monty's face, and though she saw kindness there, she didn't see any expression that he knew how to answer her question. "I see." She stood to leave.

As she turned, a large hand rested on her shoulder.

"You are never alone, Daisy."

New tears stung her eyes. "Thank you."

The hand released her, and she walked back to the villa with a heart full of heavy thoughts. Although Monty showed her great kindness, it was her father's words that came to the forefront. *God does not forsake you, Daisy. Trust him in the deepest darkness. He is there.*

CHAPTER TWENTY-SIX

BROGAN RUBBED the hip he'd landed on when Daisy threw him. She threw him with a good bit of strength and unnatural talent. He'd studied jiujitsu for years, so he knew a genius when he'd met one.

But her face, her entire appearance, was another matter. She wasn't simply beautiful. It's like he finally could see what all of the lightpeople had been talking about since they got there, only that beauty was now physically represented.

A hand presented a plate of savory food in front of his face. Lightfleet cleared his throat.

Brogan grabbed the plate and set it on the atrium table. "Lightfleet, does any of this makes sense to you?"

"You're welcome for making lunch." Lightfleet plopped onto the couch and tore into his own plate of meat and vegetables.

Brogan deadpanned, "Thank you for lunch."

Lightfleet swallowed an eager bite. "Daisy's going to be okay. Better than okay. Admittedly, it's surprising to see her like that, but she will adjust faster than most."

"It already bugged me that her presence made me invisible after we came back from Ahl. Only a few lightpeople bother to talk to me. With her looking like . . . like that, the only thing they'll ask of me is to stop blocking their view. I'm not even sure why I was pulled into all of this stuff."

Lightfleet chuckled. "Not exactly worried about her well-being then?"

Brogan shot Lightfleet an annoyed stare. "Of course I'm worried, but it's shaking the framework of my understanding."

"I'm afraid you'll have to settle for being insignificant in Elleson. Except to me, of course. Sit back and watch the show, remember?"

What Lightfleet said had merit. Maybe he should focus a little more on guarding the castle and being moral support or whatever for his half-sister.

"If it helps, I like you way better than Daisy."

Brogan chuckled. "Why is that?"

"She'd beat me in swords for sure."

* * *

MOST GIRLS WOULD LOVE to become more beautiful. In truth, Daisy had wished it as well. Now she realized that *wishing* for something and *getting it* was not always what it turned out to be. She hated the way people stared at her. Lightfleet and Brogan weren't helping either.

"I'm sorry, Daisy," said Lightfleet. "It's just so beautiful." He poked at her cheek.

"Not me, but it? My face?"

Brogan snorted. "You're great and all that. But your new face is kind of amazing." He threw a grape at her nose and watched it bounce off.

She gestured toward the door. "You can see why I never go out there without a scarf."

Brogan nodded while Lightfleet shrugged.

She rolled her eyes and wrapped a scarf around her head. "I might as well go outside."

She left the castle grounds through the main gate and made

her way to Mabel's cottage. Her quirky friend was planting something in her garden and singing.

"Hello Mabel."

Mabel didn't even look at Daisy but continued with her seeds. "You're early."

"Are you talking to me or to the seeds?"

"I've never thought to speak to the seeds." She stared down at the dirt with a quizzical expression. "Hmm."

"What do you mean by *I'm early*?"

"I wasn't expecting you until tomorrow, but it wasn't an exact notice." Her gaze finally met Daisy's just as the scent of roses wafted in on a warm breeze. "Why is your head covered?"

"To avoid all the staring."

Mabel raised a single eyebrow. "What happened to you? Come in and tell me. And please take off your scarf. It must be stifling."

Daisy followed her into the cottage. Mabel messed with her teapot as Daisy untangled herself. "You're right. This scarf is suffocating."

Mabel turned toward Daisy and dropped her teapot, which shattered on the floor.

Daisy wrapped her face again. "Mabel, I'm so sorry. Your treasured teapot!"

"Don't be silly, child. That isn't your fault." But Mabel wouldn't look at her as she cleaned up the broken shards.

Daisy found the trash bin and tapped Mabel's shoulder to indicate she was holding it next to her. Mabel jumped and nearly spilled the shards before dropping them into the bin.

"Well, I-I have other teapots . . . under some baskets." Mabel started the fire under the kettle again and seemed to forget about finding another teapot.

"You know, Mabel, I actually need to be back at the villa—"

"Of course, dear, don't let me keep you." Mabel ran from the kitchen without a goodbye.

Daisy saw herself out and closed the cottage door behind her.

The best place for her would be the woods, where no one had

to deal with the sight of her. She ran to the small gate and greeted Grovin.

"Is that you, scum-dwelling lass?" The Ahlish idioms had become a joke between them.

Her heart lightened. "Aye, ye hairy beast."

Grovin's laughter boomed. "Why are you hiding behind your scarves today?"

She sighed. "Oh. You know . . . *reasons*."

He nodded. "All the accursed *reasons*. Enjoy your woods."

The small gate clanged shut behind her. She tore off her scarves and tied them to a tree near the gate. They flounced in a breeze that carried an acute scent of fresh berries.

Sudden delight arrested her as her heightened senses told her which direction she needed to walk to find these berries. She could hear small, scurrying animals in the berry patch picking their favorites. She could see individual leaves fluttering around her, not just the wave of green blobs her poor brain used to interpret as trees. Blobs were all her eyesight afforded her before. But these leaves each had their own shape, their own glimmer of happy, reflected sunlight.

Smells, shapes, colors, sounds. Before the change, nature had whispered to her, but now stimuli screamed from every direction while her mind somehow took in each detail with delineated understanding. Rather than overwhelm her, it lifted her in delightful songs that made her forget her despondency.

In a crescendo of joy, she sprinted down a path. The wind lifted her thick hair behind her.

She ran. Her breath became more intense, but her heartbeat remained steady and powerful. She didn't need to stop and rest. She leapt over rocks, stumps, and branches without slowing. At this rate, she could smoke Brogan and Lightfleet in their next race.

While she didn't grow physically weary, she did get hungry. Very hungry. She followed the scent of berries, fruits, and edible plants all around her. She chose a particular bush and plucked pink berries from among velvety green leaves.

The berries melted in her mouth.

As she ate, she detected a scent of horse-like dander. She peered around and locked gazes with a tawny deer. It kept its head down as it backed away from her, flicking its white tail. She must have interrupted its own feast of berries.

"I'm sorry, little deer. I'm leaving now." She giggled and sprang back onto the trail to run again, this time back to the castle.

She retied the scarf around her face and hair, then greeted Grovin.

"You certainly took a long, rot-infested stroll, lass. Were you in the woods all day?"

"I was, you busybody." She laughed to emphasize that her insult was simply Ahlish flair.

That was fun. She'd do it again tomorrow.

Day after day she left the castle before yellow and explored fields, trees, and waters until purple. Grovin wasn't always the guard, but her new competency in the Ellesian language removed barriers. *Hello. What's your name? See you later. Thank you. Goodnight.*

One morning the glorious smell of bacon woke her; it had gripped her with longing even while she had slept. How long had it been since she'd eaten meat?

She shuffled into the kitchen where Brogan sat with his arms crossed next to a pile of bacon and freshly baked bread.

"I thought I might catch you like this."

She huffed, though her heart warmed at the sight him. It *had* been a while since they'd talked.

He gestured to the mouth-watering platter. "Would you like some?"

She nodded, the English word *yes* somehow out of reach. "It smells amazing."

Brogan's eyes widened.

"Have you been practicing Ellesse?" he asked in the singsong tones.

She shook her head. "It was just easier to say it in the 'Song of Dew.' "

He now sat up straight. "Daisy, how do you even know that expression?"

She didn't want to answer, afraid some other unnatural revelation might pour out of her mouth, so she shrugged.

Brogan shook his head and gestured to the plate opposite from him. "Sho ahlamon." *Bon apatite.*

She tore into the delicious food.

"Wow. Watch your fingers."

She shoved another slice of bread in her mouth. "If shust fo good." Finally, English.

"Anyway, I have a reason for stopping you before you leave."

She motioned him to speak while biting into her fifth piece of bacon.

"There's news from the front."

She set down the bacon. "Go on."

"It hasn't gone as well as they hoped. The King of Ahl has used unexpected methods, I guess."

"Is everyone okay?"

"For now, but they are scrambling to hold their ground."

Somewhat relieved, she picked up more bacon.

Brogan continued. "I also overheard the head of the castle guard yesterday. They might force you to stay within the castle walls for your own safety. I thought you should be aware of the dangers creeping through the forests."

"What?" A little piece of bacon shot from her mouth onto the table.

Brogan's lip curled in disgust. "Ew. No one is pretty enough to do that." He flicked the bit off the table with his finger.

Daisy suspected the orders were Orya's doing, and she no longer trusted his motives. She would have to leave the castle today and simply not return. For a moment she pictured Brogan's worried expression once he'd realized she'd left. He'd been the one to run into Ahl months ago to save her, and that without knowing her as well as he did now.

She swallowed. "Thank you for telling me about the guards."

"Maybe you can talk to Choral and take a guard with you next time."

She nodded and waited for him to leave for the sparring pitch. As soon as the door closed, she ran to her room.

She stretched into her dragon skins, threw whatever basic supplies she could find into a backpack, slid a note under Brogan's door, then left the villa and the castle walls. She walked into the trees with no intention of coming back.

DAISY STARED INTO THE THICK, dark forest, searching the trail far into the distance until it turned and disappeared. She would take this trail until she found its end. And when she found its end, she would find another.

She slipped off her moccasins and sank her toes into the damp earth. No restrictions, not even on her feet. She sprinted forward, dirt clods hurling up behind her. This was even better than her dreams had been while on missions for Choral. She grabbed a tree branch and hurled herself forward, flipping and twisting before she landed higher up the tree. Another few leaps upward and she was crouched on the uppermost branch.

A curious squirrel leapt close and chattered from a nearby oak.

"Am I encroaching on your territory?" Daisy asked the small creature.

At the sound of her voice, the squirrel backed away and squeaked again. A bright red bird landed next to him and commenced staring.

"You really haven't seen anything like me up here, have you?"

She swung back down through the branches to run the path again. It was easy terrain, and after many hours she reached an unmarked fork. To the left, more woods. To the right, the trail moved upward.

A purple flash told her the day would be gone soon. She should rest and choose which way to go when there was light again.

She climbed the largest nearby tree as high as she could. The oncoming darkness hid the landscape from view; she would have to wait until morning to assess her surroundings. In the meantime, she leaned against the trunk and let the cool breeze waft over her face, tendrils of her hair floating in its direction. Her eyelids felt heavy. She pulled some survival cord from her backpack and strapped herself to the branch. She could sleep here for the night, despite the rough bark against her back.

Daisy awoke as the light warmed the morning sky. To the north, the canopy stretched beyond the horizon. Warm light outlined each individual treetop. To the south, craggy mountains jutted upward.

She climbed back down to the fork in the path. Based on the location of the mountains, the path to the right led south, straight toward them. They would provide a compass of sorts, so she decided to take the path south.

At first, the steep incline challenged her, but the path turned left and leveled. As long as she wasn't climbing or descending, she knew she'd be moving eastward.

She continued for days with the jagged peaks at her right side until she ran out of woods. Abruptly. A large expanse of unending sand met her, stark against the rich forest. She didn't understand how those ecosystems coexisted in such diametric contrast. Magic, maybe? Magic powerful enough to set a boundary for the trees and the dunes?

She crouched and studied the phenomenon. A nearly solid line divided mossy wet earth from dry grains of sand.

She had no way to ask Mable about the sharp delineation, so she filed the mystery away. Where to now? North would take her to the battlefront. So she'd go south, where deep forests covered craggy mountains until a toothy tree line broke through the green felt.

She yelled, "Next stop: learning to climb like a mountain goat."

The sound of her own voice spooked her. How long had she been fixed in silence? She had lost count of the days she'd been mute like a wild beast, then laughed to herself.

No. Not *only* to herself. "Mr. Eternity, I like your world. Is it wrong that I've run away to play in it?"

She ran again. Up onto the mountain, back down into the forest. Through brush and canopy. Even back to the sands. Days were spent exploring. Watching wildlife. She even found fairies in the deepest canopy under the southeastern crags. She lay next to them, studying their speech.

She fell asleep listening to their high voices and awoke to discover them clipping her finger and toenails. One made a face as he tossed a filthy, dirt-encrusted clipping onto the ground.

"I'm sorry, fairy. I haven't paid attention to my nails."

He scowled and flew on his way.

"Are you the grooming police?" she muttered, studying fingernails that now looked much cleaner. To be fair, she'd only bathed the few times she found running water.

A cold gust of wind hit her face. A rogue snowflake twirled past her, then another. Snow fell faster and heavier, blanketing the forest within minutes. The fairies must have gone for shelter.

Was it possible to freeze to death here? How had she not noticed the cold? The humid heat of summer had still hung heavy when she left.

She would need to find shelter. There was a cave somewhere around here but in which direction? She swiveled until she remembered and ran forward. By the time she spotted the cave, six inches of snow lay on the ground. She stared down at her perfectly warm bare feet.

She picked up a handful of powder. It melted around her fingertips. Daisy marveled at how her toes and fingers remained warm and well regulated by the passage of blood. She always needed toe and glove warmers when she played in the snow back home, but now her body resisted the bite. Instead, the cold refreshed and clarified her thoughts and soothed her lungs.

"How interesting. You created us to love this painlessly— without the freeze biting our skin."

At the sound of her voice, something rustled only feet from where she stood. Daisy always heard animals before they heard her, so she flinched. A man emerged from a camouflaged, snow-covered tent. Her adrenaline kicked in, but she remained planted. Her training had taught her to make every move count.

The man saw her, startled, and fell sideways. But rather than landing on the ground, he flipped over in a crazy acrobatic way while unsheathing a small blade.

She darted her hands upward to show him she wasn't armed. She doubted she would have any difficulty deflecting an attack, but there was no reason to test her theory.

The man's eyes didn't communicate much. Maybe confusion. His deep, calm voice said, "Forgive me. You caught me by surprise." He lowered the knife as he stared at her.

"Hello, Zerek," she replied, unable to keep her lips from spreading into a smile.

ABOUT THE AUTHOR

Misha McCorkle grew up praying, reading, and drawing. She survived growing up with three older brothers by hiding in her room (with the cookies) and playing sports somewhere away from the proximity of her home.

Misha has degrees in fine arts and in the Old Testament. Now she's writing books. She redeems herself socially through sports, but really she's just a big nerdy nerd who still doesn't know how to put her makeup on right.

She's from Colorado, but not the pretty part... the part that looks post-apocalyptic. She moved to the Front Range as an adult, which is nice.

Misha believes in redemption, in forgiving people generously, in living out faith as we are each uniquely called. And since kind adults had an enormously positive impact on her teen years, she wants to give back by providing a narrative for teens that helps them navigate our increasingly complex culture.

Elleson is the first book in a series. Ready for book two? Head over to **www.mishamccorkle.com** to learn more.

Lightning Source UK Ltd.
Milton Keynes UK
UKHW010838141220
375205UK00001B/102